The Crossing

Critical Acclaim for Mark Alan Leslie's
True North: Tice's Story

"Leslie vividly describes the plight of runaway slaves ... Tice exhibits a deep religious confidence that will endear him to readers of inspirational literature. While the main plot is a work of fiction, the well-researched historical elements make it believable and even, at times, educational."

—**Publishers Weekly,** *which named True North its lead Featured Book in Booklist in April 2015*

Critical acclaim for Mark Alan Leslie's
Midnight Rider for the Morning Star: From the Life and Times of Francis Asbury

"In a world of namby-pamby Christianity, along comes a story of a man who played no games with God. The life and exploits of Francis Asbury read like the biblical Book of Acts. Mark Alan Leslie did not write 'just another book.' I couldn't put *Midnight Rider for the Morning Star* down. Neither will you. This one is a 'must read.'"

—**Frank Eiklor**, *president, Shalom International Outreach*

"...engaging, entertaining, informative and *convicting*. We spend so little time in God's Word, and have so little passion for souls! I am inspired by Asbury's life and example. Although I am one of our congregation's main evangelists, Bishop Asbury puts me to shame and challenges me to be more passionate, saltier, wiser, more effective at redeeming the time, and certainly more willing to suffer for the sake of the gospel."

—*Jamie Lash, Jewish Jewels*,
Fort Lauderdale, Fla.

"*Midnight Rider* is an exciting, exhilarating story that challenges the reader in an intense way."

—*Dr. Dennis E. Kinlaw, founder,*
The Francis Asbury Society and
past president Asbury College

"Again and again it spoke to my heart."

—*the late Merlin R. Carothers, founder,*
Foundation of Praise and author of
From Prison to Praise

"[It] is a stimulating and imagination-provoking book."

—*Patch Blakey, executive director,*
Association of Classical and Christian Schools

"An exhilarating historical novel, helping readers experience the heart and mind of this 'saint.'"

—*Chris Bounds*, *Professor of Theology/Chair of the Department of Christian Studies and Philosophy at Asbury University*

"This is a fast-paced ride and read through the new Republic with America's most influential religious leader."

—*Darius Salter*, *church historian and pastor, Richardson (Texas) Church of the Nazarene*

"If the life of Francis Asbury ever inspires a movie, the script may resemble Mark Alan Leslie's historical novel, *Midnight Rider for the Morning Star.*

—*Bill Fentum*, *United Methodist Reporter*

"A delightful, enriching and inspiring read. The Church needs to read this and regain Asbury's passion and zeal. As a Christian and pastor, I've used this book for a witness several times."

—*Pastor Randy Brown*, *Christian Revolution*

The Crossing

Mark Alan Leslie

Cover Design: Jeff Gifford
Interior Design: Melinda Martin
Editor: Deb Haggerty
Published in Association with Les Stobbe Literary Agency

PUBLISHED BY: Elk Lake Publishing, Inc., 35 Dogwood Dr., Plymouth, MA 02360

Library Cataloging Data
Names: Leslie, Mark Alan (Mark Alan Leslie)
The Crossing/ Mark Alan Leslie
290 p. 23cm × 15cm (9in × 6 in.)
Description: Elk Lake Publishing, Inc. digital eBook edition | Elk Lake Publishing, Inc. Trade paperback edition | Elk Lake Publishing, Inc. 2016.
Identifiers: ISBN-13: 978-1-946638-01-1 | 978-1-946638-00-7
Key Words: Maine History, KKK in Maine, Anti-Semitism, Black History, Bigotry, Klan, 1920s.

Dedication

This book is dedicated to fine friends,
encouragers, and devotees of American history,
Dave and Suzy Schaub.

Acknowledgments

My wife, Loy, publisher and editor Deb Haggerty, and agent Les Stobbe all have my undying gratitude. Also, to cover designer Jeff Gifford: Well done.

And libraries! What would we do without them? The state of Maine Public Library in Augusta is extraordinary, even to possessing PhD thesis papers written a half century ago, perhaps the only existing writings—outside of a *Washington Post* article—spelling out the extraordinary story of the rise and fall of the Ku Klux Klan in this very "white" state.

Indeed, few if any Mainers were ever taught about this brief and disturbing time in the state's history and the villains, victims, and heroes of this conflict. Perhaps historians of the past preferred not to confront Maine residents with the ugly facts and so, this chapter faded to "sidebar" and vanished into the vapors of antiquity.

CHAPTER ONE

A triple play! Young Joshua Craig was still reliving the game-ending, ankle-high line drive that he snapped from his shortstop position before stepping on second base to force out Bobby Jenkins who was off the bag, then drilling the ball to Jimmy Thomas at first base to catch Stevie Fowler before he could get back.

This was euphoria. He thought of the word in his 6th-grade English test Mrs. Green gave the class just yesterday. E-u-p-h-o-r-i-a. He couldn't wait to tell Dad and Mom about it—moment by moment. His anticipation of the hit, his instinctive step toward second, his—Whoa! What was that?

Something suddenly grabbed his attention, something odd, something out of place. But what? He squinted and looked up to the top of Henhawk Hill. There was a light up there and not just any old light—not a little lamp or lantern. A blaze!

For several minutes, Joshua stood transfixed, feet planted like in a pot of clay. Overwhelming curiosity paralyzed his thought of continuing on home. Dusk darkened into twilight, and as the rising moon painted yellow hues on the tree branches, Joshua could see more clearly.

It was a bonfire, and in its midst was a huge wooden cross. He could almost hear the flames crackle, and what they lit up? A chill flickered down his spine. A circle of white-cloaked, hooded figures moved around the cross, rhythmically lifting their arms toward the sky, then lowering them. There were probably a couple dozen or so people.

A booming voice carried down from the hilltop in phrases muffled by the distance. And as if a bucket of kerosene had been tossed on it, the cross flashed into a flaming ball, scorching the air. The blaze seemed to heighten the motions of the hooded figures.

Just then, a scream pierced the air. A shiver of fright flew up Joshua's back. He tried to turn to run, but his feet felt like balls of lead—heavier than the double harness for Dad's oxen. Worse still, he couldn't remove his eyes from the scene above.

At that moment, the figures stopped and huddled around the cross. Minutes seemingly passed by. The night noises of crickets and katydids had fallen silent since the scream. The faint smell of smoke reached Joshua's nostrils. Its bitterness stung his tongue.

The flame began to wane and the figures moved as one away from the cross. Suddenly, most of the ghouls in the congregation dispersed down the northeast side of the hill to Joshua's right. Again, he tried to move. Again, he couldn't. His feet were heavy blocks of lumber. A drop of sweat began to crawl from his temple down his cheek.

One small group remained behind, tightly knit as if its members were sharing a secret. Six were in the band, five wearing white robes. The sixth, draped in what appeared to be a red robe— though it was hard to be sure from this distance—towered over the others. It bent to the ground and picked up something— something shaped like—like a bedroll perhaps. Then, two of the figures stepped to the front and two moved behind the bedroll, lifted it at hip height, while the large figure and one of the others lifted lanterns to shoulder height and stepped off away from the burning cross.

The group moved with apparent urgency down the hill, never stopping, on a route between trees and underbrush. When they reached the steepest terrain, the four figures carrying the bundle turned as on an axis so that they were at the same level, then continued on their way until they were just about thirty yards or so from Joshua, the distance from home plate to first base.

The boy trembled. He felt he had been watching a story unfold in a picture book. It took several long moments for reality to register with him. But when the point struck, it did so with certainty, suddenness, and fright: They were coming directly toward him!

Joshua's heart raced.

Now they were only fifteen or twenty yards away, still heading toward the very spot on which he was standing.

Joshua again struggled to move his feet, willing them take that one motion that would free him to run. He could steal second base, even third, so why couldn't he move this moment when his life could be in danger?

Now the two figures in front were ten yards away and the light from their lanterns drew ever closer, just feet away from Joshua.

Icy fingers played taps on his nerves. Finally, the reality of their closeness struck him like a right cross, and that blow sent him reeling backwards, propelled down the narrow, winding path that led to the road about a quarter of a mile from his home.

In the last minute or two, darkness had descended on this east side of Henhawk Hill, but Joshua knew the path well and darted around its bends. Tree roots and jutting rocks—dark shades in a world of gray—loomed up at him, but he bounded over and around them. When he reached a small field near the road, he stopped momentarily to look behind him. Light from the lanterns bobbed along through the trees.

He bent at the waist and inhaled deeply, but it felt like his head was in a box, like all the oxygen in the woods had been sucked up by some inhuman monster of some sort. He stood straight and tried again. This time it worked. With relief, he absorbed the fresh air of the cooling night, then walked briskly down the road. A jumble of thoughts flooded his mind.

Suddenly, male voices sounded and horses came around a bend in the road. Joshua jumped into bushes and hunkered down, just then noticing that he held his baseball glove in a vise grip. The men were speaking all at once, but in secretive tones. Not boisterous and jocular like you'd expect from such a large group. Not a single laugh. Not a chuckle. Not a "Glad to see you tonight, Chuck" … "You, too, Roger."

Probably a couple of dozen horses passed by. A horsefly buzzed Joshua's head, and he bit a lip trying to keep from swatting it. When they'd gone, he counted to ten and stepped out. Just then, a large dark horse almost ran into him. He leaped away and fell to the ground.

He blinked and looked up at a stallion towering over him that was darker than the night. Its nostrils flared. He gulped and tried to catch his breath. He thought the face under the hood was Danny Farmer's dad but wasn't sure.

Then the rider's big fist stretched out from the white cloak and pointed an extraordinarily long, bony finger at him. Joshua looked away.

"Boy!" the man's voice boomed, "you saw nothin' here tonight, right? Nothin'!" Yep, it could be Mister Farmer, but Joshua wasn't sure. One thing he was sure of—it was a scary voice and not one to argue with. He recalled Danny sometimes coming to school all banged up and the talk around school that Mrs. Farmer sometimes sported similar bruises. Nobody's house had that many doors to run into, not even Doc Walker.

He gulped hard and murmured a "yes, sir."

"You say a word, your daddy and mommy get hurt, boy."

That shook Joshua down to his toes. The threat in the voice was easy to believe. At the moment, Joshua just hoped that big horse didn't stomp on him.

"You hear?!"

Joshua whimpered and nodded his head.

"Git off with ya', then."

Joshua made sure he still gripped his baseball glove, pulled his cap down over his ears and sprinted as fast as he could in the heavy dusk.

♔ ♔ ♔

Joshua didn't say a word that sleepless night, Sunday, nor the next day, Monday, nor even the next. He loved his Mom. He adored his Dad. The best ever.

He went to school Monday and Tuesday, yipped it up with the guys when the last bell rang at 2:30 Tuesday, planned with Bobby Spillman to go fishing after school Thursday, figured with the gang that they'd be playing pickup games all the time, like every day, when the school year ended Friday. But that night, he couldn't sleep again. He wondered what was the world's record for not sleeping. He knew Mom would figure something was wrong. Maybe even tonight she'd corner him and ask him and not be satisfied and ask him again, all the time saying, "Joshua, you're not sleeping, are you?" And "What's going on?" And finally, he'd succumb (s-u-c-c-u-m-b) and tell her.

So, that third day Joshua summoned the courage to return to Henhawk Hill. Maybe it was because some bully on a horse thought he could boss him 'round and scare him. Maybe it was because he knew his Dad was broad and strong and could whoop anyone alive, big white cloak on a big black horse or not. Maybe because these woods always held a serenity for him that he didn't want to lose forever. Heck, even the poets Mrs. Morris made the class read talked about Maine's forests, their beauty, watching nature, feeling its power, its magnificence, its creativity. Well, he didn't know about any of that fancy stuff, just that it was his playground and it weren't for anybody else to steal it from him. The other night might have broken that sense of perfection, but Joshua wanted it back. Bad.

And maybe it was because Pastor Nathan had preached Sunday about David and Goliath, the boy and the giant, facing fear when you know God's on your side, knowin' He's your protector and He has an awesome right hand. Well, it was probably all those things, though Joshua didn't sit around and analyze himself. It was time to be strong. Heck, it was time to get some sleep!

5

He knew this for sure: he was twelve years old now—old enough to help build Dad's new barn, old enough to steer a horse while it tilled a field (well, re-tilled anyhow), and he wanted to deal with this thing himself, then present the facts calmly to Dad and Mom. Before she harangued (h-a-r-a-n-g— oh, darn) him into submission.

He almost laughed in spite of himself. Plus, today was different. First, it was noontime, though the sun was behind clouds. Second, no cross was burning. Third, standin' steadfast at his side was Moe, his big German shepherd, his assurance, his sidekick against fear.

Joshua was skipping the lunch hour at school, but that was a small sacrifice. Heck, in the springtime no one's head's into learnin' anyhow. Mom called it "spring fever." Joshua simply called it "boredom." And besides, it was hot for spring—Dad said it was the hottest he remembered—and it was stiflin' in that schoolroom.

So here he was, feet planted in the exact spot he'd stood those two nights before. He'd found his footprints, molded into the spring-dampened earth. He looked up through the branches toward the place where the cross had burned.

He turned to walk back down the hill, following his trajectory from the other night. He grabbed a dead branch off the ground and began swinging it like a baseball bat as they descended. A minute later, Moe veered off the path and dashed right into a thicket of brush and alders. Joshua tugged at his overalls, pulled the strap up onto his right shoulder, and walked toward the thicket. As he got nearer he poked the dead branch at a bush in front of him and called, "Moe."

The dog growled—low, intimidating. Joshua couldn't see him through the dense bushes.

Again, "Moe." No response. No Moe bounding out, knocking him to the ground and slobbering all over his face. But there was a sound. Joshua tilted his head and listened. Moe was diggin' at the ground.

Joshua tossed the branch aside, approached the thicket and peered in, squinting to see in the darkness. Yep, there he was.

"Here, boy!" he called.

Joshua always told his friends Moe was the most obedient dog in The Crossing. Heck, the world. Now he doubted that. Not today anyhow.

Exasperated, he decided he'd find out close-up what was distracting his dog. He took a step back, readied himself and lunged through the outer crop of branches, driving his legs forward with a burst of strength into the midst of the undergrowth. As he plowed through, there was a blur of branches and boughs, then a startled Moe turning to look up at him just before he fell face-first to the ground at the big dog's side.

Joshua lay face down and caught his breath. He squeezed his fingers into a layer of winter-old moldy leaves covering the earth. Boy, Mom'd make him take a bath tonight, that was for sure. Suddenly, a putrid smell assaulted him. He jerked up onto his knees, and yelled, "Ugh-h. Yuck! Let me outta here!"

He looked down to where his left hand had dug into the leaves. Half a red bandanna stuck out of the ground. He looked a foot to the right, where Moe'd been digging. Reaching out of the earth as if to grasp the sky was a hand, its fingers gnarled and gory, caked with mud and dried blood.

Joshua screamed, screamed again, and again. Freezing shivers bristled his back and sent a shudder the length of his body. With one quick motion, he jumped to his feet, turned, closed his eyes and dove out through the thicket. landing on his back. A wave of nausea swept over him, and he vomited and vomited until his ribs hurt beyond pain and it seemed he'd voided his entire body. Moe whined at his side, and when Joshua looked at him, Moe slobbered a big lick on his cheek.

CHAPTER TWO

Jennifer Craig whisked the apple pie out of the oven with a gleeful flourish. It was a job well done—to welcome spring with apples (canned last fall) and cinnamon, a celebration to awaken the household from its wintertime slumber. She had always loved spring the most of Maine's seasons, and she had always made a point of marking its arrival with a special treat.

Her apple pies were known throughout Androscoggin County, routinely winning blue ribbons at the Maine State Fair in Lewiston. Her masterpieces never ceased to win over the judges, but no one loved them as much as Samuel and Joshua.

Joshua. That little rascal would take all for himself if she didn't watch him. "And that's why," she said aloud as she reached into the oven again, "I made two."

Jennifer brushed her long, golden hair back from her face as a smile curled her lips (Samuel said it would make the world laugh with Job to see that smile). She thought of beams of warm sunlight filling her house, pulling her flowers through the rich earth in the front yard, and these extra-warm days washing away the chilly memories of a lengthy, draining winter. Sometimes it did seem that Maine had two seasons—winter and the Fourth of July. But the last week had been extraordinarily hot and humid for late-spring.

She signed and patted her protruding tummy.

This would be a season of joy for their little family.

"Oh, yes, Elisa, you'll greet this world soon, and how it'll greet you. With beauty, love, security ..."

It was all idyllic in Jennifer Craig's world.

But "security" had barely escaped her lips when Joshua burst in through the screen door at the rear of the kitchen, Moe at his heels. His clothes were covered with dirt and pieces of dead leaves, his face was smudged with perspiration and grime, his hands and sandy-blond hair were caked with dried earth.

He stopped abruptly in the center of the kitchen floor and pulled his thin body up straight. But his green eyes were glazed, not focusing. He glared at her as if seeing through her, staring into nothingness. His mouth opened, yet no sound came out.

Jennifer's breath caught within her. Her head whirled at the sight. She placed a hand on the kitchen counter to steady herself. What began as a tingle of fear spread, sending little pricks of electricity to her extremities.

What was happening? Joshua wasn't bleeding. Was he in shock? Then the thought of terror; something had happened to Samuel! She took a step toward her son, terror gripping at her throat, and Joshua let go a blood-curdling shriek. Jennifer recoiled. It seemed to burst her eardrums.

Just as suddenly, Joshua's legs swayed, his body crumpled and he fell face-forward to the floor. Jennifer lunged to catch him, but he landed with a heavy thud, his small frame offering no resistance, no hand to break the fall.

Her son sprawled on the wood floor at her feet, Jennifer Craig gulped for air, tried to maintain a semblance of calm and to fathom what had happened to her son, perhaps to her husband, and to her shining, glorious day.

ƙ ƙ ƙ

"Catatonic." Doctor John Walker folded his stethoscope while walking down the stairs with Jennifer behind him. He took a deep breath, cautious about what to say. Could be worse. Could be better. Doc didn't like neutral and he didn't like mysteries, but in this case, being in a state of extreme loss of motor skill was at least better than the other extreme of catatonia, constant hyperactive motor activity. Being inactive might be the better thing for the boy.

"Catatonic?" Jennifer repeated.

Reaching the bottom of the stairs, Doc turned to Jennifer. "He's in a state of neurogenic motor immobility."

"Neuro—?"

"It's a psychiatric disorder, my dear."

Jennifer's brow knit.

"Think of it as being in a wide-awake coma. Joshua's in a state of deep unconsciousness that you usually see with someone who's been injured. But, I see no injuries apart from a couple of bruises around his knees. Coulda got them playing ball for all we know. My guess is something traumatized him. Sent him into shock, a state of physiological collapse."

Her eyes wide, Jennifer's hand shot to her mouth.

"Joshua's a strong boy, Jen." He put a hand on her shoulder. "Usually this condition doesn't last more than two or three days. I'll come by again this evening or early tomorrow. Until then, there's not much you can do for the boy but give him plenty of chance to rest. He'll come along."

Jennifer was fighting off tears. "What in the world could've traumatized him that badly?" she asked. Her hands were still shaking and he covered them with his own. He'd brought this girl into this world, and her husband, Samuel, too. She was like a daughter to him, especially since her parents had both died.

And Joshua? Well, he'd delivered him in this very house, tended to him through the whooping cough and measles, and had slept more than one night at his bedside one spring when he suffered with severe bronchitis. The boy had fight, like his Dad.

"There's no telling the cause, my dear," he said. "We may never know—even from Joshua himself."

Jennifer looked up at him, her eyes wide in apparent disbelief. But what else could it be?

"Mental shock, or paralysis can produce retrograde amnesia," Doc explained. "When Joshua awakens, don't push him too hard to find out what happened. Ask him, but don't push it. If he doesn't recall, that alone might alarm him yet again. He may never remember, and that may not be a bad thing."

As if anticipating Jennifer's next question, Doc cut her short. "I wish I could stay but, as you know, Clara's finally going to have that baby of hers. That's where I'm going now, and I've got to ride down to Lewiston tomorrow to pick up a bundle of medicines waiting for me at Central Maine General."

"Give Clara my love," Jennifer said. "I'd hoped to be with her through the delivery, but I talked with her a couple of hours ago, and she understands."

Pulling softly at his chin whiskers, Doc looked for a moment toward the top of the stairway and Joshua's room, and murmured, "Funny thing. Such a strange, strange thing. I *do* wonder what happened to that boy—what was done to him or what he saw. I certainly would like to know."

A door shut at the end of the first-floor hallway toward the kitchen at the back of the house.

"Me, too, Doc." The firm voice was that of Sam Craig. Doc turned to look at the tall, broad-shouldered man. He was browned by the sun, with creases in his brow and calluses on his hands.

Sam's warm, neighborly face flashed a twinkle despite the circumstances. There was a bright substance inside the young man. College-educated, with a degree in animal husbandry, Sam had returned to Cooper's Crossing to farm. "Get my hands dirty, not sit behind a desk," he'd said.

"He'll be okay, son."

"You're right, Doc. 'cause the hand of God is on that boy. No matter what did happen, I trust the Father will deliver him from the fowler's snare. But we're thankful you rode out here so quickly to check him over."

"Well, Joshua's like one of my own—same as you and Jen. I'll do whatever I can. But you're right, ultimately, we're all in God's hands—and what better hands to be in, eh?"

Sam and Jennifer both nodded at that.

"Well, I'll let Jen bring you up to date. I've got to get over to the Whittakers', or Clara's going to have that baby without me."

As Doc stepped past Sam and through the doorway into the daylight beyond, he patted Sam on the back. He looked back a moment later to wave goodbye. Jennifer had run to her husband's arms and was burying great gushing sobs onto his chest.

With a tug at his whiskers, Doc wiped away a tear. Then he was off to his 1921 Commonwealth Touring Motor Car and on his way to deliver a baby.

CHAPTER THREE

Sitting high on her stool behind the long counter, Ada Cutter wondered how to deal with this fellow standing in the middle of her store. He was such a sight. As usual.

She could barely stop herself from shaking her head and revealing her absolute disapproval. But he was a customer. And, by gosh, customers were always right. Right?

Richard Fryer, a short, squat man with a sort of twisted Southern accent, addressed no one and everyone as people milled through the Cooper's Crossing General Store.

"It's a cryin' shame," he said. "I tell ya', a c-cryin' shame a man can't set hisself up in a place and have a s-say as to who c-can or can't move in amongst him."

Fryer was ignoring the odd looks from Ada's customers. He probably thought of them as the grossly uninformed. His furrowed brow creased a bit, and his baggy clothes ruffled even more as he moved his shoulders to a half-shrug and stammered, "D-D-Darned Canucks are f-floodin' across the border, s-sittin' on our land and t-taken' our jobs. Darned if I-I-I'll hire 'em, the trash, even if there weren't n-nobody else."

Ada finally blurted out, "What if Mr. Stridler tells you to?"

Fryer turned on her. "W-Well, he won't, c-cause Mr. Stridler don't like 'em no b-better 'n me." He hesitated, then added, "'N the Whittakers now got that negra boy. Takin' up space. Breathin' our air!"

His eyes blinked quickly. It seemed he was grasping for a control button. Finding it, he changed gears into a conspiratorial tone. "Looks like there may be only one way to keep 'em in line, d-darned frogs, if they k-k-keep comin' in. And I think we m-might've found out about that already."

A new customer entered the store and Ada smiled to herself. This will end the foolishness.

Sure enough, when Fryer puffed up his chest to continue his diatribe, a big hand landed on his shoulder and forced him to turn.

By the look on Fryer's face, he knew who it was even before the firm hand settled on him, for the blended pipe smoke often swirled ahead of Robert E. Lee Stridler wherever he went.

"I think that's quite enough, Richard." Stridler's voice was a deep, stern monotone.

Fryer looked hesitantly up to Stridler's face, not quite meeting his eyes. Tongue-tied on the first syllable, he managed, "Ye-yes, s-s-sir."

"This isn't the time nor the place, and I'm sure Miss Ada would agree." Stridler spoke in a low tone, just loud enough for Ada to hear. Then he leaned toward Fryer and whispered something Ada couldn't make out. Fryer's face transformed from browbeaten to encouraged, and Ada's own brow furrowed as she wondered at the message.

Fryer lowered his eyes, and Stridler, dressed keenly in a suit and silk vest, stepped to the counter and flashed a disarming smile at Ada.

He placed his hands on the counter—the only things which betrayed his link to the land—rough calluses protruding at every finger along the palm.

"Ada, my dear," Stridler said, cupping the bowl of his pipe, "I'd like to see your selection of red cloth ribbon, if I may."

Red ribbon. How odd.

Ada walked to the end of the counter and reached up on a shelf on the back wall. The front door opened again, and she looked over her shoulder. Two men dressed in coveralls and with dirt on their boots stepped inside, waved casually to Fryer and sidled up to Stridler.

"Mornin', Bob," said one, who leaned toward Stridler. "Meetin' still on for tonight?"

Stridler pulled the men aside and murmured something to them. Ada could have sworn it was "Not so crowded in public. Sometime. Some race." But that didn't make any sense. She began to mull over the words, to decipher them.

But then she was certain she overheard "red trim microbes." She'd read about microbes and microbiology in a magazine recently and wondered why these men would be interested in science. Robert Stridler, yes. But Caleb Morse and Red Varney? She shook her head and turned to her selection of yard goods along the store's back wall.

••••

The sun was midway on its way down in the western sky. Around four o'clock, Reverend Nathan Hind thought as he sat and looked through the large window in his study. He read aloud from the first draft of the speech he would be giving during the panel discussion at his denomination's Northeast Conference: "Truth is more practice than theory. Judge all teaching by the Word and what it produces, not by how it sounds."

He had taken I Timothy 6:20-21 as his text: "O Timothy, keep that which is committed to thy trust, avoiding profane and vain babblings, and oppositions of science falsely so called: Which some professing have erred concerning the faith. Grace be with thee. Amen"

Ah, truth, he thought, there's only one truth and yet how often we so disdainfully twist it into oblivion!

He stood, stretched and looked out the window once more and gauged how much more time had elapsed since moments before when he last gazed out. Yet time was of the essence. With a normal delivery and, God willing, no complications, Clara Whittaker might have had that baby by now. And about time, after years of trying—and failing.

He smiled. But just then, thinking of Clara, something out of the ordinary played around in his mind. It pinched at his cheeks.

Something … something's wrong.

He leaned down to his desk, closed his writing tablet, and hurried over the bare floor to the outer hall of the rectory. Picking up his lightweight coat and snapping his collar tight, he stepped into the refreshing spring air outside.

"Dear God," he said, "watch over them. Watch over Clara and the child."

Nathan climbed up into his carriage, picked up the reins and snapped them with authority. His ten-year-old Alt-Oldenburger, Hatty, jumped out with vigor. Good girl. As soon as she was harnessed up, she was always raring to go.

The bustling community of Cooper's Crossing seemed like a windup rag doll freshly wound as Nathan rode down Main Street. People stopped in the midst of their chores and errands, the women nodding, the men waving "Hello's."

He nodded back. He had helped nearly all of them in one way or another over the past fifteen years, as permanent a post as any clergy would get.

Nathan's hearing was extraordinary. He could hear when children whispered from the back pews during a sermon. And so, as he rode past John and Ada Cutter's shop, he could hear the tall, stocky man inside. Perhaps wanting him to hear, Robert E. Lee Stridler said all too loudly, something about ministers needing foresight as opposed to "hind"-sight. Get it? Ha-ha.

A hearty, mean laugh—joined by another—erupted from inside Cutter's. God forbid that Nathan should ever think such evil of a man, but it was difficult to avoid in Stridler's case. And to think the man was named after the great general. In fact, if rumor served true, he was looking to form an army, of sorts, of his own. Probably just gossip, idle speculation, ear-tickling stuff. People did like their ears tickled.

Nathan directed Hatty to the furthest edge of the street. Horse-drawn wagons and carriages and a few newfangled automobiles rolled past him. There went Ivory Gorman in a brand spanking new 1922 Nash. Then Horace Mankins behind a pair of three-year-old twin Percherons. Then Donald White in a year-old LaFayette.

Nathan laughed to himself at the diversity. For himself, horses were the ticket. Hatty knew his voice. She had personality. And she loved to cuddle—something a Nash or LaFayette could never do. Plus, she'd never gotten a flat tire. Not one. He guessed the hay and grain evened out with gasoline in the cost of fuel.

Nathan struggled to think on matters other than Robert E. Lee Stridler. He turned northeast onto Harlowe Way, the road that took travelers up the east side of the Limerick and Androscoggin rivers toward Maine's deepest woods.

Progress, the development made possible by that very forest, was evident everywhere. In the pavement on the streets, the growing number of shops in town, the new equipment and railroad tracks at John Thomas' saw mill on his left.

But also, the less desirable changes. He glanced at Ilsa's Inn on the corner of Main Street and Harlowe Way, where frilly dressed young ladies took "customers" upstairs for brief "rendezvous."

Nathan didn't know exactly who those customers were, though he had heard some stories third-hand. Yet, when the log drives came in, Ilsa's was a booming place.

The drives brought a complete change of clientele around the town, even to his church. The boisterous French-Canadians who composed most of the log-driving crews were themselves a paradox.

On the one hand, they were by-and-large a fun-loving crowd who confined what trouble they caused to their own quarters. On the other hand, they'd been known on occasion to tangle in fisticuffs that bashed up more than one bar.

On the one hand, some of them indulged in liquor and loose women. On the other hand, many of them nevertheless confessed Christ as their Savior and would show up in the Cooper's Crossing Catholic Church.

They were a dichotomy and always would be.

Ilsa herself had attended Nathan's church for a brief time after she moved to town and opened the inn. Early on, he had confronted her with the Lord's Commandments.

"We are to be 'living epistles,' Ilsa," he'd told her. "What kind of epistle will you be with this house of yours?"

Ilsa had seemed dismayed, almost as if she were deaf to his sermons and blind to the words of the Bible. Her response? She didn't return to his church.

When he attempted to approach her again, she resisted. He persisted. She repelled. It appeared to be an irresistible force against an immoveable object—only he knew this battle was in the heavenly realm, not against flesh and blood.

Nathan pushed those thoughts from his mind. Except for what he considered The Seven Bleak Months, two hundred dizzying days of darkness, he had enjoyed his years at Cooper's Crossing. The first eight years, he and his wife, Elva, had labored to build up the congregation in numbers and in spirit—adding a community soup pantry, a free clothing store for the poor, a mid-week Bible study and Sunday Schools for both children and adults. A midwife, Elva had worked hand-in-glove with Doc Walker, and several of the new mothers had joined the church with their husbands and children. The church was bursting at its seams.

Then the world had spun on its axis and crashed into an abyss that held Nathan in turmoil for years. Elva and their baby had died in childbirth. Dark depression, a crushing crisis of faith, and despondency—all combined—were equivalent to being at the bottom of a waterless well.

It wasn't until he was fellowshipping with the town's Baptist pastor, Daniel Osbourne, that he was himself able to climb into the rarified air of restoration with his God.

At that moment, Nathan passed the wood-framed police headquarters and he was drawn from his reminiscences. The jail cells inside were empty now, but Nathan wondered if someday soon, they might be bulging. Needing a new coat of paint to cover its peeling brown-painted exterior, the police headquarters was in sharp contrast to Doc Walker's home next door.

While the jail rested on level land, Doc Walker's home, along the opposite side of the street, stood on a high hillock. While the jail was surrounded by a hay field for forty or fifty yards in each direction, Doc Walker's home was encircled with full-bodied elm trees, their branches filled with buds of leaves. And luscious bushes, dutifully trimmed by Laura Walker, ran the breadth of the front of the house except where a brick walkway led into the front door between the pillars.

Though Doc was The Crossing's finest and most-respected physician and earned enough money to buy and maintain the magnificent home gleaming there in the light of the sun, some of the attributes of his home reflected the doctor's philosophy and indeed the feeling The Crossing's residents held toward the man who had treated many of them from birth to adulthood.

The hedges? They were planted by Aubrey Wilson from his greenhouse operation in lieu of payment for an appendectomy Doc had performed on Aubrey's teen-age daughter. The coat of paint, new last fall, was applied by John Masters and his son in payment for caring for his wife Ann's broken arm. Some beautiful pieces of pine and oak furniture inside the house were also built and some of the wallpapering was done by Doc's patients and their families. And he wasn't averse to accepting a side of beef or pork or chickens or vegetables in payment instead of money.

In fact, when circumstances called for it, he asked for no payment at all.

"Just keep the kids growing strong and sturdy," he might say,
or "Just let me see you once in a while in church on Sundays."

ʞ ʞ ʞ

Nathan rode on beyond the village for about a mile over a
gently curving road through fields, around small slopes and past
heavy growths of trees. The sun was still warm in the sky and
drying the last remnants of yesterday's rain.

Jake Flanders, Ned Beatty, and Fred Sherwood all waved
hellos from their respective fields, where they were preparing the
land for early planting.

It was a beautiful country, this state of Maine. Nathan compared
it favorably to his native, lakeless, mountainless Alabama. But,
as he came upon the last bend in the road before the Whittaker
farm, he looked northwest at the steep hill which stood out from
the midst of the mixed forest like a king's throne. Hemlocks were
few in this woods, but here several rose high toward the blue
sky, serving as a backdrop on the north side of the nearly barren
plateau atop the hill like the back of a throne. It gave the hill a
sort of majesty.

Nathan wondered what, if anything, had happened up there
just nights before. "Father God," he said aloud, "station Your
angels around Henhawk Hill and prevent evil from destroying its
beauty."

A simple and direct prayer. After all, Jesus didn't prattle on
endlessly. He was quick and to the point. That's what Nathan told
parishioners who all too often liked to hear themselves talk when
in a prayer meeting.

The Whittaker farm encompassed hundreds of acres, including
the richest stand of pines in the countryside, but the house itself
sat nearly upon the road. If its four frontal pillars were to fall,
they'd land on the road. The house's two-and-a-half stories
contained more than a dozen good-sized rooms. It had a pair of
Dutch ovens in which Clara could cook a pig, if she wished.

And attached to the back of the house was a dream for a flower-lover like Nathan: a real, honest-to-goodness greenhouse ... not a big one, but not small, either. Until Clara adopted the two children through that foreign relief agency, she'd spent much of her time nursing and tending flowers in that greenhouse.

But over the past couple of years, she had devoted more energy to raising Ming Su and Willie. Ming Su, a six-year-old, had been with the Whittakers about two years now and had learned to speak very respectable English since coming from Southeast Asia.

Willie, a four-year-old Negro, had been with his new parents for a year—many, many miles away from his birthplace which, hopefully, he'd never have to see again. Clara and Matt had confided to Nathan that the child still suffered nightmares about the chilling, repulsive experience when his natural father was killed by white men—Klansmen—in Georgia.

A band of cloaked Ku Klux Klanners had accused Willie's father, a fair-skinned Negro, of consorting with a white woman. Hooded figures had held Willie and forced him to watch as they flogged his father, then branded "KKK" on his head with acid and finally, castrated him, leaving him gushing blood in the middle of a field. He died with Willie clutching at him, screaming and numb with fear.

His mother having died at childbirth, Willie was left homeless. The Whittakers, who had tried unsuccessfully for years to have children, decided to follow their adoption of Ming Su with a second. The result: Willie Whittaker.

Wondering what he would discover inside, Nathan rapped the door banger. In a moment, Matt opened the door and his face broke into a broad beam.

"Impeccable timing!" Matt said. "Come on in and meet the newest Whittaker."

"Hallelujah! Boy or girl?"

"The most beautiful little girl I've ever seen, Nathan." The unmistakable, booming voice from the stairway was that of Doc

Walker. "Believe me, Nathan, curly, auburn hair like her mother's and eyes as deep blue as the sea."

Doc's stout frame moved gracefully, belying his size, as he came down the stairs.

"I'm telling you, Nathan, when Jen and Sam finally got it done, it was"—he drew out the last word—"perfection."

Matt drew up close to Doc and, with a tear working its way down his cheek, said shakily, "I'm forever indebted, Doc. Clara, too."

Matt turned to face Nathan. "The baby was breech and if it weren't for Doc, we'd have lost her—and maybe Clara, too."

Nathan recalled the unease that had been troubling him this morning. So, *that* was the reason. "Well, Matt, doctors and God seem to work together very well. Especially here in The Crossing, where the two are a team."

"Matt," Doc said, turning toward the door and obviously making his departure in true Walkerian fashion that brought a smile to Nathan's face, "I brought Clara into this world about a week after I took up my practice here. I'll never, ever let anything take that fine girl from this world."

Doc tugged at his chin whiskers. With a wink and a nod, he opened the door and added, "You owe me a couple of Clara's New England boiled dinners. Now, get up those stairs to her and that wee one. I'll be back to see you all tomorrow."

He motioned to Nathan to follow him, and held the door open for Nathan to step back through and into the sunlight. When outside, Doc's face transformed from amused to introspective. Was that worry etched there?

"Okay, Doc. You were playing a role and you played it well. Now, exactly what's the problem?"

Intense, Doc leveled his eyes on Nathan.

Anxiety played in the back of Nathan's mind. He waited and waited, then blurted out, "Doc, what's the matter?"

"Oh, I-I'm sorry, Nathan. It's nothing at all to do with Clara or the baby. They're in fine condition and high spirits."

"Well, then?"

Clutching his medical bag, Doc strolled to the horse and buggy in the drive. His face remained stern and thoughtful as he tugged at his whiskers. "Nathan, I'm heading up the road to the Craigs' and I wish, when you get the chance, that you'd ride out there, too. Something very much out of the ordinary has happened to young Joshua."

Nathan took a step backward. He loved that boy like the child he and Elva never had. A bitterness attacked his stomach and he stammered, "Wh-What is it?"

"He came home delirious and very much disheveled late this morning, looked at Jen ('wide-eyed,' she described it) and fainted. He's comatose, in shock, and no one knows why. Now, I don't think anyone should *force* him to tell what happened, but you've always had a way of discovering such mysteries."

Nathan absorbed the doctor's words. "Absolutely. I'll go out there right now."

Doc hesitated, fidgeting and mulling, then replied, "Well, tomorrow would be a better time. I think he'll be more 'with us' then. But thank you, Nathan. Thank you very much."

Doc boarded his buggy, took the reins in hand, and lightly snapped them, spurring his big horse on.

Nathan watched the buggy ride out to the road and turn north and over the Squapan Stream bridge, his thoughts on young Joshua Craig, and his eyes drifted again toward Henhawk Hill.

₭ ₭ ₭

Clara Whittaker was a stunningly beautiful woman, her attractiveness enhanced by a warmness that radiated and enveloped whatever rooms she entered, Nathan thought as he stepped into her bedroom on the second floor. Dressed in a baby-blue nightgown and with her long auburn hair pulled tight and braided, she was propped up on a very large bed cradling her newborn baby in her arms.

Matt, beaming ear-to-ear, stood next to the bed, obviously enamored with both baby and wife. Cuddled up on either side of Clara were six-year-old Ming Su and four-year-old Willie. The baby's right hand was wrapped around Ming Su's index finger.

It was a sight that would remain etched indelibly in Nathan's mind.

Matt waved him into the room, then Willie nearly leaped from the bed and ran to his arms.

"Pastor Nat," he said. "Pastor Nat. We got ourselves a sister!"

Nathan bent down to pick up the boy. "My, oh, my!" he said and squeezed Willie tight. "What a thrill. New life!"

"Thanks for coming, Nathan," Matt said.

Nathan nodded, sure he spotted a tear on Matt's cheek, and looked keenly at the new mother.

"My, my, Clara. How can you look so well-rested and in control so soon after an ordeal of the magnitude I hear you went through?" he asked.

He set Willie down, approached the bed and sat down in a chair by Clara's side. "May I take a closer look at this new addition?"

Clara carefully passed him the baby. Cupping his hand behind the child's head and holding her tiny hand in his, Nathan wondered in amazement at God's creation. Such a tiny creature with such minute parts, but with everything so much in place. A scale model of precision. One word escaped his lips, "Beautiful."

"I can't help but believe you helped make this possible," Clara said, extending her hand to hold Nathan's. "We owe a lot to you—our guardian angel always with a prayer."

Nathan beamed. "You're sweet, my dear." He looked at the baby. "I remember the day this was *you*! And your Mom was laying where you are now."

"Same bed, right?" Clara asked.

"Yep. And your Dad was standing in about the same spot Matt is now." He chuckled.

"I wish they were alive to see their grandbaby," Clara said.

"Me, too. Fine people, your folks." Nathan hesitated. "Do you have someone coming to care for the children while you're taking care of yourself and this magnificent specimen of Whittaker and Linnell blood?"

Clara stirred a bit under the bed sheets. A puzzled look came over her face and her green eyes squinted as a frown creased her high brow.

"I thought I had," she said. "Ida Thurston was going to come help after the birth. She helps me with the spring and fall cleaning, you know."

Nathan nodded.

"She and Ian always need the money. But she came over just yesterday and told me she couldn't do it. She acted so very strange, muttered something I didn't really understand about her husband not approving, and quickly showed herself out. Meanwhile, Jennifer was going to come over and help with the delivery, but then that problem arose with Joshua. So, we're left in quite a predicament."

Matt spoke up. "I'm going now to see if Ann Masters can help for a while, and I can stay at home too for a week or so until Clara can get back on her feet."

Nathan's thoughts lingered on Ida Thurston and her husband, Nick, then Nathan turned his mind to Ming Su and Willie, and to Henhawk Hill and the rumored mysterious flames in the night. Only then did his thoughts wander to memories of his boyhood in Alabama.

No, no, he thought. No such thing could be happening here. Not Maine.

CHAPTER FOUR

Hank Green stood still in their small backyard, his broad shoulders bent, ignoring the solemn stare of his wife from the rear door. He had been standing there like that for some time now, in a state of distress and sorrow, recalling the past—the period when he and his brother Steve were young, and Steve was alive.

Hank and Harriet had just this morning received the news that Steve had died. Hank had listened to how it had happened, then he had told Harriet that he wanted to be alone for a while, and he had gone outdoors. He knew she was worried about him, about what he would do.

Steve was always the hot-tempered one in the Green family, while Hank considered himself easy-going. Even gentle. But the circumstances surrounding Steve's death troubled him. He was in a slow boil. Could he leave these feelings right here in the yard? He knew he'd try but doubted he'd succeed.

Beyond knowing today was Saturday, Hank had lost track of time. The house had suddenly felt claustrophobic, driving him outside. And he had wanted to be alone to cry. He wasn't embarrassed when those tears arrived. Harsh and gulping and uncontrollable at first, now they came in infrequent, short gasps.

That overwhelming grief was now secondary to the hate that tightened his stomach in a knot. He hated the man who had killed Steve. He despised all the men like them. And he'd do all he could to get rid of them.

Steve had lost his job in the mill at Lewiston and had gone to a bar, probably because he couldn't face going home and telling Trisha the news. While in the bar, he'd gotten in a fight with some French-Canadian who worked in the mill. The bartender had later claimed Steve hollered at the man because the guy's relatives were taking Steve's job and the occupations of other Americans in the mills. And, well, if Steve said it, it was darn well true.

The two had become embroiled in a scuffle, had fallen through the bar's front window, and a sliver of glass had pierced Steve's jugular. He'd bled to death before they could get him to Central Maine General.

Hank figured police would determine Steve's death was an accident and set the French scalawag free. There'd be no revenge—not by the law, anyway. But Hank knew that even if that particular Frenchman wasn't guilty, two other parties *were*— the mill owners for hiring foreigners in the first place, and the United States government, politicians, and bureaucrats for letting all these ne'er-do-wells into the country.

Canucks! They were everywhere. Lewiston, Biddeford, Rumford, Portland, Bangor, Rockland. Even here in The Crossing. Hank swore to himself. Heck, a Frenchman owned a mill right here in town—*owned* it! Here was a Canuck who owned a wood mill! And all Hank owned was this little house on this puny piece of property.

This was America, not Canada, not France, and yet some Canuck owned this wood mill! Not an American. Things were mucked up. They were really mucked up. Steve had said just that the last time Hank had seen him. *Oh, Steve—oh, God.*

𝕶 𝕶 𝕶

Harriet was deeply concerned for her husband but was trying to carry on as normally as possible under the circumstances. She was putting dinner on the table when Hank stepped into the house. Sixteen-year-old Tanya and twelve-year-old Joey were sitting across from one another. They had had their cries, or at least Tanya had. Joey had never liked his Uncle Steve. He thought him a bully.

Harriet and the kids looked up at Hank as he entered the kitchen and were silent as he sat down at the table. It was apparent the pain was still twisting at Hank's system, and Harriet wondered how he would work it out. Hopefully, the funeral would help soften the blow, help her husband cope with the loss.

The meal was silent, with one exception. "Tanya, I don't want you seeing that Letourneau kid no more. Never again." Hank spat out the last two words. Tanya began to protest, but her father's glare stopped her cold.

It was a hateful, scary stare Harriet had never seen in the man she loved. She knew her daughter well and it was obvious Tanya's heart was shattered. She wondered if Hank would now demand that Joey stop playing with Andy Letourneau, the younger brother in the family.

When Harriet stood and asked Hank if she could get him a cup of coffee, he rose. "No. I've just decided there's someplace I want to be tonight. Got a meetin' I want to go to." He pulled a ticket out of his pocket. It was about the size of a moving-picture ticket. "I'll be back later on."

"Meeting of what?" she asked as he slipped on a Mattet.

"Oh," he looked at the ticket, "just some men from around town."

And Hank was gone out the door, leaving his wife mystified, and not a little fearful.

₭₭₭

Nathan Hind sat staring at his meal. If someone had asked him what was for dinner, he couldn't have answered even though it sat no more than two feet away.

"What is it, Reverend?" The voice of his housekeeper, Hannah Brown, was overflowing with concern.

Nathan didn't feel melancholy, or stoic, but somewhere in that vast gray area in between, and he realized Hannah knew him well enough to be worried.

"What in the world is troubling you? I sit your favorite meal down in front of you, and you act as though you couldn't care less."

Nathan glanced up at her, then down at his plate of chicken cordon bleu, beet greens, and baked potato with a hefty helping of gravy on the side.

"Hannah, come sit with me for a few minutes, will you?" He pointed to a chair to his right.

This was not an unusual request—not since Nathan's wife died some six years before. Nathan often asked Hannah to sit and talk over issues of the church or community. He trusted her and her opinion. And so, she took the seat to his right.

"I'm troubled," Nathan said. "In my prayer time this morning, I believe the Lord revealed some things to me—about our congregation and the townspeople in general—that frighten me a bit. And if I'm right, I've failed to reach these people with the message of Christ: to love the Lord your God with all your heart and love your neighbor as yourself.

"I've strolled around this town for years, the faces friendly, the voices cheery," he continued. "But the last few weeks, I can almost feel something sinister lurking about. I'll sense a presence, turn about to see who's there, and I swear I have, more than once, seen a slithering dark form move behind a building or into an alley, or just disappear into the air."

Hannah furrowed her brow, listened intently.

Nathan shrugged. "Now I believe what I'm seeing is not a real person but something in the spirit world, some of Satan's legions—"

Hannah flinched.

"You think I'm crazy." It was a statement, not a question.

She shook her head. "You've preached from the Scripture that our fight isn't against flesh and blood but against spiritual forces of evil in heavenly realms. I believe the Word of God, and that's what it says. It sounds like you've gotten a glimpse into that other world."

"I think so, Hannah, and it's frightening. Here, right in our midst, in a town at peace for more than a hundred years. The worst anger I've seen here was at a town meeting, where Bob and Jerry Agee always take the opposite side of every issue." He chuckled wryly at the thought, but it was a short-lived moment. "What do you think, Hannah?"

Hannah drew in a breath. "Gotta say, I've been feeling tension around town too," she said. "Fifty-one years I've lived here. I know every soul who walked its streets, and I sense something I can't really describe. But it's dark."

"Darkness of spirit," Nathan said.

Hannah nodded and whispered, "Oh, dear."

"A portion of the conference will deal with the Ku Klux Klan and how clergy should respond."

"Oh, dear."

"It's here in Maine, not that far from The Crossing. We have to be alert."

"Oh, dear."

Nathan clasped his hands on the edge of the table. "The church has to redouble our prayers for our family, friends, and neighbors in order to save our lives and our future."

"Well, maybe you should call a meeting of the church board about this," Hannah said.

"Good idea, my dear. As soon as I get back from Boston, yes. I'll meet with Harry, Dan and Frank," he said, referring to Harry James, the pastor of The Crossing's Congregational Church; Daniel Osbourne, the town's Baptist pastor; and Frank Lajoie, the St. Joseph's Parish priest.

"We'll take on this battle head-on—and post-haste."

"Good." Hannah rose, then pointed to his plate and added, "But a soldier needs nourishment for the battle. So please dig in, Reverend, while I clean your study."

Nathan again stared at his plate, but what he saw was that dark form vaporizing before his eyes—and he shuddered.

ʞʞʞ

The Cooper's Crossing Grange Hall was immersed in a sort of semi-light provided by low-watt lights from a very high ceiling as Sam entered. Men, some dressed in suits and carrying hats in their hands and some wearing blue jeans and boots covered with dirt from a hard day's work, sat in the stiff, wooden chairs or stood in tight circles talking amongst themselves.

The place sounded like the hum of a nest of large wasps. A menacing tone.

Several men turned and waved to Sam as he surveyed the room and made his way toward the back. One of them, Todd Hamilton, had listened to the night's speaker when he lectured last week on "Americanism," and had told Sam he simply had to be here.

Sam nodded in acknowledgement. Among them were two members of his church, one railroad employee and a farmer.

A small stage, a foot off the ground and twenty feet square was pushed up against the rear wall. A lectern was placed at the front of the stage and centered about ten feet behind it were four chairs. The center-right chair looked exactly like one Sam had seen in a mail-order catalogue. It resembled one King Henry VIII might sit in, only its back wasn't nearly as high.

Sam pulled his watch from his pocket. It was nearly eight o'clock. The poster outside the feed and grain store had read:

> Informational Meeting. A high-class order for men
> of intelligence and character. A purely benevolent
> and charitable institution. The Ku Klux Klan,

Cooper's Crossing Grange Hall. White, Gentile,
Protestant People Welcome. 8 p.m.

Sam was both bothered by, and inquisitive about, the
designation: "White, Gentile, Protestant People." No Catholics?
No native Indians? No blacks?"

Interesting. Todd hadn't mentioned anything about the Klan.

Sam had kept abreast of the KKK phenomenon in Maine,
disturbed by reports and truly not believing all he'd read. Why
would Mainers, after all, feel the need to support the Klan cause?

Last November, Republican Governor Percival Baxter had
dismissed the Klan's validity. Sam had agreed and tried to dismiss
its existence, even when reading about plans in the works for the
town of Milo to allow the first KKK parade in New England. In
fact, if held, it would be the first daylight march by Klanners in
the entire country. So strange. Heck, his great-grandfather had
died in the Civil War, fighting to end slavery.

And now the news was that the Klan had purchased the
massive Rollins Estate on Forest Avenue in Portland for its
headquarters. It would build a four thousand-seat auditorium and
a sixteen hundred-seat dining hall. *Four thousand!*

He guessed he'd find out, firsthand, what this Klan thing was
all about, what lurked behind the posters and hubbub.

If it was good, well then—good. If evil, well then—good to
know. Drop it and move on.

Sam turned an encompassing gaze on the crowd. The side
entrance opened and the doorframe was nearly filled with a large
person draped in a red robe with a small white cross on the left
breast. It had to be Bob Stridler. Stridler stepped into the hall
and four men followed him in—Dick Fryer, his overseer; Simon
Foot, who owned the biggest of the two hardware and farming
equipment stores in Cooper's Crossing; Garner Fletcher, a
leading officer in Northern National Bank; and another fellow he
didn't recognize.

Fletcher, Foot, and Fryer—had to be a joke there somewhere—wore white robes. The face flaps on the peaked hoods on their heads were turned aside to reveal their faces. The stranger must be the speaker—some fellow named F. Eugene Farnsworth. He wore a dark-blue suit with a high-collared white shirt and red necktie. He also sported a Van Dyke beard that reminded Sam of a man he'd watched entertain The Crossing's townspeople when he was a child. Sam's Dad had called the guy a "snake-oil salesman." Sam didn't understand the term then. He did now.

Stridler waved Farnsworth to his side and the two men made their way to the stage, Stridler exchanging greetings with several men. Stridler ascended the stairs two at a time, and took several hand-sized sheets of paper from inside his robes.

Farnsworth, along with Foot and Fletcher, took seats on-stage behind the lectern, while Fryer stopped at the foot of the stairs and turned to face the front of the hall. Fryer looked very official. *Or officious.*

Sam, standing just a few feet away from the stage on the left-hand side opposite Fryer, scrutinized the strange little man. Fryer had arrived in Cooper's Crossing about a year ago.

Word was that he took a room at Helen Rand's boarding house on the outskirts of town but stayed only one night. The next day, he was given the job as overseer of Stridler's farm which encompassed potato, corn, and hay fields—much of the profit from which went toward keeping Stridler's pride and joy, his stable of racing horses. The mystery man—for no one knew his origins, just that he had arrived with a bundle of cash and an attitude—possessed the finest racing horses in Maine and probably the Northeast. He also owned a Duesenberg, but like many other people in the area, he preferred to do his normal traveling on one of his horses or on a wagon behind them.

Fryer seemed to be a nervous man, always twitching. His short, chubby hands were always tugging at twisted pieces of cloth, or rubbing a pebble, or jingling change in his pocket. At this moment, he was pulling at a bit of cloth, wrapping it around his fingers and tightening it by pulling at both ends. Perhaps there was a bit of masochism there, Sam thought humorlessly.

Probably in his early fifties, Fryer was a little shy of normal height, his short-cut brown hair sticking up in odd places. He always looked disheveled.

But what disturbed Sam was Fryer's eyes. Sam liked to look people directly in the eyes when he talked to them. Their sincerity, their honesty, their fakery, their hurt, and their joy were mirrored in their eyes. The eyes, he found, did not disguise the true feelings and intent behind them.

But, during his brief encounters with Fryer, even just passing remarks about the weather, Sam had never gotten a look into Fryer's beady eyes. They were in constant motion, never settling on one thing or Sam's eyes. They certainly gave no inkling of what lurked in his mind.

How did he ever get the job as Stridler's right-hand man? Maybe tonight that question would be answered.

The measure of a man was his feelings on matters and how he turned those feelings into action, and this KKK involvement could speak volumes.

A crack of wood striking wood brought Sam's attention to the stage, where Stridler was pounding a gavel on the lectern. Farnsworth, Foot, and Fletcher sat behind him, with the empty "king's throne" between them.

The noisy room was stilled in a short moment, leaving but an echo of the murmur. Everyone not already in a seat found one and stayed their attention on the tall, robust man at the lectern.

Stridler's large presence commanded respect ... respect, if not admiration. The gavel struck one last blow, bringing a final hush.

His voice solemn and resonant, Stridler began, "Friends and neighbors, thank you for coming. I believe the large turnout, even with the little explanation you've received, illustrates the need for this meeting, the need for true Americans and, as we'll prove tonight, the need for the knights of the Ku Klux Klan."

"Here, here" came calls around the hall.

"To that end, I bring you F. Eugene Farnsworth, the king klaxton of Maine's Ku Klux Klan."

Stridler took a step backward and waved Farnsworth forward while he himself settled into the large seat behind him.

Farnsworth effused confidence. He smiled as if he were about to checkmate a chess opponent. No notes. No need, apparently.

He placed his hands on either side of the lectern, scanned the room, leaned forward and dug in.

"It's been four years since the end of World War One and this country has never needed the Klan more," he said. "Indeed, Maine has never needed the Klan more. Economic distress. Worry over Catholic subversion of American ideals. The loss of Protestant political and economic prominence. The forfeiture of a thousand farms a year and the resultant rural-to-urban shift in our population ... It's all disillusioning, isn't it?"

Scattered responses upheld this assessment.

"And we're here to address those fears. Yet, just the other day Governor Percival Baxter dismissed the validity of our fellowship. The man indolently declared that 'level-headed citizens of Maine will not allow themselves to be influenced by such an organization.'"

Farnsworth took a deep breath. "Well, I say to Percy, Please, dear man, remove your flimflammery from the public discussion! Open your eyes and you will see the truths of the Klan's concerns. They're displayed every single day.

"Rotten politics ... Aliens in our country ... liquor in the speakeasys ... threats against our Bible ...

"Face facts, governor, because the rest of us 'common folk' must live with these facts every hour of every day."

Several men shouted agreement.

Sam twisted uneasily in his seat. He liked Governor Baxter. In fact, he'd voted for the man who had been a friend of his father.

"Politics?" Farnsworth said. "The cheapest thing you can buy in New England today is a politician!"

Roars of agreement met this declaration.

"But the Klan—the Klan can *not* be bought."

More roars.

"Another thing that *can* be bought? And that illegally as well?" He hesitated, drawing out the tension … "Booze. No other state in the Union has such a blot upon its history as Maine in regard to liquor."

Oh, oh, Sam thought. That'll win supporters in any group nowadays.

"Aliens? Foreigners? What harm they?" Farnsworth was full into the swing of things now. "I can show you the tombstones of the murderers of our Presidents—and they're *not* in *Protestant* cemeteries!"

"No, they're not!" several yelled. A shiver flew down Sam's spine at the sound.

"Wake up, Mister Baxter. This so-called *infamous* Ku Klux Klan is going to elect the next governor of the state of Maine, and we are not going to stop there."

Fists shot to the air.

Farnsworth seemed to rise to the tips of his toes to gain an inch or two to his modest height. "We shall see you, Percy, replaced by a true man of honor, of grit, of substance: Ralph Owen Brewster!"

Cheers rang out all around Sam, reverberating off the tin ceiling.

"And soon afterward, we will elect Hodgdon Buzzell of Belfast, the first member of our Belfast klavern, the Maine State Senate President!"

Hoots and applause.

"Friends, you're no doubt aware that the Klan is active from Kittery to Fort Kent, from Portland to Bangor, from Augusta and Gardiner to Rockland, and even in towns like Dexter, Milo, and East Hodgdon way up in Aroostook County.

"Every day three thousand five hundred men are joining the Klan across America. That's three thousand five hundred!"

Applause carried like a wave over the crowd.

"Why?" Farnsworth asked. He settled back down and lowered his thunder to a calm breeze. "Because men—men like you—" he pointed a finger around the hall, "are waking up to the fact that the future of America, of the white race, of morality, and of our position in the eyes of God lies with the success of the Klan."

"Here, here's" again echoed through the hall. Sam looked about him at the cross-section of men. Most were listening intently. Heads nodded. A few eyes were even moist.

Lowering his voice, Farnsworth said, "Now, thus far, your chapter is small one in number but, Exalted Cyclops Stridler tells me, its members are stout in heart and in their desire to better your town and our society. To those knights among you, I say, your principles will be shown to be true, you will grow in strength and numbers, and that growth will make the Cooper's Crossing klavern more aggressive and progressive."

Farnsworth's eyes bore into the crowd.

"And with an indomitable desire to achieve success against the evils that are jeopardizing our existence and our livelihood."

Applause exploded.

Farnsworth breathed deeply. "Thousands across this beautiful state are joining us because they now realize that we must join together if we want to preserve our state's beauty and keep it in our hands rather than have it fall into the hands of aliens.

"Aliens who serve another God—and pray allegiance, *not* to America, but to a man on the other side of the world. Aliens who have never risked their lifeblood in this country's defense. Aliens who have come here uninvited and unwanted by the great majority of Americans!"

Jeers and howls met this outcry.

Farnsworth straightened his back and drove on, "The very reason we exist today is because we're threatened by outside forces, outside movements that will twist our lives if we don't take action. We exist today because the purity and leadership of the Anglo-Saxon civilization must be protected against the havoc that may be wrought by the wave of immigration from Ireland, from southern and eastern Europe and, most of all, from Canada."

Sam averted his eyes from the man on stage. *I've apparently been too isolated lately to* not *have noticed this sentiment growing.* He shrugged, a heavy weight on his shoulders.

Farnsworth wasn't done. "The Klan exists today," he declared, "because the mongrelization of the white race is a dreadful peril, and we must face up to it and stop it. We exist today because American land should be owned by those who founded, fought for, and created—with muscle and desire and blood—this free country. We exist today to protect America against the invasion of aliens and Roman Catholics, Jews and, yes, Negroes! Negroes here in Maine? Yes! It was all of three years ago, in 1920, that NAACP chapters were formed in Portland and Bangor, and the one in Bangor succeeded in prohibiting parts of our movie, *Birth of a Nation*, from being shown! An excellent movie. A powerful movie. A necessary movie. Censored!"

Boos bounced off the ceiling and hisses filtered through the crowd.

The hair bristled on the back of Sam's neck.

"We exist today to stop the aggression of the Catholic Church and the government's part in that belligerence. Not only Jews, but Catholics as well have increasingly objected to the reading of the King James Bible in our classrooms. The Bible!" He threw up his hands in dismay. "And yet our state legislators continue to ignore our pleas to stop granting aid to Catholic schools. Catholics who disdain our Bible. All of this leads to taking the Bible out of schools completely. Imagine our children being raised without the word of God!"

This must be what drew Todd, a faithful churchgoer, to this meeting, Sam thought. The crowd was in full hoot now. Anger boiled throughout the hall.

His voice reaching a crescendo, Farnsworth pounded a fist on the lectern and boomed, "And we exist today because tomorrow—yes, tomorrow may be too late!"

Farnsworth's body slumped, then his shoulders. There was a noticeable metamorphosis in the air. His face maintained a tension, but he emanated an appearance of control. *Snake oil.*

No question, this fellow knew both the situation and his place in the order of it.

Sam continued to gauge the crowd. Farnsworth held them in the palm of his hand, like a baseball pitcher does a baseball. If he wanted to throw a fastball, he could. A slider, he could. Indeed, he had just thrown a curveball of historic proportions.

The proof was the faces in the crowd. Like one, they exhibited a startled acceptance of all he'd said. Each sentence was a revelation.

Seconds later, Sam sidled out of the building. He doubted anyone noticed, for all their attention was on the man with the Van Dyke wearing the red necktie.

When he had mounted his horse to trek back home, Sam heard one pair of hands clap, then another, then an explosion of applause.

KKK

Inside, Stridler watched and waited as Farnsworth accepted his fill of the praise, then pressed the palms of his outstretched hands toward the floor to quiet the crowd. The seconds ticked on, however, as a steady murmur combined with clapping hands. The dream was coming true. Again. Here in Maine. So far north of his roots. So far north of where he would have believed it possible. A rebirth. For the Klan. And for him.

When the din subsided Farnsworth turned aside, and Stridler nearly leaped to his feet and strode to the man's side.

"The Klan lives!" Stridler said.

"It does indeed!" Farnsworth responded.

"Thank you, Eugene," he said. "For your honesty, for your forthrightness, for telling hard truths we might not want to accept but must."

He clapped as Farnsworth took a seat and the hall again broke out in applause.

After a long minute, Stridler stood behind the podium and, in a voice of controlled force, declared, "Yes, French-Canadians—Roman Catholics all of them—are threatening to overthrow our government to replenish their Pope's coffers. Their loyalty is to the Pope, not the country that feeds, clothes and nurtures them."

A sound of confirmation mingled through the crowd.

"These Frenchmen are bringing all sorts of ills down upon us." Farnsworth's voice bristled with contempt. "To our south, in Lewiston and Biddeford, they're taking the textile jobs created by true Americans and meant for true Americans. To our north, lumberjacks from Canada are chopping down our trees, pocketing much of the profit from our woods, and bringing liquor and sin with them."

Stridler looked at his watch. "And when are they coming?" He looked back up. "Soon enough! Lumberjacks coming right here to Cooper's Crossing, filling our beloved town with wickedness."

Again, boos circled the hall.

Stridler barged on, "We cannot continue to tolerate aliens taking American jobs and the wealth that rightfully belongs to the white race to those who didn't toil to make that wealth possible."

Stridler bowed his head and asked, "Looking around you, and it need not be too hard, what dangers do you, dear friends, see threatening to crush and overwhelm the Anglo-Saxon civilization?"

A cacophony of answers rang out. A number of fists shot up in the air.

Stridler smiled to himself. *Going well.*

He looked up and pointed at several men who had called out answers. "Right. Right. And right! Foreigners, alien dogmas and creeds, all pressing down upon us and trying to slowly push native-born, white Americans into the center of the country. If we don't fight back, at some point in the future we will ultimately be overwhelmed and smothered!

"The answer lies with you, Ike Dawes, and with you, Hank Taylor." Stridler pointed to the two men. "I've only been here a short time, but I know both of your grandfathers and great-grandfathers sweated and toiled all their lives to bring life to the land you're farming today. Do you want to lose that land to an alien?"

"No!" the two men answered in concert.

"And the answer lies with you, Silas Clark, and you, Cecil Chamberlain." Again pointing at the men he had singled out of the audience, he asked, "Are you willing to refuse the purchase of goods from your stores by aliens? Are you willing to give a little for the cause you know to be a good and just one—yes, a just one in the eyes of God? God, who commanded we not worship idols and graven images. God, who said 'Call no man "Father"?' God, whose demand is ignored by these one-and-the-same Roman Catholic French-Canadians.

"And you," Stridler said, his eyes moving over the entire assemblage, "are you willing to commit yourselves to doing something to help turn the scheme of things in favor of the true, one-hundred-percent Americans, to maintain solidarity of American tradition and the American family—"

Rumbles of affirmation.

"To fight against such evils foisted upon us from these French lumberjacks?"

It felt like the walls were shaking.

"Yes, immorality, bootlegging, and sexual permissiveness on the very streets of Cooper's Crossing!"

Now the floorboards wobbled under restless feet.

"If you're not willing, then we can pack our bags this moment. We can move away and leave behind all of what we and our forefathers have worked and strived for."

Shouts of "No!" echoed around him.

Stridler stiffened his shoulders. "But if you *are* willing, we can overcome our challenges. We can maintain the Caucasian race as the dominant race in this country, and the values and virtues of old-stock America as those representing all our people."

The hall boiled with raised voices. All positive.

"And we can assure ourselves of a future—an outlook of prosperity, freedom of choice and religion and speech. And—" Stridler raised a clenched fist high, "and a future blessed by God!"

Cheers rang through the hall. Not a man in the room was seated.

Stridler turned to look at Farnsworth. They exchanged smiles. The Klan has arrived, Stridler thought. And is firmly entrenched.

When, after a minute passed, the applause died down, Stridler motioned to Simon Foot, then told the crowd. "I'll now turn the lectern over to our klaliff, or vice president, to explain the structural aspect of our organization and how people may join."

ꗏ ꗏ ꗏ

Foot took his place at the lectern as Stridler stepped back to the throne-like chair in the center. From his feet to his long and narrow nose on his long, narrow face, Foot looked like someone had taken an average-sized person and put him through a wringer, lengthening each appendage and each feature. As if his character would be incomplete without them, very large ears graced his head and a high forehead receding to thinning hair.

Scattered applause greeted Foot. He squinted, looked out over the crowd, tried to stop the quiver of his hands and cleared his throat. He'd never addressed a large assemblage. Indeed, a board-room meeting of nine made him quake. But he gathered himself and began, "Th-thank you. I'm, ah, I'm going to try to keep this part of our presentation brief. There'll be plenty of time to, ah, to expound on it further to those who express m-more interest."

"Klansmen have more than six million brothers from Georgia to California and from Texas to Wisconsin," he said, and as soon as he opened his mouth, he felt an odd transformation. He could do this. He knew his stuff. So, like Stridler, he could exude leadership.

He squared his shoulders and continued, "As a fraternal order, the Klan is unparalleled. As a beneficiary organization, it is unsurpassed. As a force supporting laws that protect unspoiled Americanism, it exceeds any association in the history of our country.

"Because its ideals encompass those of native Americans in all our states, the Klan has structured its membership by regions," he said. "At the top of the pyramid is Colonel William J. Simmons of Alabama.

"Colonel Simmons is the Imperial Wizard and oversees the Invisible Empire. In reforming the Klan, he has divided it into state realms, each of which is headed by a King Dragon. Each realm has provinces, all led by Grand Titans. And within each province are the individual klans, or klaverns, encompassing a city or town, each klavern being presided over by the Exalted Cyclops.

"Officers in each klavern are entitled klaliff for vice president, klokard for lecturer, kludd for chaplain, kligrapp for secretary, klabee for treasurer, kladd for conductor, klorago for inner guard, klexter for outer guard. But the most important link, the invaluable, irreplaceable force behind the great strength of the Ku Klux Klan, are the klansmen."

Stridler's low-toned voice behind him urged, "Get on with it, Simon."

He nodded and stepped up his tempo. "Klansmen, themselves, distinguish us as America's most high-class order. Therefore, we ask ten questions of all potential members."

Foot held up his right forefinger, then the middle, then the ring, as he rattled off the questions:

"Is the motive prompting your ambition to be a klansman serious and unselfish?

"Are you a native-born, white, Gentile, American citizen?

"Are you absolutely opposed to and free from any allegiance of any nature to any cause, government, people, sect, or ruler that is foreign to the United States of America?

"Do you believe in the tenets of the Christian religion?

"Do you esteem the USA and its institutions above any other government—civil, political, or ecclesiastical—in the whole world?"

Men around the hall were nodding their heads at each question. On to his left hand.

"Will you, without mental reservation, take a solemn oath to defend, preserve, and enforce the United States and its institutions and government?

"Do you believe in clannishness, and will you faithfully practice the same toward klansmen?

"Do you believe in and will you faithfully strive for the eternal maintenance of white supremacy?

"Will you faithfully obey our constitution of laws, and conform willingly to all our usages, requirements, and regulations?

"And, finally, can you always be depended on?"

Foot let his eyes wander over the faces in the audience— nearly all of them he knew, many he had loaned money to, then concluded, "A person must be able, with his hand on the Bible and the fear of God in his heart, to answer all ten of the questions affirmatively in order to join the Klan. Loyalty—to America and the Caucasian race—and dependability—to do what the Klan asks of you—are absolute necessities."

Backing up a step from the lectern, Foot turned to Garner Fletcher and asked, "Now, Fletch, will you enlighten the people on the initiation fee?"

ꝅ ꝅ ꝅ

Fletcher, already on his feet, walked jauntily to the podium. At six-foot, he was a big man, brawny. Tight muscles bulged beneath his robes. He made sure any new acquaintance knew he starred on the wrestling team at Harvard.

Fletcher was sure about one thing; he would not mince words. "I'm the Cooper's Crossing klan's klabee or treasurer. And, as you might have guessed, it takes a great deal of money for the Ku Klux Klan to fight this battle for America," he said. "Involved is a great amount of organizing, printed matter to carry our message, and the few salaried people who can devote their full time to the fight.

"However, amazing as it may seem, we ask very, very little from those who join our ranks. A one-time initiation fee of ten dollars for lifetime membership. That's all.

Turning, Fletcher nodded to Stridler.

ꝅ ꝅ ꝅ

Stridler approached the front of the stage and stood beside the podium. *Time to close the deal.*

His hands at his side, his voice dripping with sincerity, he said, "It's a solemn task we face, and we need your help settling the imminent problems we've exposed her tonight."

His voice swelling, Stridler declared, "But we must face it. We can no longer turn our backs in hopes the problems of our society will disintegrate. They are no illusion, no mirage confronting a dying man on the desert. They are very, very real and they challenge all of us who are very much alive now, but will remain alive *and content* only if we take action—action against encroachment on our land, our morality, our religion, our great country, and our supreme race."

Stridler stood quiet for a moment, then in a calm voice added, "Only with your help can we conquer the dreaded woes we've described. Think over all that has been said, consider the ten questions our klaliff listed, and ask for God's assistance in your decision. That done, contact one of us or a klansman you know.

If you fulfill our requirements, arrangements will be made for your 'naturalization' as a klansman."

Stridler turned on his heel and strode off the stage, Farnsworth joining him at his side. Like the Red Sea, the crowd fell away on both sides, making way for their departure. Fryer joined them, with Foot and Fletcher trailing close behind. Hands reached out to greet them and he and Farnsworth accepted affirming pats on their shoulders.

All around the hall, men stood, talking excitedly in little clutches. *Sweet victory.*

Stepping outside, Stridler laid his eyes on his big Appaloosa mare, Brisia, tied to a hitching post and chomping away at a bag of oats hanging before her. Brisia, named for Briseis, the woman Achilles loved in Homer's *Iliad*. Back home in the South, a woman had been Stridler's Achilles heel. He wouldn't allow that to happen again. And Brisia, his prime transportation, was his constant reminder of that resolution.

Yes, all is right with the world.

₭ ₭ ₭

Sam unsaddled his horse in the barn and began to brush him down. His mind raced with whispers of what he had just heard at the grange.

"The purity and leadership of the Anglo-Saxon civilization must be protected" ... an "invasion of aliens and Roman Catholics and Jews" ... the "mongrelization of the white race."

"What in the world is happening, Lord?" he asked aloud. "We haven't learned from history?"

As if an invisible force were pushing him, Sam dropped to his knees, compelled to pray, to plead: "Father God, deliver this community from evil forces, from lying spirits, from demons of hate and bigotry and selfishness. Speak by Your Spirit to the people in this town to flee from evil speech. And please, God, reveal the true nature of the Ku Klux Klan to everyone. Deliver, especially, the leaders of this movement out of the hands of the enemy. And may You be glorified, Lord, in our lives. Amen."

CHAPTER FIVE

The tantalizing aroma of venison and eggs frying on a skillet wafted into the woods surrounding the small clearing where the meal wagon was hitched. Emile Francoeur breathed it all in and smiled. He rolled up the sleeves of his red-checked flannel shirt, pulled his green flannel pants up over his belly, tightened the suspenders and bent over the large open fire. He was tending three oversized skillets, one filled with venison, one with bacon, and one with scrambled eggs.

When ready, he'd place them in one of three big cylindrical containers hanging over a second fire. Biscuits cooked on another frying pan hanging over the fire.

Emile was thankful that it was spring. The cold of the long winter was past and the clouds of black flies, no-see-ums, and mosquitoes that accompanied the mid-summer months were yet to appear. The spring and fall—with their beauty of life and colors—coddled him in a powerful fondness for these woods through the years. He rubbed his balding head and recalled he had a full head of red hair when he first took to lumberjacking.

Emile looked through a thin line of trees bordering the clearing to the west. Beyond them flowed Alamoosook Stream, roaring with swollen spring-thaw waters from Gooseye Mountain to the north and Hemlock Mountain to the east.

Just a few miles to the south, Alamoosook flowed into Limerick River which grew deeper and wider and in turn joined the Androscoggin River six or seven miles further at the town

51

of Cooper's Crossing. The end of the spring log drive was, therefore, within sight, for Cooper's Crossing was the destination of the logging crew with whom he worked.

The muffled crunch of a branch breaking under pine needles came from the trees just to the north of the clearing. Emile turned to look. It would be the crew checking in for breakfast—and none too soon.

He walked to the stove and removed a tray with two dozen of his buttermilk biscuits. Everyone's favorite.

"Hey, hey, Emile. Leave it to you. You found a perfect site—right next to the stream." It was the loud, carefree voice of Jigger Jacques. As usual, Jigger was the first man into the clearing. Count on Jigger; first to sharpen his ax, first to begin chopping down the trees, first to ride the logs downstream, first to tackle a log jam. Small wonder he had been the pride of even the Bangor Tigers—the best of the world's lumberjacks.

Emile looked over his friend and shook his head in awe. That Jigger was in his fifties showed only in the lines of his leathery face, aged by sun, the cold, hard work and Maine's harsh wilderness. He was the spryest man in camp, and although small, he was the most wiry and toughest of the muscle-bound lumberjacks in the crew.

One by one, two dozen lumberjacks followed Jigger into the clearing and strode expectantly toward the wagon where Emile was preparing to ladle out their breakfast. They'd been working for more than two hours—since the sun rose over Hemlock Mountain—and they were ready for a couple of servings each of Emile's tasty grub, especially those biscuits.

"Mangé vu. Dig in, men," Emile said as they formed a line at the wagon. Speaking to no one, he asked, "How far upstream are you?"

The answer came in the thick French of Andre LaRoche, the drive foreman, who earned the respect of his men as much by the work he did at their side as by his knowledge of the woods and the rivers.

"A couple hundred or so yards," LaRoche said. "This would be the perfect place if we hadn't run into trouble at Ripogenus Rapids. By God above, I swear those rocks are bigger and more jagged every year I run this stream."

He shook his head in apparent dismay. "No matter how high the water's runnin' they're always high enough to cause a jam. Next time, we're gonna bypass 'em. We'll haul the logs below Ripogenus by wagon. Springtime or not."

Andre stood in the middle of the line, his crew grumbling agreement.

Yvan Rousseau, a huge man who towered over the others, declared, "I'd rather haul those logs all the way to Limerick River than try to run those rapids again. That's the biggest log jam I've ever seen on any *stream*. I had a stick of dynamite ready, but then Jigger. Well, Jig—"

"The Jig," Andre interjected, "got right down in there, gave a little nudge to just the right log, and when that wall of wood came down on him—"

"He just hopped aboard like he was gettin' on a train headin' south," Yvan chortled.

"Yessiree, Jigger," said a young man standing next to him, "I believe you could ride the bubbles of a bar of soap to shore in a hurricane."

Everyone broke out in laughter and words of agreement.

Emile watched his friend's response, figuring it would be memorable. He passed Jigger a plate of food and a mug of coffee. With the flicker of a smile and devilishness in his eyes, Jigger stepped out of line and replied, "Yep, Monty, maybe so."

Holding his plate in the palm of one hand and the steaming mug of coffee in the opened palm of the other, Jigger danced a jig. Not a crumb of food spilled. Nor a drop of drink.

Grinning, he repeated, "Maybe so."

ʞ ʞ ʞ

Monty—born Albert Lamontagne, a name shortened to "Monty" the first day he stepped inside the one-room schoolhouse in St. George, New Brunswick—got his own plate full of eggs, bacon, venison, and biscuit and black coffee and joined Jigger on the trunk of a blown-down oak tree at the edge of the meadow nearest the stream.

Monty was the youngest of Andre LaRoche's crew. He had joined it early in the winter. Not quite twenty years old, he was strong and willing, but, the woodsmen soon found out, green as a month-old sapling.

Jigger had immediately taken him under his wing, taught him to use the two-man saw and hitch up a log sleigh. Last week at Spoon Lake, he'd shown him how to build a boom as the crew moved its bounty of logs across the lake to its outlet at the Alamoosook.

Monty not only was grateful for the help and attention, he looked up to Jigger as the supreme logger and riverman. All the men said he was the best, and when Jigger had a few belts in him he was prone to indulge in his own bit of self-flattery.

The standing joke about Jigger was "Give him a second and he'll take an hour." He could—and regularly did—regale the crew for hours on end over a hot stove on a winter night.

Looking at Jigger devour some venison dipped in honey, Monty recalled the day, shortly after Monty had arrived, when Pierre Bonanfant showed up in camp. A broad, tall man, Pierre was half-French, half-Indian—his mother being a Passamaquoddy from way Downeast in Maine. His long, sleek black hair was tied in a ponytail, and he wore deerskin pants, shirt, and moccasins.

Dropping a homemade backpack to the ground, Pierre had asked Yvan where the foreman was, then had approached Andre and asked for a job.

When Andre asked if he had experience, Pierre declared in French, "My daddy was a lumberman, a great lumberman, and he taught me all that is known. I've run the Penobscot, the St. John, and the Kennebec rivers, and I've logged from New Brunswick to Moosehead Lake." He pointed to his head. "In here is the Frenchman's knowledge of lumbering and the Indian's wisdom of the woods."

Overhearing the conversation going on just outside the log cabin in the middle of the camp, Jigger had set down his jug of potato brew, jumped from inside the cabin through the door and roared, "Injun'! I can run faster, move sideways quicker, jump higher, squat lower, shout louder, trim a tree swifter, and spit further into a wind than any man in camp."

Then, with just a bit of deference to Andre, he had proceeded to tell Pierre he had a job if Pierre could beat him just once in ten tries at the lumbering sport of his choice. When Pierre chose ax-throwing, Jigger released a low, snide laugh.

Monty carved a bull's-eye target on a tree thirty feet away, then stood with the entire crew stood behind Jigger and Pierre to watch.

Jigger gaped a wide smile at Pierre, hefted his ax, drew it slowly behind his ear, took aim, then let the ax down to his side. He turned, looked up at the much taller Pierre and asked, "Sure you don't want to choose another contest, like racing me to the river and back? You're so tall and," he gestured to the younger man's legs, "so long-legged."

Pierre shook his head.

Jigger shrugged. "Okay, then."

Monty wondered how this would turn out. This Pierre was twice Jig's size.

Jigger again hefted the ax, winked at Pierre, then turned and let the ax fly. The ax head flipped once, twice, three times, then thunk! Square in the center of the bull's eye.

Pierre's eyes lit up, obviously stunned.

Then Pierre took aim, stepped forward and with a fierce effort released his ax. Monty let go a relieved breath as the ax stuck the base of the trunk, three feet below the bull's-eye.

"Best of five?" Jigger asked.

Pierre nodded and the next three minutes saw Jigger pierce the bull's-eye within inches of each other throw. Pierre's efforts went left, right and high, the last one clipping a hunk of bark off the tree.

Jigger exchanged looks with Andre, then faced Pierre with a glimmer in his eye. "Know what? All or nothing on this next toss. You go first."

Pierre erased a defeated look from his face, and Monty guessed what was to come.

Jigger stepped aside as the as the big newcomer straightened his back, breathed deeply, raised his ax and let it sail. It went straight and true and buried into the heart of the tree, a foot below the bull's-eye.

Jigger moved into place, grunted something in French that probably only Pierre could hear, then whipped the ax toward the target. It flipped twice, then grazed the tree, skipping into the earth several feet away.

"I guess you've earned your place in camp, son."

"You didn't have to do that," Pierre said.

Suddenly fully sober, Jigger replied, "No. But I needed to find out if Jean-Louis Bonanfant's little boy really did learn all he was taught. If you're half the logger and half the man with half the heart of your daddy, then you're welcome here."

Andre stepped forward and stretched out his hand toward Pierre. "He's right."

Monty and the rest of the crew had gotten a new colleague and learned a bit more about their Jigger.

ꝛ ꝛ ꝛ

As the days passed by, Jigger told the crew about Jean-Louis, who had taught Jigger his trade the same way Jigger was tutoring Monty.

Fragments of that story spilled out when Jigger was "well-oiled" and sitting down with the big half-Indian, a dozen years his junior. "That daddy of yours," Jigger said one day. "That daddy of yours was as strong as an oak. He'd walk a felled pine barefoot, and kick off every branch from top to bottom."

The men laughed, but Jigger knew they half-wondered if what he said was true.

His favorite story? Jean-Louis and he were entering a work site in Wytopitlock in Aroostook County—or, to Mainers just The County—where a giant of a woodsman was chopping down a tree.

"Jean-Louis walked up to the man," Jigger said, "and told him, 'That ain't the way to do it.' The fella growled at him, flexed a muscle that would scare a bear and handed him his ax as if to say, 'Prove it.'

"Well, Jean-Louis shook his head, took his own ax and with one swipe, felled the tree. That Mainer just stood there in awe, dumbfounded, not knowing what to say for the longest time. 'squitoes flew in and out of his mouth it was so wide open. A squirrel coulda nested in his beard without him knowing, he was so comatose."

Jigger raised himself up to full height and continued, "Finally, he asked, 'Where'd you learn to do that?' 'The Sahara Forest,' Jean-Louis answered. To which the man said, 'That's the Sahara Desert, isn't it?' Jean-Louis looked at him crossways, like he was inspecting a simpleton, and replied, 'Yeah, *now*.'"

Today, Jigger felt Pierre was as close as a brother, for Jean-Louis had been like Jigger's adopted father before Jig went off to Michigan for a few years to work.

In fact, he looked at the whole crew as family not only working together but spending the fruits of that work together.

🕮 🕮 🕮

Jigger felt obligated to share the learning experience he had received from Jean-Louis. And young Monty was his ideal pupil.

The time was drawing near, Jigger told him, when they'd reach Pocomoonshine Mountain, and just beyond that, Cooper's Crossing, the final destination.

In Jigger's book of destinations, both had their strong points. But Pocomoonshine? Ah-h, it had a *special* eccentricity.

"Suzie Cooley," Jigger said softly, almost mystically. "Suzie's what's at Pocomoonshine Mountain. Suzie and her specialty, that is."

Jigger took a slug of coffee and pointed a finger at the black liquid inside. "Bitter, right?'

Monty nodded.

"Add a few drops of Suzie Cooley's specialty—" he leaped into the air and pirouetted, "and this coffee'll slap you awake in the morning and cuddle you to sleep at night. Phew!"

Jigger pulled his shirt up to his chin and pointed to his hairy chest. "This was bare until my first swig of Suzie's homemade whiskey."

Jigger looked about him to his fellow crew members. "True, right?"

They all nodded and laughed.

Jigger then turned his attention back to Monty. "They can have their gold rush out there in California. Here in Maine? It's Suzie Cooley's potion. It'll make ya' dance like a flamenco and sing like a canary. And it'll grow hair on your feet so's you'll never have to wear boots again."

Drawn in by the joke, Monty automatically looked at Jigger's bare feet and remembered how he'd looked with astonishment when he first saw Jigger walking on new-fallen snow, barefooted. Monty had discovered Jigger seldom wore footwear, even caulked boots at river-driving time.

A soft, "Oh, mon Dieu," slipped from Monty's lips and he looked up. "But I thought the way you all mentioned Suzie Cooley's name with reverence, that she was, you know, a woman of, well, another sort."

"'Another sort,' indeed!" Jigger replied, "Half-squaw, half-white woman. She lives on that mountain, grows taters and herbs, and digs roots, then combines 'em all in this big still." He lifted his arms wide. "Her customers come from all over, and I'm proud to say I'm one of her oldest and best. Yep, Suzie's 'another sort' all right."

Pierre chortled and declared, "But, Monty, seeing Suzie herself is as much an experience as drinking her potion."

Jigger shot Pierre a warning look and Pierre took notice and continued quietly, "What I mean is she's tiny and old and her skin's like baked leather—"

"But it's as tight as bark on a tree," Jigger said

"Probably those roots she cooks up take away the wrinkles," Andre said with a laugh.

"If you were blindfolded but for seein' Suzie," Pierre said, "you could tell what time of the year it was by what she was wearing. As the temperature goes, so go her clothes. In the midst of winter, she must wear eight or ten dresses. And as the weather gets warmer, off come the dresses one at a time until in the midst of summer, she's down to one. Yep, old Suzie's somethin' special."

"A stick of dynamite," Jigger concurred, but already his mind was recalling Cooper's Crossing, the thriving community situated at the fork of Limerick and Androscoggin rivers. A place with neat, large farms on its outskirts and fine, well-kept houses tucked within the trees just skirting its Main Street. A picture of serenity. But a place that also offered the sweet joys hankered for by loggers who had been away for months cutting down and moving logs to The Crossing's two sawmills.

"Now, Cooper's Crossing—that's a place." Jigger winked at Pierre, lowered his gaze on Monty and, taking a mouthful of scrambled egg, said, "Don't compare to Bangor, mind you. I mean, Bangor's got its Exchange Street with great backhouse bars and cathouses. But, The Crossing's got Ilsa's. And Ilsa—well..."

Jigger turned to Pierre with a twinkle in his eye, then began to sing with Andre, Yvan and the others joining in:

"Came into Cooper's Crossing the eighth day of June,
Walked into the town with the full of the moon,
Stalked the length of Main Street and this was my doom,
I paid a call on sweet Ilsa's saloon."

Breaking into laughter, the crew boomed on:

"I boldly walked in and stepped up to the bar,
And a dashing young beauty says, 'Have a cigar.'
She says, 'You're a logger, right well do I know,
For your muscle is hard from your head to your toe.'"

As they finished, Jigger looked straight ahead to the nearby stream with a look of recollection in his eyes. Abruptly, he hopped to his feet, scaled his near-empty tin dish into the meadow, jumped like a kangaroo through the bit of woods bordering the stream, and leaped out into the boiling torrent, landing on a log.

"Yahoo, Ilsa, I'm coming!" he hollered. "I'm coming!"

But Jigger struggled to maintain his balance on the wildly turning log. Just as the men stood and cheered him, with the suddenness of a lightning flash, Jigger's feet went out from under him and he flipped backwards into the rushing, crushing current. He gulped a deep breath of air just as he was yanked under the water. Logs galloped around and about him, banging his head and shoulders with deadly velocity. He struggled to get above the water but didn't know what direction was up. A great force of water gushed into him and cracked his head against a rock.

🐾 🐾 🐾

When Jigger went underwater, Pierre shared a look with Monty beside him. They leaped up and raced to the stream.

Pierre reached down and broke a long alder off at its base. "Grab my hand!" he yelled at Monty.

Monty wrapped an arm around a riverbank tree and stretched his hand to grab Pierre's spare hand. Putting one leg into the stream, Pierre extended the alder out over the rushing water near where Jigger had fallen. Not a sign of him. The water was frigid. It would steal the breath from anyone falling into it.

"Dear God," Pierre called, "I've never seen him fall. Help! Please, God!"

Others of the crew had run to the stream.

"Where is he?" barked Andre.

"Don't know. Maybe further downstream," Pierre hollered. Andre and others ran down the streambank, struggled through alders, searching the roiling waters. Still no sign.

"God?" Pierre called, looking heavenward.

Suddenly, a hand appeared out of the water and grasped the very end of the alder. "Got him!" Pierre screamed. "Got him!"

A moment later, Jigger's eyes, and then his mouth, surfaced and he gasped loudly for air. He didn't even have the breath to talk. He didn't need to. Adrenalin surging, muscles bulging, Pierre yanked with a might he didn't know he possessed, and the alder slid along and past his hip, and Jigger's body along with it. As Jigger got near the shore, Andre and Yvan reached out and yanked him onto dry land.

Pierre looked skyward and said a thank-you.

ƙ ƙ ƙ

Shivering uncontrollably and out of breath, Jigger looked in wonder at Pierre. "Mon Dieu! Mon Dieu, Pierre! Did you see him?" he asked.

"Did I see who?"

"The man? The angel?"

"You're not only loco about women," Pierre said, "you're loco, period. You almost just died, man."

"No, I'm serious. Honest to God. Thank You, God. Thank You, Jesus!" Jigger shouted.

"He's hysterical," Andre declared. "Get him some blankets, somebody, and bring him to the fire."

Arms wrapped around Jigger and pulled him along to the cooking fire. He shivered—from the cold but also the memory of the one who saved him from death.

Sitting there holding blankets about himself, Jigger looked around to the others. "I'm not loco," he said. "I was drowning. The current was tugging me under to the bottom. I couldn't fight it off, couldn't get to the surface. Logs were all around and above me, banging at me." He rubbed his sore right shoulder. "And the cold stole my breath.

"Then I looked up—" Jigger looked to the heavens and tears burst from his eyes. "God, thank You. I love You!" he said.

Then, his eyes piercing the others one at a time, he went on: "Then I looked up and a man bathed in brilliance reached down to me. He reached down and began to pull me up."

Jigger stopped and looked squarely at Pierre. "The next thing I knew, I was grabbing that stick, and then I was looking at your beautiful mug."

Pierre sighed.

"You believe me, don't you, Pierre? Andre? Yvan?" Jigger looked at the other men.

"Yes, Jigger," said Yvan. "I believe."

"Me too," Andre said, and the men standing around the fire all chimed in in an almost melancholy way.

"Well, that angel saved you for a visit to The Crossing," Pierre said. "One of Ilsa's girls will treat you to a nice steamy bath."

Pierre laughed but Jigger looked seriously at him. "No, Pierre, not for me. Not ever again. That angel didn't speak to me. But in that instant I knew. I knew I was done with sinnin'. I'm going to be a changed man. A new man. You go ahead, but you'll be goin' without me."

CHAPTER SIX

Garner Fletcher slapped down the ledger, his frown deepening. He twirled a pencil through his fingers, forefinger to pinky and back, to his pinky and back. Then snapped the pencil in two.

If only his bank were doing as well as the Klan was nationally. If only …

If only the state of Maine were doing that well. Fat chance. The tale out of the state capitol was that the fools in the Legislature were voting to use taxpayer dollars to fund Catholic schools. Catholic! With his money! If only …

Perhaps the bank's goals, and those of the state, weren't as honorable as the Klan's. That might explain the problem. He wondered how his Dad would respond to such a thought. His Dad. A tear worked its way down his cheek. Perhaps …

His Dad had died just a year ago, after suffering how long? Fifty-eight years. A lifetime! Fifty-eight years in pain from injuries sustained fighting in the Civil War. He'd been shot several times in a battle against a platoon of black men and Cherokees who were fighting for the South.

Oh, his Dad would indeed agree with Garner: the KKK was right in opposing the dissolution of white America. No doubt …

It wasn't hateful. No. Garner considered himself a good man. He didn't hate the blacks or Indians. He simply hated what they were doing to the white race and nation.

He didn't want anything bad to happen to the Jews and blacks and French-Catholics. He merely wanted to live separately from them. He had his own religion and wanted it unassimilated, his own philosophy and values and wanted them undiminished. He wanted to prevent these outsiders from integrating into white, Protestant society. He wanted to strengthen the bonds of Christian fellowship. To continue, here in The Crossing, the great things the white race had accomplished in Europe.

His Dad had fought to preserve this great nation, and after suffering for decades, had died to this purpose. How could Garner do less? He knew plenty of his Harvard classmates, especially those on the wrestling team, particularly those whose fathers gave their lives for the country, would agree. His colleagues in the business community, if fully informed, would concur. Wise men would stand on the side of the Ku Klux Klan.

And, despite some misgivings, so would he. So would he …

ꝁ ꝁ ꝁ

It was going to be a fine year, a mighty fine year. The crops were going to just burst out of the ground and be nurtured by just enough rain and pulled out toward the sky by plenty of sun. A bumper year for farmers. So said *Farmer's Almanac*, and Sam Craig didn't know what those Geigers down there in Lewiston had going for them, but their almanac was always predicting the seasons right on the nose. They'd predicted a God-awful winter, and sure enough, The Crossing had gotten one of its worst ever. And now the farmers would collect their dues. They'd sure enough earned them.

But the first order of business, Sam thought, was to repair those rotting boards in the hayloft before Joshua or someone else stepped through them. When Joshua regained consciousness, that is.

Sam cast his eyes down and shook his head, his thoughts on his son. Joshua, in his own world where some mysterious force or something seemed to be guiding him through a maze of dreams and nightmares, keeping him awake but in a mesmerized state.

Luckily, Jen was able to get liquids down him, Doc's special concoctions of vitamins, protein, and whatever else was necessary to sustain the body.

Joshua had yet to speak, but once in a while would gasp, his eyes wide, as if seeing something terrifying. The boy was absolutely in a hell in his own mind—a hell created by who-knows-what.

But Sam stood firm in his faith, alongside Jen, trusting God to pull the boy through.

Sam stepped over to the stall and brought his workhorse, Mike, out to where he could harness him up. Tightening the straps, bridle, and traces, Sam stroked the big gelding's neck. Mike had lost his winter coat and was sleek and as richly brown as an otter.

Mike was a fine horse, performing all his duties well. A mild-mannered riding horse for Joshua when the boy was younger. A rugged working horse in the field when that was needed. Today's wagon full of lumber would prove to be one of his heaviest loads, so Sam made a mental note to buy some lumps of sugar in town to reward him upon their return.

Sam hitched the horse to the wagon and, with a flick of the reins, started off down the road toward Cooper's Crossing. A mile later, Sam eyed the big white house on his left with pillars adorning its front.

Matt Whittaker was in the drive, working on his plow. A picture of brawn and breadth, he was on his knees, his shirt sleeves folded up to his elbows, tools spread out around him and his working hat lying upside down on the ground beside him.

Matt was pulling a long bolt out of his hat—like a magician and his rabbit—when he noticed Sam. "Mornin', Sam," he hollered.

Sam waved, then pulled Mike up at the end of the drive. "That's the new plow you got last year, isn't it?"

"Yeah. I kick myself for buying it out of the catalogue. But I'll give Simon Foot a piece of my mind when I see him, too. Cheap steel. I wouldn't be surprised if I could bend it myself."

You could bend *most* steel, my friend, Sam thought.

"I planned to break in some new pasture for corn this year for the cows and eating, but I wouldn't dare try it with this plow. Lord's will get my hardware and equipment business from now on. To heck with Foot."

"I gotta tell you something about Foot," Sam said, "but first things first. How's Clara and the baby?"

"Both are doing fine, thanks. How about coming in and saying hello? I know Clara'd love to see you. It's been a week or so since we've seen either you or Jennifer."

Matt took a step toward the house, but Sam motioned for him to stop. "No, no, Matt. I know what it's like after a woman's had a baby. She can use all the rest she can get. In three or four days, Jen and I'll get over to see her and the baby."

As Sam spoke, a little black boy ran out from behind the house, followed close by an Oriental girl a bit taller and slenderer than the round-faced boy.

"Daddy, Daddy," the boy called, "Suzie's after me. She says she's gonna git me and toss me in a bucket of Clorox and dye me white."

With this, young Willie Whittaker ran behind his father, putting Matt between him and his sister, and hugged Matt's legs.

Matt laughed and addressed the young girl, who'd pulled up short in her chase. "Now, Ming Su," Matt lectured, "that wouldn't be nice at all and you know it. How'd you like it if someone bigger than you tossed you into a vat of dye and turned you red?"

The girl looked at her father and then to the ground at her feet. "But, Daddy," she said, "that's exactly what Danny Thurston said he was gonna do to me. He said he was gonna pour his momma's bleach on me to make me normal."

"'Normal,' did he say?" Matt asked and turned a quick look at Sam to underline the remark. "Okay, kids, that's enough of that. Now go on off and play—and play something else, please. And don't you worry, Willie, no one's going to change your color. We love you as you are. Don't we, Sam?"

"Sure do. Head to toe!"

The boy looked at Sam and giggled. "Love you, too, Uncle Sam!"

Matt knelt, kissed the boy on the forehead and sent him off to play with a soft slap on his bottom.

Turning back to Sam, Matt asked, "Did you hear that? *Normal.* Things are happening here. Strange stuff that I thought'd never come about in Cooper's Crossing. We've known most everyone around here all our lives, right? But some people seem to have a new attitude about us."

"Just what do you mean, Matt?" It was a rhetorical question, for Sam already knew the answer, as if it were at the tip of his own tongue—a menacing answer to an ominous question.

"Well, it's funny. It isn't as though it just happened yesterday or the day before, but it seems to be coming to a head really quick, and spreading as fast as it can. For instance, I woulda had this plow fixed and been out in the fields with it right now if it weren't for Ida Thurston. She told Clara a month ago—she assured her again a couple of weeks ago—that she'd come over when the baby was born and take care of the kids and the house and cook some meals."

"I know."

"We were going to pay her for her trouble. Then, just a couple of days ago, she told us Ian wouldn't allow it."

Sam shifted uncomfortably on the bucket seat.

"Now if that wasn't the strangest thing—so I decided to take a ride over to the Thurstons. Darned if Ida didn't act as if I'd brought an army of ants with me and they were all climbing up her skirts. She mumbled some unintelligible gibberish about Ian not approving and her having to stay home with the kids. She seemed spooked, if you know what I mean."

Sam looked up the drive to where Willie and Suzie had disappeared.

Matt read his thoughts. "Yeah, Willie's seen the ultimate worst of this first-hand. The scars are deep."

"I know he's had nightmares," Sam said.

"Nightmares, cold sweats—"

"And now that horror threatens us even here in Maine."

"Who would've guessed?" Matt said.

Sam nodded. "Well, I'll tell ya'," he said, "I didn't have to guess after last night."

"Oh?"

"I went to that meeting of quote 'the world's greatest secret social, patriotic, fraternal order,' unquote."

"You didn't."

"I did." Sam read his friend's astonishment. "To check it out, Matt. Just to make sure I was right about it."

"And?"

"Creepy, to say the least. It was weird to see people dressed in bedspreads and dunce caps up close and personal. I mean, if you want to start a Protestant version of the Catholics' Knights of Columbus, would you dress up like that?"

Matt laughed.

"And I'm afraid there was a lot more yet to come when I left."

"You mean you left right in the middle of it?"

"Yeah."

"Why?"

"I knew what was coming, Matt. You've read some of the reports about the Ku Klux Klan, right? Back in the 1800s they had the Negroes and Jews to hate on. Here in Maine, there aren't many Willies around, so their main targets are Catholics and Jews—'unAmericans' taking American jobs.

"In fact, Bob Stridler called it a battle against an invasion—*invasion*, mind you—of aliens and Jews and Catholics. They want to maintain America as the land of the free, as long as 'the free' are Anglo-Saxons and Protestant. I'm surprised they haven't narrowed it down to descendants of the Mayflower Puritans."

"Maybe that's the next step," Matt said without cracking a smile.

Sam couldn't help but laugh. Just like Matt, to try to lighten the mood.

"But, Matt, this all means they're against those two beautiful kids of yours."

Matt shook his head and said, "Sam, I want to believe the best. I've known most of the people in this town most of my life. If I didn't go to school with them, I've done business with them or gone to church with them. They wouldn't do anything to Suzie and Willie, would they? They're just kids."

Sam hesitated, thought again for the previous night, then replied, "I wouldn't have believed it if I hadn't been there myself, Matt. It was astonishing. Stridler had them raising the roof."

"If that's the case," Matt said, "a lot of people could get hurt. Think of how many Catholics we have in town."

"And coming to town," Sam said. "The river drive's gotta be near."

Matt's face twisted, a look Sam first saw when they were kids playing Cowboys and Indians and Sam snuck up from behind a tree and had the draw on him.

Sam said, "I'd keep a close watch out if I were you, Matt. For you, Clara, Suzie, and Willie."

"Right."

Sam turned to his horse, then remembered what he had wanted to share with his friend and looked back. "I thought you should know. Simon Foot's one of the leaders."

"Oh." Matt didn't look surprised.

"I don't know how far they've gone here, or how far they will go," Sam said. "But I think Stridler and Simon are willing to go as far as they think they must."

Matt stepped back from the wagon as Sam picked up the reins. "Any change in Joshua?"

"No. It's like his mind is in Never Neverland, only his Never Neverland is infested with monsters. He doesn't talk. Just sleeps and stares. But we feel the Lord has told us he'll come out of it."

"We pray it's sooner than later." Matt reached up to take Sam's left hand."

Sam accepted his friend's consolation.

"Tell Jen that Clara and I both send our love and pray it isn't too long."

With a nod, Sam snapped the reins and Mike took off into a steady gait, pulling the wagon toward town. He rode on, scrutinizing the woods and fields as he went, checking the wet areas for signs of fiddleheads, noticing Nancy Flanders digging dandelion greens. Squapan Stream meandered parallel to the road, and Sam compared its high-water marks to those of previous springs.

Shortly, he neared the town and its Main Street. Leaving a stretch of woods behind him, he rode into a clearing with Aubrey Wilson's blacksmith and saddle shop on his left, at the corner of Harlowe Way and Main Street, and with Ilsa's Inn on his right, kitty-corner on the two streets. Across Main Street was the Cutters' hardware store, a feed and grain store and the Community Church flanked by Nathan's big, newly painted parsonage.

Sam pulled the reins to the right, steering his wagon past Ilsa's and Frank Thomas' sawmill. Sam had never seen eye to eye with Thomas, whether it concerned the way tax moneys were spent in The Crossing or how appropriate the weather was to the time of year. If Sam spoke up at the town meeting and called for more money for the schools, Thomas asked that it be diverted to the sheriff's office. If, at the church board meeting, Sam spoke out in favor of Bingo to raise funds, Thomas would declare it "the devil's game."

The two men had never come to blows, but Sam had been sorely tempted. And he certainly wouldn't deign to give him his business.

The wagon's wheels bumped over railroad tracks, jolting Sam out of his thoughts. The tracks crossed the road heading north where they split, with one set of tracks bearing to the right and into Thomas' mill and the other set bearing northwest across a trestle over Limerick River and on to Jacques LaBonte's saw mill. That was Sam's destination.

Just fifteen yards after crossing the tracks, Sam came to the bridge traversing the Androscoggin just below the forks where Limerick River joined the Andy. At that fork, the Andy was flowing southeast and the Limerick southwest and when they converged the waterway flowed southerly.

LaBonte's mill was nestled at the north of the forks between both rivers, connected to Cooper's Crossing by the railroad trestle over the Limerick and the narrow bridge over the Andy.

At the end of the bridge, Sam steered the horse onto a road heading north, then twenty rods away turned again over the bridge to the mill. Whereas most of the stores and shops in The Crossing were on the east side of the Andy, the part of the village on the west of the river contained mainly homes and St. Joseph's Catholic Church. It was the residential area of The Crossing's village.

The waters of the Andy frothed as they rushed around and over the rocks below the bridge. The joyful smell of freshly sawed wood greeted Sam as he rode over the bridge. He recalled the days in his youth when he worked much of his spare time when not in school piling the boards into empty boxcars, filling their bellies before they headed back downstream to Lewiston for new homes there and to Bath and Brunswick for the great wooden ships.

That experience had whet his appetite for another exciting career—for every several months the log drives would come in and along with them came the brawny, boisterous, fun-loving lumberjacks—a group of free-spirited men with not a worry in the world, who drank every last drop of life from every moment of every day—not to mention every last drop of every bottle they got their hands on along the way. Sam coughed a laugh in spite of himself.

When Sam graduated from high school, his first act had been to buy a pair of caulked boots and an ax and head north into the woods to find the lumber camp of foreman Alfred Pleau. He stayed with Pleau for a year; twelve months that taught him just how demanding a job lumbering was—sun-up to sun-down six days a week, fighting black flies and mosquitoes in the summer and bitter cold in the winter.

But it was also a year that created memories to last a lifetime and friends to last forever. It also brought him a hero (in a strange sort of way)—Jigger Jacques. A tough, wiry little man who could accomplish amazing feats. Stories Sam had heard about Jigger that he naturally assumed were exaggerations, turned out to be eyewitnessed truths.

Jigger was an enigma. He'd been in who-knows-how-many brawls, yet didn't have an enemy in the world. Normally warm and friendly, he could turn cold as ice when facing inequity of any kind to any person, familiar or stranger.

And physically? He was the epitome of a lumberjack. Maybe five-foot-nine, he could slam down an ax with the force of Paul Bunyan.

LaBonte's mill saw was buzzing and men were busy carrying lengths of wood to the mill yard when Sam reached the end of the bridge. He pulled Mike up at a hitch in front of the office, which was contained in one room at the center of the large saw building. Immediately, Jacques LaBonte burst out of the door, waving.

"Sam, my boy," he called, "you've come for your lumber. And for a visit, too, I hope." A big man, as tall as Sam and just as broad-shouldered, Jacques had black, curly hair and a full beard sprinkled with gray. Sam figured Jacques would turn seventy before his hair turned gray. When you don't worry, you stay young, and it seemed Jacques didn't have a care in the world. He'd live forever.

"How about we visit while we load my wagon?" Sam replied. "I've got a lot of work to get started on, and planting isn't too far away."

"Okay." Jacques took Mike's reins and led the horse and wagon toward the lumberyard. Sam kept pace beside him and noticed an unusual, troubled expression on the Frenchman's face.

"What's wrong, Jacques? I sense something very thick in the air. As a matter of fact, that seems to be the atmosphere nearly everywhere I go lately."

"A lot of things are worrying me today." Jacques pulled up short and turned to Sam. "I've got a bad feeling about it, Sam. Strange things are happening."

"That seems to be the phrase lingering on some people's minds lately," Sam said. "'Strange things happening.' Everyone's saying that. That is, except maybe the people causing those strange things to happen. Just what are you referring to?"

Scratching his beard, Jacques turned to walk on and explained, "Business is getting worse and worse. People who've been regular customers for years—Ted Beatty, Cecile Chamberlain, Royce Whitney—aren't coming to me anymore. They're going to that snake across the river. I know it's nothing to do with my prices, I still look the same, and it isn't as if I stopped takin' baths. And it can't be that I don't get the orders ready soon enough, or that my house is in the wrong part of town, or that I don't go to church any more.

"I just can't understand it, Sam. Then, to top it all off, there was some vandalism on the railroad trestle and we had to close it to the rail cars for three days while it got repaired. And five days ago, Jean Bonneau disappeared."

"Jean Bonneau?" Sam hadn't heard a thing about LaBonte's yard foreman going missing.

"My one suspicion is that his disappearance revolves around something bad." Jacques leaned in close to Sam. "He was sleeping around with a certain person's wife."

Sam stepped back.

"But," Jacques said quickly, "I know he and she didn't run off together because I saw her in town at Ada's yesterday. Now, you tell me: What's happening and why?"

Sam looked Jacques in the eye, consuming this new morsel. Bonneau had appeared to be such a good and friendly guy. But an affair with a married woman? Sam never considered that he was an adulterer. And evil does lead to evil. Perhaps in that lay the answer. Perhaps the woman's husband was suspect. Who else would want to do anything to him? Suspicious, very suspicious. So much happening in Cooper's Crossing and all at once.

"If what you tell me is true," Sam said as they stopped at a stack of two-by-six lumber, "then I *think* I know what's happening. And I can tell you why, too, but you won't like it and neither will a lot of other people around here. But they may be outmuscled."

Picking up a ten-foot length of lumber and loading it aboard his wagon, Sam continued, "It seems we're in a new era—an era of hate and mistrust. I've read about it in other places—even as close as Portland—but I never thought we'd see it here in The Crossing. Now we've got it, we'd better watch out."

"You never were one to walk all around Robinson's barn," Jacques said. "Tell me exactly what the devil you're talking about. Why should anyone hate or distrust me?"

"Very simple and straight-forward. You're French-Canadian, and that's two strikes against you when just one strike means you're out. It means you're French—there's strike one—and you weren't born in the United States—that's strike two. And a third strike is that you—or at least most French-Canadians—are Catholic.

"Your ancestry's all wrong, Jacques. That's what's wrong. The Ku Klux Klan's made it out of the cities—out of Portland, Bangor, and Augusta—and it claims people who aren't native Americans and who aren't Anglo-Saxon Protestants are a threat to the country.

"What you've experienced so far, I'm afraid, are the first flare-ups. And since the spring log drive must be nearly here, I'm coming to think—just since this morning I'm coming to think—that the real battle is very near."

Sam looked with apprehension at Jacques, waiting for a reaction.

One moment passed, then quickly and intensely, lines of anger marked a face not used to their cruelty.

"But people get hurt in battles," Jacques said. "They die. And little ever gets resolved. What, Sam—what have I done? No, I wasn't born here, but I've lived here for twenty-one years. I've walked the woods of every part of Maine. I've fished its streams and swum in its lakes. I've paid for the land my mill's on and have worked hard, and I mean hard, to build my business. I've made friends. They haven't cared that I was French. They haven't cared that I wasn't born here. So why should they care now? And what matter is religion? Our God is the same God. Our Savior is the same Savior."

With a swift, violent movement, Jacques brought his arm down hard and smashed his closed fist on the pile of wood beside him. His voice suddenly low and distant, he said, "I don't understand."

𝕶 𝕶 𝕶

Riding back home along Harlowe Way an hour later, Sam thought of the letter he'd received from his brother who was living in Georgia.

"You wouldn't believe," John had written, "how downright hateful they are down here toward some people. If you're Jewish or Negro or Oriental or Italian or Irish, for that matter, you're going to have trouble. Why, the colored can't even eat or go to the bathroom where the whites do."

This kind of bigotry was raising its head again, reaching epidemic proportions in other parts of the country, but it was in its infancy in Maine. Sam'd heard reports that Klansmen were running for mayor in Sanford and Bath and Rockland. But something had to be done to stop it in The Crossing.

Sam pulled up short in his thoughts as his eye caught a movement off the side of the road where an embankment fell toward Squapan Stream. He squinted in that direction. Sure enough, strange as it seemed, down in the midst of alders stood an old Morgan stallion, his back covered with a homemade Indian-style blanket.

The horse seemed to be coughing, regurgitating, its head hung low next to the stream's rushing waters that were swollen with the spring runoff.

"Whoa!' Sam called to Mike, tugging on the reins. He jumped down from the wagon. As he reached the opposite edge of the road, he noticed through the gray shadows and the tangle of branches below him that a person stood on the far side of the horse.

A raspy, neutral voice grumbled, "Now, calm down, boy. Drink some water." With that, the person drew the horse's head down to the stream, revealing that it was Suzie Cooley.

"Suzie," he called, "spring surely is here if you're coming to town."

Obviously unaware anyone was watching her, Suzie jerked her head up. "Oh. Oh, Master Craig. It's you, is it? My, aren't you a sight. Handsomer and handsomer every year. If I weren't twice your age and if I were twice as pretty, I'd sure try to lure you to Pocomoonshine."

Sam laughed. Suzie straightened her dress and Sam judged, from the thickness of the clothes about her, that she had shed down to three dresses. *She's a landmark to the weather.*

A multi-colored floral print with a deep-blue background was the outermost dress this spring day, fitting with the deep-blue sky and the freshness felt by the cool air and shown by the new light-green grass and the tiny buds on the alders surrounding the woman.

Her coy smile and the bemused shine in her eye belied Suzie's age, told by her weathered, Indian-skinned face and her short-cut black hair speckled with the salt of long winters and work-filled summers and falls. Strong, callused hands were signs that her work was more than household chores and more even than planting spuds in the spring and digging them up in the fall. Those hands telegraphed the source and difficulty of their labor, but they also signaled a strength that stretched beyond their bones and ligaments to the rest of the aging woman. It was the strength gained through years upon years of living alone in the mountains, struggling to provide for, care for and protect herself.

But Sam guessed there were more complexities that the hands did not reveal—the obstacles, fears, and prejudices facing a half-Indian girl whose white father had died on a log drive on an unknown river twisting through the vast forest of the Midwest. When she was fourteen, she had lost her mother to pneumonia, and she was left with a two-room shanty on the side of a mountain with just two rocky acres cleared for planting. That was two acres that, along with the roots of the plants surrounding the mountain, would later provide liquid for a recipe she would perfect into the best moonshine this side of the Penobscot River.

At this moment those hands were caressing the horse's head and Sam asked, "What seems to be the matter with your horse?"

"His thievery's finally caught up with him," Suzie answered, leading the horse through a twisting path out of the alders and up the hill to the road. "Old Jake here believes himself smart, whereas he's really a smart-aleck.

"Master Craig, this boy's got so sneaky and sly that he's got hisself in a pickle. He's an alcoholic."

Sam fought off a chuckle that fought to come out of his chest. Then offered, "Oh, really?" and reached out to help Suzie up the final step to the road.

"It's true." She shook her head in apparent dismay. "At first, I thought it might be Randy, a raccoon in the neighborhood, who's been gettin' into my vat where I age a lot of my, uh, recipe. I keep it in the ground in a nice, cool pine grove. I knew it weren't no person 'cause no one would dare. They know me too well to try.

"But, just when I was about to tie that rascal up by his hind legs and give him old tarnations, this fool horse comes stumbling out of the woods, trying to stand straight and whinnying *Auld Lang Syne.*"

She put her face directly in front of Jake's and declared, "Crazy horse."

The horse waffled his lips and snorted.

Sam broke out laughing, and Suzie joined him. Reaching into a satchel draped over Jake's back, she pulled out a small, unmarked bottle apparently filled with liquids of her own concoction and handed it to Sam.

"For being such a nice young man," she said, "and so handsome." She patted his cheek and winked. Then, nimble as a teenager, she grabbed Jake's mane and pulled herself atop him. A moment later, she rode off toward Cooper's Crossing with a backwards wave of her hand.

Sam stood there, shaking his head and watching her ride off, a smile stretched from ear-to-ear.

💠 💠 💠

Dear Lord, this is Your child even more than he's mine. Please, oh please, restore him to us.

Tears trickled down Jennifer's face as she ran a damp washcloth over Joshua's forehead. His eyes were open, but apparently unseeing. This was her first truly harsh test of faith since she could remember. Worried about Joshua's neurological whatever-it-was and whether he would awake "normal," if he awoke at all, she reflected on what had been an idyllic life.

She was raised by loving parents, married her high school sweetheart, bore a son she adored, cherished her life and home in the country, attended a faith-filled church with a wonderful pastor, and possessed a large group of close friends. What more could a woman ask for?

"Nothing," she said aloud, startling herself just as a knock came at the side door.

She stood, gently squeezed Joshua's shoulder and walked to the door. What a wonderful surprise, she thought as she looked out the window of the door. A gaggle of Joshua's friends stood on the porch, worry and expectation written on their faces.

She opened the door, smiling despite her worries. "My, you're a very sober-looking group," she said.

"Hello, Mrs. C.," said Tommy Mullen. "We've come to see if we can visit Josh. We heard what happened."

"That's very thoughtful, boys." Jennifer's eyes embraced them all. "He's still not responding, but maybe you all can lift him out of it. Just one thing: Be positive around him. Speak only positive things, fun things."

"Yes, ma'am," Tommy replied, and a chorus of "Yes'ms" trailed along after him.

Jennifer opened wide the door and four, five, six, seven teenagers gingerly entered the house.

It's as serene as I've ever seen these boys, Jennifer laughed to herself. Tommy, Hank, Petey, Todd, Danny, Bobby and Abe. Joshua's Three Musketeers (Tommy and Abe being the other two), plus five—all members of his baseball team, The Raiders.

"It's right through to the living room, boys," Jennifer said. They all knew their way. The Craig home—indeed the fields, forests and hills surrounding it—was a favorite haunt for all the boys, especially The Three Musketeers. They'd play Cowboys and Indians out in the woods, then scramble back to the house for the occasional molasses cookies fresh out of the oven. Samuel and Jennifer were a second father and mother to Tommy and Abe, as were their parents to Joshua.

In double file, the boys walked to Joshua's bedside, then spread out around it.

Shoulders convulsed on a few of the boys. Tommy and Abe pushed back tears. But they all kept their composure at seeing Joshua in such a state.

Tommy reached down for Joshua's hand.

"Hey, J," he said, "the gang's here. The Raiders are ready to raid! We just need your big bat."

Abe piped up. "Yeah, we were all at practice and Coach Rider told us why you weren't there. So here we are. Can't play without a shortstop, J. Can't play without you." Abe started to stammer and his lower lip shivered. He turned away, stifling a tear.

"J, it's me, your better half," chided Hank, who as the second baseman was Joshua's double-play partner. "Hard to make that pivot to first when no one's there to throw me the ball. So, well— so, hurry up and wake up, will ya'?"

"Yeah," chimed in the whole gang.

Todd, who was standing at the foot of the bed, grabbed Joshua's foot through the sheet that covered him and gave it a little shake. "Right, and you and I gotta get goin' on that background for the church play, ya' know. We've been proca, prosac, priscrat—well, we've been putting if off too long. Pastor Nat'll get on us for that."

Jennifer couldn't help but chuckle at that, but then she had to bite her lip to stop from crying that her boy wasn't able to do any of these things right now. She turned and went out to the kitchen to fill some glasses with milk and a plate with corn muffins she had baked earlier. They were still warm, she thought as she piled them up. Still warm—and for no explained reason a renewed torrent of tears came gushing from her eyes.

A minute later, she returned to the living room, with a tray full of the goodies for the boys. "I'm going out to hang the laundry, boys," she said. "Here's a little something to get you through the afternoon."

"Thanks, Mrs. C.," Tommy replied, and the others echoed him, turning to the tray.

"Stay as long as you'd like," she said. "I know it will do Joshua good to hear your voices. A prayer would help, too, boys."

"That's something I *know* we can do," Todd chimed in with a smile.

CHAPTER SEVEN

Sam stood in the hayloft, leather gloves on, tossing bales of hay down below. He was down to sixty bales and prayed he had enough to last until first cut.

His thoughts continued to return to Joshua and Jen. This was particularly difficult for her. Sam could busy himself with myriad outdoor chores every day, but Jennifer was consigned to the house with Joshua hour after hour.

Exhausted each night from the heavy and long work preparing for the planting season, Sam usually fell asleep when his head hit the pillow. But he had awakened more than once in the middle of the night to find Jennifer had left his side in favor of the overstuffed rocking chair next to Joshua's bed in the den.

In the meantime, Joshua was not only missing out on school, but also on what he seemed to love the most, next to baseball, that is—working the land. The boy loved the woods and animals. But, most of all, Joshua loved the earth, had a special feel for it.

Sam had once happened upon the boy in one of the fields after the ground had been harrowed but before it was planted. Joshua was kneeling on the ground, grasping two handfuls of rich earth. The boy looked up at Sam and exclaimed with a touch of wonder in his voice, "It's amazin', isn't it, Dad? All those vegetables can grow from little seeds just plunked down into the ground?"

"Yes, them and the weeds, too," Sam had joked.

Joshua had returned his attention to experiencing the feel and texture of the earth and the moisture and potential for life it contained.

Later, Sam had stopped the boy while they were forking hay down from the hayloft onto the barn floor below to be placed in the stalls for feed for the livestock.

"Listen, son," he said, "I'm happy that you love the land, that it's special to you. Of all the things you might have inherited from me, from my genes, I'd be happiest if that were it. This land around us has kept the Craigs from being hungry for three generations—four now.

"You said this morning that it's amazing how plants grow in the soil. Well, it is. And it's fascinating to watch it happen. And you could get a lot of meanings from it. But there are just two things I want you hold onto, always. Love the land, but don't expect to get no more from it than what you put in.

"And that, son, is the rule for all life as well. You have a good feel for the land. It's a part of you. I want you to have the same feel for life in general and your friends and family in particular. In all you attempt, in all you do, in all you foresee and dream about, you should possess love for those around you and you should give if you expect to receive in kind."

Sam, who had bent down on one knee, straightened up and pulled his pitch fork from the bale of hay where he'd stuck it when he began talking.

Joshua, who had been sitting with his legs dangling over the edge of the loft, swung them up onto the loft floor and looked up at his father. A smile tugged at his lips and put a bright gleam in his eyes. "Thanks, Dad. You're really somethin'."

"So are you, son," Sam replied. "Now, why don't you run down to the pasture and bring in Mike and Luella? This is about the last of the hay we've got here, but it's more than there is out there in the field this time of year."

Joshua jumped to his feet, sprang over the ladder and slid down its rungs to the ground below with such speed that it nearly frightened Sam. Ah, the boy was growing up. But not too fast, hopefully, to learn what must be learned about farming—and human nature.

Sam stared at that very same ladder and wondered if the boy would ever slide down it again.

ʞ ʞ ʞ

Nathan Hind sat in his buggy, urging his horse on. The Craig farm was too a bit far from town to walk. That distance, however, certainly didn't seem to restrict anybody from traveling there for a visit. The house—warm, inviting, friendly—reflected the traits of its inhabitants. Both possessed a magnetic force, drawing men and women, townspeople and country folk alike.

Nathan had been in the home many times, either socially, or to plan a church affair with Jennifer or a church committee. As a hostess, Jennifer was unsurpassed and she preferred to have the committee she chaired meet at her home, where she could properly display her hospitality, rather than in the rectory.

In fact, Nathan preferred the Craig household to the rectory. Oh, he liked his parlor and enjoyed his den, but the Craig home was unique, special. The furniture wasn't untouchable, but comfortable. The house wasn't immaculate, but clean and "lived in." Its friendly, intimate air, welcomed anyone who entered its doors. It seemed to say: "Sit down, relax, put your feet up, make yourself at home, let us get to know you."

And the people, he thought, the people—they embodied the good qualities of the New Englander. Sam and the earth were inseparable. To think of one was to think of the other. Sam had once said to him, "It was the few extraordinary men who brought us to where we are and it will be a few more extraordinary men who will take us to those stars up there." He'd pointed to the heavens. What a dreamer.

A humble man, Sam was not speaking of himself as one of those extraordinary men, but he could have been. College-educated and brilliant, Sam could be one of those few extraordinary men, Nathan thought, if only he wanted to be. But he didn't. Sam loved the land, and with it he would stay.

Jennifer was indeed his perfect mate. She was Mother Earth. Sam had told Nathan that his wife's love made him feel whole.

When Nathan had taken his pastorate in The Crossing fifteen years ago, it was every young man's dream to gain Jennifer's hand. It was also their folly, for she belonged to Sam. They wed before they were twenty while Sam was still in college, and three years later Nathan baptized Joshua. Since then, Jennifer had grown, filled out as a woman and as a person—whole, comfortable with herself as an integral part of the world around her.

And there was Joshua. If his spunk and spirit could be bottled and sold, it would gain a man a fortune. The boy lived with a vigorous energy that was contagious, and he seemed to have inherited those mysterious life forces unique in both his parents.

Nathan left his horse and buggy at a water trough near the barn at the end of the driveway. On his way to the kitchen door, Jennifer burst through it to see him. She was tired, it was obvious, but she flashed a brilliant smile and threw her arms around him.

"Hello, Nathan." Her voice was mellow, subdued. Jennifer sensed relief.

He squeezed back. "Jen."

Tears welling up in her eyes, she said, "Thank you so much for coming. Come on into the den, Nathan. We moved Joshua down here so he'd be closer to 'the action,' and we wouldn't have to climb the stairs so often."

Nathan followed Jennifer down the corridor and into a room on the left. The room faced south and was getting its last bit of the noonday sun. Joshua was half-sitting, propped up on a pile of pillows. He stared straight ahead, expressionless, his big, brown eyes missing their usual sparkle.

Moe lay at the foot of the bed.

Jennifer turned to Nathan. "Moe's been keeping vigil over his young master. Whenever Joshua stirs or makes a sound, Moe whines and moves up closer to Joshua and nudges his arm or licks his face."

Nathan knelt and patted the dog on his head. Moe mumbled a response and wagged the tip of his tail in a slow twirl.

"He's run into the parlor or kitchen to get either Samuel or me to come back with him to the den," Jennifer said. "It's like he wants to show us some new development. But each time we get here Joshua's in the state you see him in now."

Nathan reached for the boy's hand. It was warm but limp. "How is he?" he asked.

"The same. Off in space somewhere. Doc said it's simply a waiting game. But it's a waiting game I'm not prepared for."

"Jen, that's the report of the world. I came with the report of the Lord, the Great Physician. Are you ready to pray?"

Jennifer sucked in air deeply—and sobbed. Yes, she was obviously ready to pray.

Nathan pulled her to Joshua's side, laid a hand on the boy's head and started calling unto the Lord.

Later, sitting on the sofa beside the bed, Jennifer said, "All I want is to see a little sparkle return to Joshua's eyes, a bit of that mischievousness. I miss that."

"He has his moments, doesn't he?" Nathan smiled.

Jennifer returned a faint grin. "Yes, he does. I remember one time I confronted him on Main Street in The Crossing. He was standing at the corner of Mutton Lane yawning these great, cavernous yawns. When I asked him what on earth he was doing he pointed to his friends Tommy and Abe, stationed further down Main Street. 'We're doin' a survey, Mom, to see if yawns are catchin',' he said. 'See, whenever a car or horse goes by, I yawn. Then Tommy down there sees if the driver or rider yawns, too.' He turned and called to Tommy, asking the results. 'Ten out of twelve so far,' Tommy hollered back. 'Looks like it's contagious, all right.'"

Their laughter was subdued.

"He's such a funny kid, a good kid," Jennifer said. She caught a sob and held it back, but couldn't stop its successor.

"That he is, Jen," Nathan said. "That he is." He put his arms out and Jennifer let her tears flow onto his shoulder.

ƙ ƙ ƙ

Sam noticed the reverend's horse and buggy in front of the barn and thought the visit was just what Jennifer needed. A number of friends had stopped by, but sometimes their visits were more of a burden on Jennifer than a help. Nathan Hind was different.

When Sam entered the den, Jennifer was cleaning off a little end table that was pulled up next to the bed to be used as a dinner tray, with two or three different kinds of liquids in glasses. Funneling the liquids into Joshua's mouth was the only way to give him nourishment.

"Hey, sweetheart," Sam said. "Any change?"

Jennifer turned. "Oh, hello, darling. No, no, there isn't. Look who's here to visit us, though."

Sam shook his friend's hand. "Maybe with another voice calling up to God, we'll win this battle a little quicker."

"Well, God says He listens to the prayers of a godly man. So, if you have three of us, maybe He'll listen more intently. And, remember, Scripture says, 'One will put a thousand to flight, and two will put ten thousand to flight.' Do the math, Sam: The three of us can put a hundred thousand demons to flight. So, what do you say we do that right now? Besides, if not now then it won't be for another several days."

"Another several days?" Sam put his hand to his forehead. "Of course. Your conference in Boston."

"I've got to be there. But while I'm gone, a young minister from Augusta will take my place. A likable young man—not *too* almighty, I don't think." He chuckled.

86

"Well, we'll miss you," Sam said. He was being earnest. What would they do if the worst happened with Joshua—and Nathan were not there? But, oh, it wouldn't get any worse, would it? Sam blew out a breath.

Nathan stood up between Sam and Jennifer. "Let's all pray together for this child we love so much."

Holding hands in a circle at the foot of the makeshift bed, the three adults called forth praise and then prayer to the Lord, beseeching Him for a quick healing, casting away the enemy of the boy's soul and covering him in the blood of the Lamb who removes sins and cleanses all who believe in Him from sickness and disease.

When the finished, Nathan caught Sam's eyes in his. "The breakthrough will come soon. Before I return."

CHAPTER EIGHT

With his buddy, Ted Newsome, at his side, Hank Green strode down a path beside Stridler's home toward a large white barn. White? Stridler had apparently disregarded the traditional red and had the barn painted with one particular scheme in mind. It was snow white with every conceivable border trimmed with a foot-wide red strip. Painted in red, also, and in a bold Gothic type, a sign over a side door declared: "Cooper's Crossing Klandom Hall."

"This way, m-men. C-come this way." Richard Fryer, his eyes darting back and forth between Hank and Ted and glancing beyond them to the wooded road, herded them toward the large structure.

Anxious nerves fought heightened excitement within Hank. Mixed with lingering pain from his brother's death, he knew the combination would test his emotions tonight. They were going to run high just as they had two nights ago, when Stridler had mentioned the men in the mill towns that had lost jobs to aliens.

Fryer waved them through the door. Inside of the door was a small enclosure—a sort of entranceway, four by eight feet wide, used as a checkpoint. A person in a white robe with a one-inch-wide strip of red ribbon and hood, sat at a table to the right. At a point just above the person's forehead, the hood was emblazoned with an emblem with two interlocking C's one above the other, above three horizontal K's, side by side. Laying before him was a spiral-bound, opened book containing lined pages nearly filled with signatures.

The man told Hank and Ted to write down their names, ages, addresses, and length of residency in Cooper's Crossing.

Newsome replied, "But I live up by Pocomoonshine Mountain. Does that mean I can't join?"

"Well, I shouldn't have specified The Crossing. The entire area is actually under our klavern," the man said. "Go ahead and sign and go on into the hall through the door." He pointed to the opposite end of the small room.

Hank and Ted entering their information in the book, then stepped through the door. The place was startling. Kerosene-drenched torches locked into braces every ten feet apart lit up blood-red walls around the entire barn. A single row of perhaps a hundred small windows near the roof-line mirrored the flames.

Hank had expected that seats would be set up in rows filling the hall. Instead, the room contained a huge, oval-shaped grandstand three seats deep. At the far end, the oval shape was broken by a ten-foot-high platform.

Looking through the grandstand, Hank noticed the rows of seats he had anticipated. The seats, most of them filled with plain-clothed men, were in rows in the middle of the hall. Those seats were surrounded by the grandstand, much of which was filled with white-cloaked figures all standing.

"Gee, Hank," Ted said, "this is kind of spooky. I don't know if I want to go in there."

But as he spoke they were approached from behind by a man dressed in robes of reverse colors—red trimmed by white.

A deep, authoritative voice from behind the hood said, "Gentlemen, if you will, you may make your way to the inside seats through that gate there, straight ahead."

Stridler.

The voice alone, the voice that mesmerized the other night, seemed to propel Hank and Ted toward the gate. Hank watched

Stridler as he made his way to the rear of the hall and climbed a steep stairway to the top of the platform.

A moment after ascending the stairs, Stridler stepped directly to the front edge of the platform, looked at a large cauldron four feet in diameter set on the floor below him, and tossed something from his hand. A flame burst several feet high out of the cauldron with a boom, startling Hank and, he was sure, all the unsuspecting men sitting in the center seats.

"The torch is lit, the battlefield is before and around us, and we are called to join the fight!" Stridler's explosive, commanding voice bellowed across the hall. He pointed to the men seated in the middle.

We all look like helpless animals surrounded by gladiators.

"What you see around you, men, is a brigade of the army of the Klan—an army of the finest Americans who have proven they're ready to defend this land and guide it to a prosperous future void of the evils now crowding our borders."

Stridler's air of omniscience was evident as he continued, "The Klan's battle against these transgressions is already being waged, and successfully, in the South and the Midwest and the West and along both coasts. But it has actually just begun. A long fight is ahead before we eliminate our enemies and the sins they carry with them.

"To win, we need more numbers, more brothers. We must build a veritable wall of defense, and our immediate job is to do that here in our klavern so that we may better organize our strategy and carry it out with more efficiency.

"In other klaverns, recruitment is done in a more personal, secret level. But I believe we're in a more sensitive territory where every man knows full well the effects of the enemy of which I speak. If there had been any doubt, then the public meeting the other night would have alleviated that. Therefore, I'm sure those of you who have not joined have come here this evening intending to do so, and probably have brought your ten-dollar klectoken with you.

"Will you, please, then, beginning with the front row, file to your left and toward the back where our klabee will collect your klectoken and sign your name to the membership role? If you're not joining us, please leave the hall immediately."

𝕶𝕶𝕶

The men stood and filed their way toward the rear. Considering his options, Hank wondered if anyone here had decided against joining. No one was leaving the hall. Were they afraid to, or were they committed to joining?

What would happen if someone left the hall? Ted, for instance, had told him he was unsure about the whole thing. And now all these men had seen each other. They obviously knew where everyone lived.

Hank cast a questioning look at his pal, but Ted simply shrugged a look of acquiescence.

They both remained in line, signed their name, and coughed up the ten bucks, which emptied Hank's wallet and, he guessed, Ted's as well.

A half hour later, the Cooper's Crossing chapter of the Ku Klux Klan had another hundred or so recruits as Hank, Ted, and the others all answered "yes" to the ten questions regarding their worthiness to join the Klan.

Standing in a semi-circle at the rear of the inner ring, surrounded by the grandstand, Hank, Ted and their fellow new members looked at Stridler on the platform.

Stridler, lifting his arms in an arc, said, "Welcome to our brotherhood, the most magnificent, patriotic, fraternal, beneficiary order in the world!"

Loud cheers responded.

When the noise quieted, Stridler continued, "Now, please join your fellow klansmen in the grandstands. As fellows, we sit in an arena with no head except this speaker's stand. We're equal.

We work together, plan together, and carry out our God-ordained duties together."

Hank, Ted and the newly initiated climbed up into the grandstands, finding seats as Stridler explained the design of the robes they would be having made.

Then, taking an abrupt turn, Stridler declared, "For as klansmen, we must wear the same robes, readily recognizable as members of the same army, collaborators in actions that will annihilate the evil around us.

"While the problems we face here in Maine are unique from those of our colleagues in other corners of the country, we're together in the same basic quest: building a stronger America and a purer America by reclaiming the land and the morals of our forefathers for our fellow Anglo-Saxon Protestants. We must negate any possibility of continued mongrelization of the white race, or it will not be only us, but generations of our descendants, who will suffer the grave consequences. The white race will be castrated—robbed of our manhood, our inheritance from our ancestors, *our* ancestors."

The full house of klansmen howled in offense.

"Frenchmen swarming into our land will bring with them an impure race. Yes, they will come unless we stop them. And unless we do stop them, there will be other effects.

"You see, with few if any exceptions, the French are also Democrats and Catholics. The Democrats we could survive with, but the Catholics?—No!"

More howls.

Hank shifted uneasily in his seat. He'd voted for Democrats a couple of times recently. A neighbor was a Catholic and, he thought, a pretty regular guy.

He looked up to watch as Stridler paused, pursing his lips and turning his eyes to scan the entire assembly. Bringing his right arm up and clenching his hand into a fist, Stridler exclaimed, "The French Catholics, the Roman Catholics, have a goal in mind and they'll stop at nothing to accomplish it. They want to destroy all non-Catholics and they want to claim title to America. They've tried ways, are trying now, and I'm sure, will devise new avenues to pursue their goal."

Stridler's face was turning red with anger.

"During the World War, they tried to take control of the country. By deserting the ranks of our armies, they sought to have us lose the war—"

Cries of foul.

"Yes, they did! Their goal? To weaken our leadership so much at home that they could take over the reins of leadership in our government!"

Jeers.

"Yes, ninety percent of the deserters in the war were Roman Catholics!"

"Fiends!" someone screamed.

"But—" Stridler shook his fist, "they've been more—yes, much more—perilous than that. We possess evidence that they were the force behind the assassination of President Lincoln!"

Murderous declarations.

"They backed Leon Czolgosz in his assassination of President McKinley!"

Calls for the Pope's head.

"And they collaborated in a devious plot that resulted in President Harding's death just past!"

Clamor broke out around the hall and hooded figures jumped from their seats, shouting, "The bums!" "Death to them!" "We can't let them get away with that!" and slurs that couldn't be repeated in mixed company.

Stridler, forcing his voice over all the others, bellowed, "No, fellow klansmen, I hadn't even told you this, had I? But I've just learned, from information handed down by the Imperial Wizard himself, that it is so.

"You have a right to be perturbed. You have a right to be frenzied. These are not just shallow words of intent of the Roman Catholics. They are a true and venomous evil among us that we cannot handle with words alone. We must take action just as they are. And we must take stronger action then theirs—even heroic feats."

Reaching inside his robe, Stridler pulled out a pamphlet and said, "These pages illustrate how violent the Roman Catholics mean to be. Copies will be passed among you for distribution outside these walls. The Knights of Columbus, that bastion of Catholic hatred, has its members pledge this oath in which they promise to hang, burn, boil, flay, and bury alive all non-Catholics!"

Hank shivered at the thought. *Flayed! Can this* really *be true?*

Stridler tossed the pamphlet into the flaming cauldron below him and continued, "Now, I ask you: Are those just empty words? We have proof that they're not. We have evidence that in other parts of the country (perhaps soon to start here) every time a boy is born to a Roman Catholic family, the father adds a rifle and ammunition to his local church's arsenal."

As Stridler spit out the last word, a zealous explosion and outcry followed. Around him, Hank noticed several stand up on their seats, raising clenched fists in the air. One cried, "Let's go and seize that arsenal! Now!"

A guttural roar of agreement surged through the crowd, and one man leaped from his rear grandstand seat to the floor behind and, running to the wall, grasped a torch from its brace.

Hank stood but was knocked to his seat by men rushing past him. Ted reached down and offered his hand to pull him up.

"Let's go!" Ted said as others rushed toward the grandstand gate to leave and march on the Catholic church. Hank hesitated, thinking of the consequences, and was thankful when Stridler's powerful voice interrupted the stampede.

Standing on the same spot he had occupied at the moment of his last statement, Stridler folded his arms in front of him. He didn't need to raise his hands to accent his words. His voice was enough.

"Stop!" he said, then paused a moment. "Return to your seats, please, fellow klansmen, for I'm not yet finished and you have, for the moment, jumped the gun."

The crowd, some dressed in robes and some in street clothes, stopped its mass motion toward the gate and looked up at Stridler. Hank angled to get a look at the klavern leader. The flickering torches touched the faces of the newly appointed klansmen, lighting up cheeks while placing eyes in shadow, illuminating teeth and chins while darkening brows in a menacing way that, in Hank's mind, resembled night-creatures rather than humans.

At the same time, the flames licking at the blood-red walls brought an orangey tinge to the sea of white robes. Then the sea broke up and flowed apart. Robes moved back to the grandstand seats, slowly at first, then with a noticeable rush—a haste similar to that of a crowd at the silent movies hurrying back to its seats to catch the second half of a show after intermission.

𝕶 𝕶 𝕶

Stridler allowed himself a moment to ponder the power he had over these men who returned to their seats at a mere word from him, these men who were metamorphosed from an audience into a mob and back with a word. He'd been learning to harness this power when he was a klansman back in Alabama. But it wasn't completely alien to him, and he wasn't about to turn his back on its possibilities. Those prospects were just too great.

Besides, the meaning of his cause far transcended the five dollars he received for every man he enlisted—though that would have been cause enough for him. The Cause was existence, a right to hold what you'd earned, and to destroy anti-Americanism and anti-Godliness.

He told himself that The Cause far surpassed money and power, and for it to be fully effective, it had to be handled with the care and thought of a master chess player, which Stridler was. Since the chess game had just recently begun, the pawns had only been moved in front of the king and queen, and Stridler was prepared to move ahead with the knights in a flank action but not to begin a full-frontal assault with queen and bishops.

That gambit would have to wait—not too long, but for a while at least—unless there came an unexpected opening. The other night's misstep with the Frenchman had caused a minor furor, but Stridler's steadfastness to The Cause, and his ability to pass on that commitment, had preempted the problem.

His eyes surveying the hall, Stridler said, "I love your spontaneity, but you move a bit too soon, klansmen. We must learn from our mistakes, especially if we want to pick up the tempo of our crusade. We must be hasty only when the situation warrants, and learn to plan ahead, to chart our every step, its consequences, and the reactions and counter-reactions to it."

Heads nodded in sober solemnity.

"Therefore," he continued, "our campaign from this point will be planned in general by our officers, along with the klavern, klorago, klexter, night-hawk, and klokans. For the newly initiated, as you'll find in the literature handed you when you signed up, these are our inner guard, outer guard, person in charge of candidates, and board of advisors. This group will formulate our plans, our future. And so, I call this meeting to a close, to be followed by a meeting of this committee. You all will be advised of our plans very soon.

"But—" Stridler leaned forward, "*do* hold tight to that hostility. The Catholics among us are, indeed, an enemy armed for warfare and we cannot wait long to act. Just not tonight."

The room lapsed into silence, a cold purposeful silence.

In the midst of it sat Hank. Stridler didn't notice him for he was overshadowed by a crowd of men standing, testosterone pumping in their veins, anxious for action—just the way Stridler planned it, he thought, smiling.

𝕜 𝕜 𝕜

Ada Cutter was taking inventory of the fifty-pound bags of grain and the five-pound bags of seed in the storage room in the back of the store. They had a healthy supply. Thank God, they'd made an extra-large order, praying all the while that it would be a prosperous spring.

Several new families had moved into the area and bought farmland. Then others, like Matt Whittaker and John Bean, were planting more of their fields than in the past. Perhaps Matt was considering he had one more mouth to feed now. And how terrific *that* was! she thought, recalling her talks with Clara and how Clara and Matt so wanted a child of their own.

Ada could hear her husband, John, speaking to Nathan Hind in the store, trying to discover exactly what the minister was looking for. He'd made a last-minute stop into the store to buy a new spring coat for a trip to Boston. His horse and buggy were outside and he was packed to go. This was his last stop and then he'd be en route to Lewiston, where he'd catch a train.

Ada didn't envy the reverend. She didn't envy his being able to visit an historic city like Boston. And she didn't envy his leaving Cooper's Crossing. To her, The Crossing was bliss— blessed with rushing rivers, near the wilderness and nature, yet not too far from the bigger cities.

There was beauty in this land. Its splendor had kept her close to her hometown all her life and it still kept a grip on her in spite of recent hints of malice—sometimes submerged, sometimes otherwise.

Those hints bothered her, but she didn't dwell on them, dismissing them as scurrilous talk from the likes of Richard Fryer and a handful, if that, of his cronies. Besides, Fryer wasn't from hereabouts. He came from out of state somewhere, probably a place that didn't want to lay claim to him.

At any rate, Fryer's speeches would have to be made elsewhere, outside her store. She wouldn't allow that kind of talk in her store again if she had to take a shotgun to the runt of a man. Thank goodness Mr. Stridler came along the other day. Now, there was a gentleman, a fellow of distinction, sure of himself who didn't have to degrade French-Canadians or Catholics. He needed none of that to assure his place in the world. Self-assured. That was the word.

"Ada. Ada, will you come out here, please?" It was John.

Ada rushed from the storage room, and there were John and Nathan. *No emergency.*

John nodded at Nathan and, with a jocular smile, said, "Being a man of taste, our pastor has narrowed his choice of a coat down to two. And knowing that you're a woman of exquisite taste, he has requested your opinion."

Ada smiled to herself. In much more meaningful ways than this, Nathan always seemed to make everyone feel that they were important, that their attitudes and feelings were significant to people besides themselves. A dear man. Sad, he was alone, a widower. His wife had been so wonderful, a perfect companion for a minister.

Nathan pulled on the coats, one after the other. Ada chose one that was three-quarter length and the deep-blue of Moosehead Lake at its deepest part—the blue she pictured the ocean to be. "Of course," she said, "the other looks very becoming on you, too, Nathan. But the blue brings out your eyes more and too, it's ten dollars while the other's twelve."

"My darling lady, in matters of apparel I trust your judgment above all others," Nathan replied, "except One, of course." He glanced heavenward. "You're absolutely right. I'll take this one."

Nathan shook off the coat and passed it to Ada.

She was ringing up the sale on the cash register when the front door opened, ringing the bell hanging from above. The doorway was filled with the large frame of Robert Stridler and a breeze from out-of-doors carried a waft of sweet-smelling smoke from his pipe into the store.

Dressed in a black riding coat with knee-high boots, jodhpurs, and a round-topped black hat, Stridler looked every bit the country gentleman. The riding crop he carried in his right hand was a perfect touch, and one instantly knew it was not a costume but an outfit worn by someone who knew its implications and carried them well, someone bred in the gentleman's class—certainly a trait rare in Cooper's Crossing territory if not this entire portion of the country. It was more fitting of Georgia or Kentucky.

Perhaps Kentucky was the origin of that look. He did buy some of his horses there.

"Good day," Stridler said in a low but powerful voice, tipping his hat to Ada. He turned to Nathan and John and said to the minister, "Looks like what I've heard is true about your trip to Boston, reverend. That *is* your buggy outside with the bags in it, isn't it?"

The pleasant look suddenly vanished from Nathan's face. He nodded agreement.

Smiling, Stridler asked, "Exactly how long will you be gone, reverend?"

"Until next Monday." The response was flat. Ada could feel the atmosphere change, tension thickening. Stridler displayed an air of affability as if he were on stage, while Nathan seemed, for no apparent reason, to be seething. The minister's face was frozen, like stone chiseled into an expression of distaste.

Stridler, unperturbed, maintained his smile and said, "Well, I hope you have a safe and enjoyable journey." Then he added, "We'll be sure to take care of the town while you're gone. Protect it from its sins, you might say."

Nathan turned to Ada, gave her a ten-dollar bill, took the box containing his coat, said, "Thank you, Ada—John," walked up to Stridler and stood nearly on the big man's boots.

The reverend, nearly a half-foot shorter, looked squarely into Stridler's eyes and declared in a voice obviously knew meant for only the two of them to hear but poignant and strong in its intonations: "Mr. Stridler, I believe I know what you're about. And I think you know how I feel about it.

"Christianity entails more than catch-words and proverbs and memorizing the Ten Commandments. It embraces an inherent decency and a respect for all men God has made, rich or poor, black or white."

Nathan's lips thinned. "You've been attending my church regularly since you moved here. But it seems all the words of my sermons have been lost on some people, you included. Yes, Mr. Stridler, I'm sure I know what you're about. I can feel it when we're in the same room, and I can sense it when you're across the street. The Spirit of God knows the spirit of the evil one."

Nathan, his body rigid and his teeth noticeably grinding, continued, "There are some sins, Mr. Stridler, that are not easily washed from your hands; sins that are not forgiven in the eyes of God without repentance; and there are some people who, if their ways are not mended, will burn forever in the fires of hell."

Ada had never seen Stridler speechless before, but he stood there dumbfounded.

With that, Nathan stepped to the side and walked around Stridler to the door.

Finally, Stridler turned and said, "Yes, you're right. We do understand each other, reverend, but I'll never fathom your reasoning, and I plan to continue attending church every Sunday for the rest of my life. Don't fall into the trap of the Pharisees. They thought themselves greater than the multitudes."

Nathan, who had stood back to Stridler while he spoke, turned with a stern glare. "It's a long way to heaven, Mr. Stridler— longer than you may think."

He opened the door and calmly left.

Ada and the two men watched the pastor board the buggy and snap the reins, then Stridler approached the counter, and asked Ada if she had any more of that pretty red ribbon she had sold him before. She mustered a crooked smile and nodded assent.

CHAPTER NINE

Jacques LaBonte stood facing the road through the wide barn-like doors. His back was to the anvil and to the heat of the fire where Emile Cote was shaping a horseshoe with a hammer. The shoe glowed red where Emile held it over the flames burning red-hot from the billows.

"So now it's been five days, and still no sight of Jean," Jacques said. "No one seems to know what happened to him. He's just disappeared."

"That's not like Jean." Emile slowed his hammering to hear Jacques' tale.

"No. He's very conscientious. The only time he's ever missed work was when he had to go to Quebec when his pappy died."

Emile left the horseshoe on the anvil and approached Jacques. Wiping the sweat from his brow and tugging his pants up over his big belly, he pointed at a figure walking along on the other side of the street and asked, "Why don't you tell Sheriff Wright about it? Maybe he's heard something about Jean. Perhaps Jean was out cutting firewood in the woods and had a heart attack or some kind of accident. We could organize a search party for him."

Jacques started to shrug off Emile's suggestion, but then hesitated. It was a good idea.

"I think I will," he said. Taking a quick step toward the open door, he turned for a moment to say, "But, if you find I'm missing for a while, or if my dog wanders over to your house looking for food because no one's fed him, or if you notice no lights on in my house for a long time some night, check it out, will you?"

Emile's mouth twisted as if he'd swallowed a lemon.

Jacques read his objection and blurted out, "Jean being missing may have more to do with things besides his philanderin', Emile, and I may be next. So, you keep in mind what and who we talked about if that happens—okay?"

Emile combed his fingers through his curly black hair and nodded his assent, but warned Jacques, "Protect yourself with that little gem I got ya' for Christmas a couple of years ago, if need be."

Jacques gently patted the bulging pocket in his spring coat and replied, "Thought of that already. Thanks."

In a second he was gone, hurrying toward the bridge in the direction Sheriff Wright had been heading.

When Jacques reached the bridge, he found the sheriff gripping the handrail and looking north, upstream on the Androscoggin River to its confluence with the Limerick. The waters were really riled. Turbulent, double-faced waves kicked up where the two rivers met. Though the worst of the waters from the spring thaw were past, there had been a lot of snow the previous winter and its effects were still being felt.

The sheriff glimpsed Jacques' approach from the corner of his eye and declared, "Plenty of flow for a good log drive."

"Sure is." Jacques pulled up beside him and rested his elbows on the rail as he, too, gazed upstream.

"They should be coming in any time now, shouldn't they?"

"Yeah. Word is Andre LaRoche's crew's pretty close, somewhere on the Alamoosook just north of Pocomoonshine Mountain."

Sheriff Wright expelled a guttural cough. "I imagine they'll make a brief stopover there, eh?"

Jacques nodded.

"Not much I can do about it," the sheriff said. "I guess Suzie makes the best hard liquor around and it'd take a heap of a man to resist such a delight when he's so nearby." The sheriff hesitated a second, then added, a smile on his face, "Even if it's illegal."

Jacques chuckled, then turned serious. "Listen, Will. I think we've got a problem. Fact is, it's probably a lot more than that, but I've been waiting before tellin' ya' 'cause I was being hopeful. Now, it seems, is not a time a person can afford optimism."

"Someone fiddlin' with the railroad trestle again?" Sheriff Wright turned away from the river and devoted his full attention to Jacques.

Jacques frowned. "No, it's not the trestle. Worse than that. Or, then again, may be nothing at all."

Jacques bent down, picked up a handful of pebbles and jounced them in his hand as he straightened. Picking the largest rock from his palm with his right hand, he turned and heaved it upstream in the direction of his mill which stood at the point sixty yards away. The rock plopped into the river halfway to the mill.

"It's Jean Bonneau," he said, keeping his eyes on the spot where the rock had disappeared into the river.

Sheriff Wright nodded.

Jacques continued, "Jean could have thrown that rock all the way to my mill. Incredible throwing arm. You know how good a pitcher he is."

"Yep. Sure is."

"Well, do you recall last year when we had the annual Cooper's Crossing Fourth of July baseball game and we played Hiram Mills?" Not waiting for Will Wright's nod, Jacques went on, "Jean was supposed to pitch that game."

The sheriff interrupted, "Jacques, what're you getting at? I thought something was wrong today, not last year."

"Hold on. I'm gettin' there. Now, the point is Jean didn't pitch that game—he didn't even come to it. And beyond that, Will— and this is between you and me—the wife of a certain Cooper's Crossing businessman didn't attend the activities for a certain amount of time that day, either. Matter of fact, Jean and this certain woman didn't attend the game and celebration because they were attending to other matters of another sporting nature—together."

Jacques paused to let what he'd said fully register.

"Oh," Will said softly, "I see."

"Now, point one is this," Jacques said, "Jean and the woman he was with have become a pretty permanent fixture—on the sly—since last summer. Point two: The woman's husband is a very vengeful person, and on top of that may very well have learned about the affair. Point three: Jean, who is usually punctual to the minute, has now been missing from work for five days, and I've heard no message from him. Point four: The Ku Klux Klan's now in town, and the Klan supposedly looks down on this type of, ah, activity. And, point five: the woman's husband, being the type that he is, may very well belong to the Klan.

"This all said, Will," Jacques continued, "the consequences could be grave."

"Agreed." A thoughtful and pained expression was carved on the sheriff's face. "And maybe rightfully so, too, though that would break the law. But we've lived with the people of The Crossing all our lives, Jacques. We've gone through school together and helped each other through jams and tragedies and what-have-you. Do you really think anyone, let alone a whole group of people, in this town would do something really dreadful? Like kill Jean or something—?"

Jacques nodded. "I do."

"Well, my friend," Will patted Jacques' shoulder, "I'd have to have some mighty hard evidence—much more than Jean's not showing up at work—to pursue the matter."

"Word is, down South where they're real strong, the Klan's good at tar 'n feathering and railroading people out of town. Maybe they did that to Jean."

Will bit his lower lip, tugged his hat down tighter on his head, then said, in a conciliatory tone, "Okay. I'll look into it. I'll ask around. But you've got to tell me who the woman is. I've got to know that. Adultery and murder in The Crossing? Jeez, Louise!"

As a wagon filled with lumber from Frank Thomas' saw mill rolled by them, Jacques leaned over and whispered into the sheriff's ear.

𝕶 𝕶 𝕶

Robert Stridler stood in the widow's walk atop his house, surveying the fields and woods and buildings encompassed by the land he called his, the property he had transformed from a barren, unproductive thousand acres to a farm boasting fields that during the summer were lush with corn and potato plants, a pasture where the best purebred quarter horses grazed nearby a string of stables, hundreds of acres of pine, beach, birch, spruce and fir.

Disregarding a cool spring breeze, Stridler wore a white cotton chamois, its top buttons undone. His dark gray jodhpurs were tucked into riding boots. But while the outfit portrayed an aloof gentility detached from labor, his hands betrayed the fact that while loosening up one of his fillies, he hadn't been able to resist riding across the road to the fields where his workmen were plowing the soil. And, while there, he'd helped adjust a plow, then paid a visit to one of his potato houses that stored spuds for the upcoming planting.

The stock of spuds was so high that he'd told Fryer to prepare another fifty acres for planting, bringing the total to five hundred acres. Another fifty would be readied for corn, both early for the livestock and sugar-and-gold for eating and sale.

Fryer had been quick to agree—one of his redeeming qualities—but seemed to be displaying even more peculiar little ticks, a nervous twitch of the left eye and of the cheek, a nibble on the lower lip. Even years before, Fryer's nerves always seemed to be on edge, but lately he had appeared to be getting worse. His eyes always moved when he talked to you. His stuttering was getting increasingly worse.

The situation might create a problem and, considering the plans for the immediate future, this was absolutely no time for peripheral issues. Something might, just might, have to be done about the good ole boy from Kentucky if he didn't begin to control his nerves in some way.

Fryer was in a demanding job, but everyone had to learn to cope with the strains of their careers and families and social and community duties. Fryer had no family, so he was a step ahead of most people. He'd have to be watched very closely, though.

Stridler turned his attention from the corn and potato fields across the road and looked around him at the compound surrounding his large captain's house. He had found a perfect location.

This estate was much like the women he had held on his arm now and then—beautiful, enticing, luring, and alluring.

But, sadly, the women could never become a part of it. They'd spoil the mission. They'd sooner or later feel they must compete with it. And they'd lose. They'd lose because they'd hold demands over his time and his affection—and his time, his affection, indeed his life, belonged to this farm, to this klavern, to this ideal and his pursuit of it. His devotion couldn't be parceled out like that.

His back to the road and facing the rear of the house, Stridler looked to his right. Between the house and the driveway stood a small, one-story building just big enough to house his little-used Duesenberg—which was one of the first models made in 1921.

Double swinging doors centered the building. They were smaller than but similar to those of the barn located directly across the driveway. The barn served mainly as a storage area for the hay for his horses, nearly all of its ground floor filled as well as the loft.

The roof of the barn stood as high as that of the house on which Stridler stood. It had been the first structure he'd built after buying the property. The barn that had stood there was old and its roof had sagged, and Stridler had been determined to have a barn sufficient for his needs.

Everything on this farm, just like back home in Kentucky, would be capable of fulfilling any needs he might have in the future. His credo was to beyond his current requirements and maintain a balanced and not overly optimistic look on the future. And he'd lived well by that credo thus far—foreseeing one major crisis of his life far enough ahead of time to escape any dire consequences—especially of the magnitude that could have befallen him.

A meadow behind the house and the barn stretched westward for one hundred and fifty yards. Most of it was open, but corral fences partitioned parts of it. In the very middle of the field stood a long stable containing two dozen stalls—a dozen on each side—with a walkway running down the middle.

Each thoroughbred enjoyed his own stall separated from floor to ceiling by partitions, with a Dutch door on the outside wall and a gate to the inside walkway.

A stable boy was busying himself unloading a flatbed truck carrying a couple dozen bales of hay he'd transferred from the barn. He was the only human being in sight on this side of the farm, and the scene reminded Stridler of a John Marin painting.

The muted tones of the spring scene were like the misty, diaphanous touches left by Marin's brush. The purity of nature was captured in a mysterious bond—a concatenation of sunlight and wind interacting over the meadow and trees.

Throughout the pastures, the grass was sprouting up bright green, resembling a velvet carpet. Later the black-eyed Susans, Indian paintbrushes, and buttercups would dress up the fields outside the corrals with brilliant, singing colors.

Beyond the stables and the field stood a narrow windbreak of trees, their limbs tipped with fresh buds of new growth, and beyond that the Androscoggin River, flowing full and fast.

The river was magnificent this time of year, roiling, muddling the reflections off its waters. It was narrow at this point, perhaps only fifty or sixty yards wide. He remembered standing on the riverbank just the day before, astonished at the water's speed and force.

It made him wonder how on earth men could physically stand atop rolling logs and ride them down such churning waters.

But he'd rubbed that wonderment from his mind when it occurred to him that he was bordering on complimenting a group consisting largely of immigrant French-Canadian barbarians. Damned drunk sinful frogs. That described them, and that sort of crowd deserved no accolades, no recognition of merit, no matter the nature.

At the thought of the log drivers, he looked to his left, to the "other" barn on his land, his latest addition to the Stridler estate. Built lower to the ground, the KKK headquarters was longer than the other barn. It wasn't as conspicuous, either, being tucked behind a line of trees separating it from the road. It also had no large front doors, but was entered or exited through just two traditional-sized doors on either lengthwise side. Further distinguishing it were the three- by three-foot windows, red-tinged, spaced along the walls near the roof.

That barn was one of his true prides. It epitomized the fruition of his move to Maine. Yes, everything had evolved so that it was very much as it had been at home. People had accepted him as a neighbor, friend, and eventually a leader in what he regarded a short time by Yankee standards. He was growing potatoes and corn instead of wheat, but his first love, his horses, remained integral to his life.

And although Fryer was a shadow of the man he had been, the appearance of the security chief from the old klavern had not yet proven bad fortune. Fryer's worst point was a tendency toward outspokenness in public places. Acceptable in Kentucky, not here.

But, yes, he had all the necessary ingredients for a fulfilling life—land bordering on a river and near a railroad for transportation of his crops; fields in which to grow those crops;

meadows on which to raise his horses; woods for beauty and harvest; and all the spiritual requisites a man of white Anglo-Saxon heritage, upbringing, education, and religion could want.

Stridler looked at the red-trimmed white barn, nodded to himself, and grinned. That barn was a key piece to it all—a place to congregate, to speak out and be heard, and to formulate action for the most just of all causes. It was a shrine which, by its architecture, reminded a klansman when he entered of his oath of obedience, secrecy, fidelity, and klannishness, and of his commitment to uphold the American ideal.

And, most important of all, it reminded each and every one who entered it of his obligation to preserve the sacred constitutional rights and privileges of the church and state, liberty, free public schools, free speech and press, the pursuit of happiness against encroachment, and the all-importance of white supremacy.

He dismissed the fact that besides, he made a lot of money running the klavern. Sure, his take from the dues was considerable, but it truly wasn't a factor. No—never.

The actions planned in that shrine were more important than money. They'd have an everlasting effect on the people of Cooper's Crossing and all of Maine.

The national Klan had determined it would establish itself across the country and saw Maine as a bellwether state. Indeed, the motto was "As Maine goes, so goes the nation."

So, when Stridler ran into his "troubles" in Kentucky, a plan emerged with the KKK hierarchy.

Edward Clarke and Elizabeth Tyler, owners of the Southern Publicity Association of Atlanta who engineered the Klan's comeback, put their heads together with then-Imperial Wizard William Simmons.

A day later, as Stridler—then Simon Kennedy Duke—hid from authorities, they determined to help him "disappear" into the far reaches of the country under a new name. They'd go to such lengths for the grandson of an officer of the KKK when it was organized in Pulaski, Tennessee, in 1865. Hey, even his middle name (Kennedy) was given him after Capt. John B. Kennedy, Klan's first Grand Magi.

And so, he was sent here to Cooper's Crossing. His klavern's klabee, or treasurer, in Kentucky was president of the bank where he held his fortune, and was able to secrete most of it to Duke-Stridler. It was more than enough to bankroll his new endeavors. And the Kentucky authorities never looked beyond their own borders for the man wanted for arson and manslaughter.

His past a faint memory, Stridler saw the major tasks before the Klan as containing and repelling the immigrant tide and maintaining control of Americans' lands, jobs and money.

But other evils existed that needed confrontation, and though they were of lesser stature, they should be dealt with first. Destroy the lesser enemy before tackling the greater and, in doing so, you'll gain strength and confidence. That was how Stridler viewed it, and he'd found no opposition, neither to the idea of it, nor to his "initial point of attack."

Liquor and immorality were the targets. Liquor, he preached, was an instrument of the devil. It resulted in demonic mischief and satanic pleasure-seeking. Sex was meant to be confined to spouses. Divorces, philandering, adultery, promiscuity, profanity—they all precipitated even worse behavior, and therefore must be erased.

Before the last meeting, in a special session of the klokann, the executive committee, Simon Foot had said, "We've gotta do something to set an example."

After the chatter of agreement, Stridler had snatched the opportunity. Yes, examples would be set, he declared, both in the countryside—on Henhawk Hill and on Pocomoonshine Mountain—and in the middle of town, at the Catholic church. Then everything would come together in one glorious uprising—good over evil!

CHAPTER 10

The hulk of Pocomoonshine Mountain shouldered out of the forest floor to the east of Alamoosook Stream. The trees, bared all winter, were gaining body with the new growth of spring. Rare patches of snow lingered here and there on its slopes, hidden in the shadow of large trees or rocks.

With a deep breath, Jigger inhaled the distinct odor of the balsam fir trees all about him. He had one eye on the path and was flipping pages of the little Bible he held in his hand.

With Pierre on his left and Monty on his right, Jigger strode down a wooded trail on their way to visit Suzie Cooley. He felt aquiver with anticipation at his annual encounter with the quick-witted little woman he'd nicknamed "La Femme de la Montagne," The Woman of the Mountain.

"Here it is," Jigger said and stopped in his tracks. He pointed at the right-hand page. "Here's that spot I was readin' this mornin'. It's in Proverbs, chapter 18, and it says: 'But there is a friend who sticks closer than a brother.' Who d'you think that is, Pierre?"

Before Pierre could answer, Jigger spoke up, "It's Jesus, my friend. Jesus. The One who saved me out of that stream. He's the One it's talkin' about. As close as your dad and I were, Jesus is closer. As close as you and I are, He's closer. I love this book!"

Pierre laughed. "I can tell that, Jig. You seem like a new man."

"I am," said Jigger. "I am. I—" At that moment a light wisp of smoke stole his attention. It reached the treetops, then dispersed into the breeze. Not heavy smoke, but constant, and it came from where Suzie's camp lay on the side of the mountain.

Jigger's eyes widened, and he grabbed Pierre's arm and pointed to the smoke.

"Somethin's cookin'," Pierre said.

"But it's not food," Jigger finished. He stuffed his Bible into his pocket and broke into a run through the woods.

Shifting his attention back and forth from the smoke to the ground ahead of him as he ran, Jigger measured the distance to be a quarter of a mile to Suzie's camp. The smoke wasn't getting thicker. That was good. He couldn't see any flames. That was even better. Or, perhaps the worst could be expected. Perhaps there was no more to burn, the camp just a pile of smoldering logs crumbled on top of one another.

More important, what about Suzie? Was she all right?

Jigger increased his pace to a sprint down the trail, leaving the younger but bigger Pierre and Monty behind him.

As he ran, Jigger's mind raced as well. What would he use to fight the fire if indeed there was anything left to fight? He'd left his ax back at camp. Would they be able to contain the fire to just the land immediately around Suzie's cabin? What if the flames reached the trees close-quartered around it? He listened. He couldn't hear Pierre and Monty.

Did the others of the crew behind them see the smoke and were they running as well? And what if they did see it, and they were racing, too—would they get to the camp in time to prevent a forest fire? Would they be able to stop it without shovels, axes, any tools at all to battle it with?

Jigger hurdled a "squirrel's bridge," a small birch tree whose top had been bent to the ground by wind or ice, and entered a pine grove. The cabin was just ahead, on the far side of the grove and past a clump of fir trees.

His heart thumped against his chest. Cold, harsh air constricted his lungs, but his legs felt fresh, like the churning wheels of a locomotive. He mustn't waste time. His body couldn't falter, not now.

Then, as Jigger ducked and ran between twin firs, the sight slammed him like a sucker-punch. Devastation but—*Merci Dieu*—no flames. Jigger bent forward, putting his hands on his knees, and inhaled deeply.

Suzie's cabin, its connecting shed, even the outhouse twenty yards away, were leveled except for the remnant of a chimney. Charred wood a foot deep on the ground, black smoke lofting out of the debris in puffs and spurts, but not a body in sight.

Walls and ceilings and floors of charcoal, chunks of blackened beams, the rubble of furniture and personal belongings, but still not a body in sight.

The ground surrounding the structures was singed from the heat and sparks that had hissed through the air, carried by the wind— the breeze of the night before, Jigger guessed. But, again, he saw no Suzie, and anxiety seized up within him like a corkscrew. The muscles in his throat constricted as he straightened up, forced his legs forward, and tried to look more closely—for a sign, a piece of clothing, one of her many dresses—anything, but hopefully, nothing.

Heavy boots broke twigs on the ground behind him. Jigger didn't turn. His purpose was singular. Find Suzie. And he prayed that when he did, she wouldn't be lying dead in the desolation that had been her home.

His comrades gasped when they entered the site. Jigger walked around the perimeter of the disaster, intent on uncovering a trace of or a clue to Suzie's whereabouts.

A line of shattered glass blackened by smoke lay on the ground where the shed had been. Jagged shards of glass surrounded large pieces of what had been jugs—probably filled with Suzie's potion, which had exploded from the intense heat.

The potion! The still! Jigger looked away from the rubble and up the slope behind the cabin site, some thirty yards into the woods. Yes!

The trees were bare enough that Jigger could see part of the equipment between them. He stepped off in that direction. As he walked closer, he could see it was more like wreckage. Twisted tubes of copper and steel sprung towards the sky. What once was a tin cylinder three feet high now lay in a bent, crunched heap with large, gaping holes gouged into it. A whitish clear liquid fell in slow drops from a hole at its base where it lay against the ground and a large stone.

It was grotesque, really, like a gigantic spider, its legs broken and gnarled. As his head spun with wonder at who could have wreaked this havoc, he heard a noise.

He bent an ear. Something between a whimper and a laugh. Human. Jigger looked to his left and, no more than ten feet away, sat Suzie Cooley. A birch tree propped her back. Her arms were tight behind her and tied to the tree.

Her face and clothes were covered with soot, smudged by tears. Her hair was tangled despite being so short.

Jigger rushed to her and when her eyes met his, they revealed anguish.

"Hello, Jig," she said softly. A touch of gladness offset the sadness in her voice. She offered a pained smile. "Mind helping a lady out of a fix?"

Jigger leaned down and began untying the rope around Suzie's arms.

"Hey, Madame Suzie." Pierre sounded astonished and relieved. He took off at a dead sprint from the cabin site up the hill, the others following him.

"It seems ever I'm in a bind, I kin count on you," Suzie said to Jigger as she wriggled her hands free of the rope he'd loosened. She rubbed her wrists and winced at the pain where the rope had chafed her skin. "Ever' time, you's there, Jig. I was thinkin' in the middle of the night as I watched this place smolder that you'd be along. An' here you are. It was good timin'."

Jigger chuckled. "Can't seem to stay away from ladies in distress," he said.

He gently turned her hands over in his and investigated the rope burns around her wrists. The skin was broken and the blood had oozed to the surface.

"Alcohol to kill the germs, salve caked on them. That oughta do the trick," Jigger said.

"Let a real medicine man take a look at this injured Injun." Pierre leaned in and gave Jigger a slow but firm push.

Pierre pulled a small inch-high jar from a bag hanging from his belt and dug his fingers into the jelly inside it to apply it to Suzie's wrists.

"Exactly what happened here, Suzie?" Jigger asked.

𝕜 𝕜 𝕜

Suzie wasn't sure she wanted to relive the worst night of her life, not even to Jigger, one of her most favoritest people on earth.

She pulled a handkerchief from Pierre's pocket and wiped it across her eyes, rubbing away the soot and tears and with them the look of anguish. Her eyes opened wide as she looked up at Jigger. It was like he wasn't even there. She was seeing the top of her chimney over his shoulder.

Hours ago, there was a roof around that chimney. Then she opened up.

"It was 'most exactly how my ema told me it had been years ago, way back'n the white man come to America and begun takin' our land," she said. "She told me tales, to learn me a lesson so I'd know the ways of the worl' of the white man, not knowin' they gave me nightmares."

Sudden pain shot up her hand where Pierre was applying the salve and Suzie winced.

"Sorry," he said.

"It's okay, Pierre." She smiled and offered him her other bruised wrist, and he again dug into his tin of salve.

She turned her attention back to Jigger. His soft brown eyes belied his rough exterior. A good friend. The best. One she could tell her story.

She continued: "Last night was one of them nightmares, Jig. Just a few differences. Instead of men wearin' coonskin hats and carryin' long rifles, they wore tall, pointy hats with flaps that covered their faces and they carried axes and sledge hammers and big sticks like them there baseball bats."

The thought of it made her squirm. Jig rested a hand on her shoulder, reassuring her, comforting.

Suzie took a deep breath and went on, "These men? They's covered with long white sheets trimmed with red. And 'stead of swarmin' down on a few Injun huts or teepees, they's comin' down on me!"

She cringed and a shiver flew down her spine. The crew had all gathered in a circle, listening intently, their faces twisted in anger.

"I was sittin' next to the fireplace, sewin' up one of my dresses—the one you always liked, Jig. The bright red one with the blue 'n white snapdragons."

Jig smiled and nodded.

"Then I heard some scufflin' outside and, all of a sudden, the door busted open and a whole crowd of these big white sheets swarmed right in on me. It was like a hive of bees. I-I didn't have a chance to even scream 'fore two of 'em grabbed ahold my arms and dragged me outta the door. They hauled me right out into the yard to another one who was even bigger than them-uns and he was wearin' red, like the devil."

Oh, for sure, he was the devil, or the devil's helper.

"And he started up talkin', no, preachin' t' me. But I didn't really hear much of what he was sayin' 'cause behind me I could hear bangin' and crackin' and splinterin' and all kinds of noise and I knew they was breakin' my cabin to pieces. And someone was takin' Jake, my horse, out into the woods. But I do know the big 'un was sayin' somethin' about my potion, and the next thing

I know they's pushin' and pullin' me up the hill here, and then they's tyin' me to this here tree."

Were Jig's eyes turnin' red?

"Then the big 'un says, 'I want you to have the best seat in the house, squaw, so's you can see both shows at once.' Just then, a group of 'em rushed up the hill, carryin' those big hammers and axes, and they started bangin' and pullin' holes in the barrels 'til it was just one big heap of scrap. Just look at it!"

She turned to survey the remains of her still. The men around her gasped, grumbled, swore. A couple of them left the group and walked toward the remnants of her still.

That contraption had been her pride and joy, not to mention the source of just about all the money she had ever earned.

ʞ ʞ ʞ

Jigger couldn't equate Suzie's loss with anything he might lose—unless someone burned down a forest, or if God made a river run dry. The still had been that important to her, he knew, and something had to be done to rectify the situation.

He'd read the Scripture about too much drink being bad, but old Suzie didn't deserve this from anybody. There had to be something they could do to help her.

Jigger reached down and helped Suzie stand, took her arm in his and led her up the hill to the still.

The ground was charred in a circle around the apparatus, and the trees at the edge of the circle were darkened with smoke. The flames must have been high and hot. Lucky the trees didn't catch fire, Jigger thought. And as he and Suzie stepped onto the blackened earth, she broke the silence.

"It wasn't enough they broke everythin' up," she said. "They had to burn it too. One of 'em brought a coupla jugs from the cabin and poured 'em all 'round here. And the big 'un, he brought a match out from inside those sheets he was wearin', and puff, this whole place lit up." Her hand flew up into the air. "A giant candle. The flames reached the still and, whoosh, went right up through the tubes, shootin' fire out the ends like a dragon snortin' flames."

Jigger shook his head. Who'd do this? And to Suzie?

Suzie continued: "Thank the Great Spirit the grass is young and green and everythin's a little moist. But I'm sure they would've stopped the fire from spreadin' over the mountain—'cause probably some of 'em are from t'other side of Pocomoonshine."

Jigger broke in, "You think you might know who it was who done it? Any of 'em?"

Suzie, her arm locked with Jigger's, shook her head slowly. "I might. And I mightn't."

Then she turned, tugging Jigger along with her, and putting an arm out for Pierre, began trudging back down the hill toward the cabin site.

"Whoever it was," she said, "burnin' the still weren't enough. I thought they's gonna bash up the cabin and leave it at that. But, the big 'un, after lightin' the fire at the still, turned nice and calm and walked back past me down the hill, noddin' to me as he went by—kind of like a how-do-ya'-do, ma'am?"

As he, Suzie, Pierre and the others behind them moved on, Jigger figured they were probably retracing the steps of "the big 'un" down the hill.

"I could see his every step," Suzie said. "I think he planned it that way, t' tease me."

As they reached the edge of the blackened ground surrounding the cabin, Suzie stopped quick and made an abrupt left turn, saying nothing but, loosing herself from Jigger and Pierre's arms, hurried a short distance up the slope of the land.

Then, kneeling on the ground, her back to the men, she pulled several dead branches from the earth and tossed them behind her. A moment later, with a shout of glee, she stood up straight and turned around.

"Well, he mighta tormented me, and burned my still and my cabin. But all ain't lost." She held her hands up high, each holding a jug of cloudy liquid. "Come on, boys. Let's indulge 'fore I start cryin' agin."

Jigger looked warily at Suzie, something moved in the trees behind her. "I don't think you'll be cryin' right now, Suzie, not when you see what's behind you."

Suzie turned to look.

"Jake!" she cried, then ran to meet her horse who made his way out of the trees.

"I shoulda known you'd come back, 'n straight for the liquor hole, too, you ole rascal." She threw a hug around the horse's neck and kissed it hard on the nose. Jake responded with a snort and long-tongued lick across her neck.

Jigger and the others roared with laughter and a new mood took hold.

Suzie guided the horse back to the men, passed a jug to Jigger and said, "What's holding up this celebration, anyhow?"

Jigger passed the jug onto Pierre, plopped himself down on the ground at Suzie's side, and pulled her down beside him. "You boys go on ahead with Suzie's potion, if you will. But take it from one who has drunk some of the best of 'em under the table, it'll come to no good."

Jigger turned to Suzie, "We've got to find you another line of work, Suzie. Somethin' else to bring money to Pocomoonshine Mountain. Let me tell you about sin and death, and about man givin' over his mind to hard liquor."

Hearing this, Pierre set down the bottle as well. But Andre grabbed its neck, took a couple of long swallows, pulled it quickly from his lips, and let loose a gasp. "Whew-w-w, Suzie, that's mighty fine potion," he said breathlessly. "Darned if it don't get better ever' year."

Andre passed the bottle along to Yvan and the big man guzzled the liquid like it was water. But Pierre focused his attention on what Jigger was telling La Femme de la Montagne.

Jigger turned, pointed to Yvan and said, "Someday, someday you're gonna pour something you shouldn't down that gullet, and it's gonna light up your innards like a light bulb and you'll go ka-boom. No more Yvan the Bull."

"One thing my daddy taught me, Jig," Yvan replied, "was to never begrudge a man his booze."

"Oh, I wouldn't do that. I love you for what you are, Yvan, even when you're tighter than bark on a tree. I just want you to live with me—and the others who know the Lord—forever, my friend."

Jigger turned to Suzie. "What we don't like, Suzie, is men who ain't men at all. We don't like those who destroy other people's property and tie 'em up and leave 'em for the black bears. And we're gonna do somethin' about it."

🕶🕶🕶

Suzie said nothing, just watched Jigger through a cloud of fatigue. The adrenalin rush that had sparked her party mood had suddenly drained away, and not even her potion could disperse the fog before her eyes or the ache in her muscles.

She really wanted to listen to more of what Jigger wanted to share with her, but she shivered despite the sun shining through the treetops and branches, and she wrapped her arms around herself as if against the cold.

Retelling the experience had helped, but the dreadful fears lingered. Those ghostly figures loomed over her in her cabin. They dragged her to a terrifying view of the destruction of her home. Could she ever shake the horror of it all?

At first, a stunned semi-consciousness had gotten her through the night and into the early-morning hours—time passing like a wisp of wind through the Pocomoonshine pines.

Then Jigger'd appeared. Dear Jig. And he'd made it easy to be reconciled to the fate of her circumstances.

But she couldn't keep her barriers up any longer. She was too tired—much too tired. Mumbling something about no more extra dresses to put on to keep her warm, she shuddered.

Just before falling off to a deep sleep, she felt Jigger catch her and cradle her in his arms. The last she heard was Jig saying, "We've gotta do somethin', boys. We gotta do somethin'."

𝕽𝕽𝕽

The pale light from a setting sun met Suzie's eyes when she awoke from a deep slumber. She didn't know if it was the sunlight or the sound of an ax cracking hard against wood that brought her the final short distance out of her sleep. The sky through the trees overhead was the light blue of the top dress she was wearing, her favorite color. Warmth and comfort enveloped her. She looked down to see that she was bundled up in a plaid flannel blanket and deerskin. Her head rested on a rolled blanket and she lay next to a large elm tree.

It took a moment to fix her location as near the base of Pocomoonshine perhaps forty or fifty yards north of her cabin, or what had been her cabin.

Then she focused on the source of that unremitting sound and an odd accompanying noise, perhaps a grating, no, a sawing. Looking downhill at the small clearing, Suzie lurched into a sitting position, and in a moment, she was standing, stunned.

At the left edge of the clearing lay a pile of twenty-foot logs stacked five feet high and eight or ten feet wide. Two standing poplars served as bookends to keep the pile in place.

At the beginning of what looked like a long assembly line, two men were taking one of the logs off the pile and carrying it toward two large wooden x-vises stuck into the ground so that when a log was placed in the vises, one end of the log in each vise, the log was held in place along the ground. There were three pair of these vises, each manned by two burly lumberjacks.

When a log was set in its place, one man stood at each end and, broadax in hand, began hewing the log down to a foot from the end. After hewing two opposite sides of the log, the men began cutting dovetail notches for the corner of the cabin, using cutout pieces of scrapboard fit into the notches to insure they were all cut the same size.

While these six pair of men chopped away, the wood chips flying about them, to their right was another link in the assembly line. A big heap of four-foot logs rose several feet off the ground, tossed there to await a skilled dissection.

Suzie watched one, whom she recognized as Ernest Plourde, work with a dexterity that betrayed his summer occupation as a carpenter.

Ernest had slit his log in half and then quartered each half, leaving all sections still standing upright on the ground. Using a steel wedge and go-devil, he quickly split the heart of the tree out by working on one section at a time. His muscles bulging inside his shirt and a calm, unhurried expression on his face, made it impossible to tell how long Ernest had been working, cutting floorboards. Since mid-morning when she went to sleep?

He deftly, and with amazing speed, split each section into four equally thick bolts, then tossed all the bolts into a growing pile behind him and the other two men working beside him.

Apparently, Ernest's concentration made him oblivious to the goings-on behind him. But the scene pulled Suzie like a magnet down the hill. Tears welled up in her eyes, blurring the image of her new home, but not before she had impressed it in her mind.

Several small boulders, their top surfaces chiseled flat, served as the foundation, lifting the cabin a foot off the ground. The sills were skillfully quarter-notched with the end logs. Six large sleepers had been lap-jointed into place, and several men were placing the dovetail-notched wall logs one upon the other. The walls were four feet high all around the cabin.

It seemed to Suzie that the woods, the nature around the small clearing, had already accepted the structure as part of the forest. It was a pure frontier cabin, its logs looking and even smelling of wilderness.

Oh, the smell of chopped birch!

So much better than her old cabin.

Suzie didn't look to her right, south of the clearing. Her mind's eye knew what lay there: the ashes of her life. Nothing saved from the hot, glowing flames of the night before. Her work, her few treasures had been reduced to cinders in a tinderbox.

In the midst of the construction stood Jigger. Pierre was doing something Suzie couldn't make out at one end of a long log, and Jigger had his ear to the other end. Jigger straightened up, said, "Nope. Won't do. Got a rotten spot in the middle somewhere." And as he looked up at Pierre, he spotted Suzie.

"Well, if it isn't the sleeping princess of Pocomoonshine!" he hollered. In a second, he started scurrying up the hill as the others called a welcome to her. Nearly the whole crew was there, she estimated, guessing that only those at the tail end of the log drive poking along stranded logs weren't in her clearing at that moment.

"Jig, what on earth you doin'?" she said as Jigger approached.

"We figured you gotta tell Sheriff Wright about all that happened, but that won't help ya' any when it comes to findin' a place to sleep. So, we decided we'd better git the pitch out of our britches and git started."

She threw her arms around him and reached up to kiss him on the cheek. Jigger turned and motioned toward the clearing.

"This crew can work pretty fast when we put our minds to it," he said. "Besides, we're only a hoot 'n a holler away from The Crossing. Even with a day off, we'll still be the first drive into town. Guaranteed."

Tears worked their way down Suzie's cheeks and she gave them free rein. She could cry 'til her body was dry!

Then, relief surging over her, she laughed aloud and jumped into the air.

When she came down Jigger pointed an accusing finger at her, then said, "Mon amie, don't exert. You need some more rest."

"But I want to help!"

"Your smile's our help." He patted her arm. "Now sit yourself right back down, Suzie, and enjoy watchin' us build your cabin.

We've got all the logs we need. All's left is to notch 'em and lock 'em together. When we get to The Crossing, we'll buy windows and maybe some bricks to top off the fireplace. We saved some of the bricks from the other cabin, but not enough 'cause of all the mortar stuck to 'em."

With that, Jigger turned and started back down the hill, singing, "Who makes the big trees fall kerthrash, and hit the ground a heck of a smash?"

From the clearing below came the chorus, "'Tis Johnny Ross and Cyrus Hewes, 'Tis Johnny Ross and Cyrus Hewes, 'Tis Johnny Ross and Cyrus Hewes."

Andre continued the song, "Who gives us pay for one big drunk when we hit Bangor, slam kerplunk?"

"'Tis Johnny Ross and Cyrus Hewes ..."

CHAPTER 11

The blaze crackled in the fireplace, Richard Fryer standing before it, agonizing as he observed the red and yellow flames. A painful reminder, they leaped into the air like writhing coral snakes flicking venomous tongues in all directions. The fire generated a unique hum-m, like an inner wind.

Fryer reasoned that fire was a force that, gaining size and momentum, became master of its master.

Wood turns to charcoal and then ashes. Is that what had happened to his life?

In his thoughts, Fryer never stuttered. In his thoughts, he was like he had been—back in Kentucky, before The Troubles. In his thoughts, he was unscathed by the past, clear-headed, unfettered in his speech. In his thoughts. In the past ...

But today was today, wasn't it? Fraught with its own distasteful complications, reminiscent of his past. Again, the past ...

Fryer stood on the skin of a black bear, gazing at the flames, wringing his hands, impervious of his surroundings in Robert Stridler's richly decorated den.

Like the wood engulfed in flames, his thoughts were consumed in the night before at Pocomoonshine Mountain, and to years before that, to a time that he'd never forget, to a different time of year and a different time of day, in a place a thousand miles away from Cooper's Crossing.

Fryer was on horseback, surrounded by a throng of white-robed figures riding horses adorned with gold sheets trimmed with red and with white crosses emblazoned on each side. The riders' eyes peered out through small slits in their hoods. They were hollering at first, then quieted to a murmur and became attentive.

There were enough klansmen to fill the field, and the ones around him strained to peer over their comrades and hear their Exalted Cyclops. It was difficult to see over the pointed hats. But it was easy to hear The Voice of their leader. The Voice and its command over its audience were unmistakable.

"... time to seize and extinguish the transgressors of the Puritan code, time to claim that the rightful law is the rule we set forth as the legal owners of this country in the eyes of Almighty God."

The voice of Simon Duke, now known as Robert E. Lee Stridler, rose like an airborne vessel, above the crowd of klansmen. "Fire kills disease, disinfects all it touches and cleanses places rife with vermin."

Picking up a torch with a long, wooden handle that had been driven into the ground, Duke cried, "Fire! Fire will be our ally tonight. It will march with us, klansmen, and with it we will ruin the sinners who soil the reputation of our community and of the great state of Kentucky. We will begin to exterminate the hovels that the Negroes are living in on land that they bought which should remain under white control. Owning property is a privilege of our superior race."

Duke's huge white Arabian rose up on his hind legs, lifted his front legs high and pierced the night air with a hardy whinny. An impressive sight.

Then the klavern leader declared, "If things progress as they now stand, Satan will rule this country. So, we must curb that plight now, starting tonight!"

Duke reined his horse around and marched at a fast military gait toward the neighboring street. His torch lit his silhouette in yellow and stood high in the darkness as a beacon, guiding the mob toward its unsuspecting victims. Into the street and then along it, past the residential homes on the outskirts of the city, the klansmen followed Duke. Fryer was now at his side.

Several klansmen, also holding torches, were in place on the edges of the crowd, the light forming an outline for the mass of riders and lighting up the white robes between them. It resembled a white tide swarming down upon the core of the city, like a hive of angry bees toward the block housing the Ike Snow Saloon and the velvet-on-velvet rooms of Grace's Place.

Almost across the street stood the police department, encased in brick walls and an abundance of small, barred windows behind which were mainly black men. Fryer spotted the chief of police standing inside the main entrance, his arms crossed, watching the horsemen descend *en force*.

The chief's face revealed interest but not concern. He was an undeclared sympathizer. It was agreed: what they were doing was right, and they were helping him clean up the city—sort of a legion of deputies whom he didn't have to pay. If they overdid it a bit, he didn't have to take the heat. After all, officially, he was out of town traveling to the county Sheriff's Office.

ꝃ ꝃ ꝃ

The chief scratched his fat chin and smiled ever so slightly. Officially, what the klansmen were about to do was deplorable.

He hitched up his pants over a belly that was fighting a losing battle with his latest diet, then turned to walk toward a side door leading to an alleyway. This was a fine moment.

A minute later, he rode his horse away, in the direction opposite Ike Snow's Saloon and Grace's "house of relaxation." A shame, he thought, that slight smile widening.

The chief was disappointed that he wasn't able to witness the upcoming half hour or so, unable to see the "judgment" the klansmen were about to lay on the city's "sin block."

A pity.

He rode toward the county seat.

Later that night, he'd learn the "judgment" had somehow spilled beyond the "sin block."

City officials and even state law-enforcement officials would have tolerated fire and destruction.

But when it turned to blood-spilling and unintended havoc?

Well, even the best of plans …

ĸ ĸ ĸ

At the head of the mob, his arm holding the torch high, Duke turned his Arabian to face his followers. With his mount walking backward as they approached the wide front porch leading inside Ike's, he bellowed over the noise of the snorting horses and clopping hoofs: "Fellow klansmen, here's where we take our stand as the champions of morality. Because our laws and our courts have failed, we're alone are left to preserve American ideals and keep our city's morals. Onward!"

With a snap on the reins, Duke turned and rode up the steps, onto the porch and through the swinging door into Ike's.

ĸ ĸ ĸ

Men at tables throughout the room and at the bar turned at the sound of hoofs on wood and the door cracking open. They gasped at the sight of the large horse, its rider and the torch with kerosene-fed flames looming in the doorway.

Beneath long flowing robes, the rider bellowed, "Since you refuse to repent, drunkards, we must cleanse you and this place."

He swept the torch around in a circle over his head and urged his horse into the center of the room. A score of hooded riders squeezed into the bar beside him, their horses clomping on the wooden floor.

Tables and chairs toppled. Glasses and bottles crashed to the floor. The bar's patrons, stunned into silence, stumbled to their feet to flee the stampede.

One man, drunken fright glazed in his eyes, tripped over a fallen bottle and fell, head-first, through the large window at the front of the barroom. The glass splintered and burst out into the street as he hit the wooden planks on the porch.

Duke rode to the bar and, reaching forward, used the butt of his torch rod to knock the neatly stacked bottles of liquor from shelves on the bar's rear wall. The thundering crash of bottles accentuated the turmoil in the small building.

Screaming, "No! No!" the bartender dove for the floor behind the bar for protection.

So many horses and riders crowded into the room that they stood shoulder to flank. There wasn't enough room. Something had to give.

It did. Moving aside as one horse bumped into him from behind, an old man, his white hair awry, lost his footing and fell to the floor. At the same instant, a young chestnut stallion bucked high in the air and when its hoofs came down, they hit square on the temple of the old man. His scream just before he was struck pierced the room and brought people in other downtown buildings to their windows.

It triggered the swarm of horsemen into action that engulfed the entire center of the city, with Ike's and Grace's being the teeming hub.

Led by Duke, the klansmen drove the customers from Ike's, then touched their torches to drapes and tables as they left the tavern. Alcohol that had been spilled from scores of fallen and broken bottles fed the flames that destroyed the business that liquor had made possible.

Fire caught on Ike's walls and strewn furniture and flicked at the pant cuffs of the old man who lay dead on the floor. Duke spurred his horse on and directed the other horsemen to spread out in groups around Grace's next door.

The three-story building stood high and proud—its Victorian architecture resembling a time of honor and knighthood. Light shone through its windows on all three floors, through rich red draperies on the first story, and lacy, feminine imported curtains on the upper levels.

As he had done at Ike's, Duke rode his Arabian through Grace's front door, splintering it, and into a large parlor bustling with activity. Women screamed. Duke saw several men run down the stairs and down a hallway toward the rear doors of the house. He knew they wouldn't get far, and a tar-and-feathering awaited them all.

A smile touched his face beneath the linen he wore, and he began his declaration against sexual sin. But, as the word "whores" parted his lips, a rifle fired and a bullet tore through Duke's robe and his left shoulder.

The blow nearly knocked Duke from his horse. He cringed in pain, blood gushed from the wound, and he turned to the direction of the rifle shot. There, by a side door of the parlor leading into a rear room, stood Grace, her eyes flashing, her look angry and determined. A tall red-head in her 40s with the face of a Broadway star and startling turquoise eyes, she possessed the aura of a noble lady. A modest but stunning red dress flowed from her shoulders, and in her hands, she gripped a rifle.

Duke winced from the sharp, burning pain in his shoulder, but managed to bring his right arm back and throw his torch like a dagger at the woman. The torch flipped end over end, its burning top aiming directly at her. She swept quickly toward the door to escape, but her long, flowing gown dragged behind her and the torch's flame caught it. Fire flared quickly up its length, fed by the motion as she rushed into the back room. Shrill screams rang through the house as Grace disappeared through the door.

Duke grimaced and pulled his horse toward the front entrance to leave, to search out a fellow klansman who was a doctor.

As he made his way through the door, he noticed beside him the short rider aboard his aging quarter horse. It was Fryer. Fryer's eyes caught his and held them for a long moment. No hood could hide the expression or the feelings behind it. Fryer was terrified.

Moments later, the entire house was ablaze and within ten minutes, flames were shooting skyward through the roof. A feeble attempt by the city's fire department failed to extinguish the blaze, and it jumped from both Ike's saloon and Grace's to neighboring stores and hotels. The entire city population turned out into the downtown streets, arriving as the klansmen rode toward the outskirts and their secret meeting hall.

₭₭₭

Fryer heard all the stories afterward. Some townspeople had just watched. Others started a bucket brigade from the watering troughs to the burning structures. Some merely stood, tortured in anguish, and wept aloud. A woman cradled a small child in her arms and turned to watch and pray as her husband jumped through the flames in a doorway to run to their second-floor apartment to rescue another child left behind. As he jumped through the flames, he was lost to sight in a cloud of smoke that filled the building, taking it over, assuming command—an indignant landlord come to take his property to the fires of hell.

Despite the destruction, the klansmen's furor against sinners continued to run amuck in the following weeks, claiming other victims, including the young, unknowing, innocent. But Duke? He was ferried away to parts unknown, two counts of murder and several more of manslaughter among a dozen or so charges against him.

Now, peering into the fireplace, the memory was emblazoned on Fryer's mind. It had all happened so quickly and uncontrollably. Chasing away the demons had turned into burning away the city—or a portion of it.

Though most of the town fathers and police officials favored the Klan, they couldn't accept such an incident without punishing its instigator. It couldn't be swept under the carpet like lesser crimes. There was a difference between burning a city and cutting out a black man's tongue, which was all right if, for instance, he insulted a white woman or argued with his superiors.

But Duke's family was wealthy and influential, with friends and associates in high places, Imperial Wizard Simmons among them.

Within days he had disappeared, his estate liquidated, his livestock and land sold.

It had taken Fryer two years to convince Klan leaders to let him know where Duke had gone.

Meanwhile, the authorities turned a blind eye—from the police chief to the sheriff to the district attorney, the judge, and even the US senator. They looked the other way when the few passionate anti-klansmen began an all-out search for Duke. They remained mum when asked to call for a regional or nationwide alert for the killer. They waited for time to take its toll, as it always did. For memories to fade, for anger to soften, for even the diehards to, once and for all, give up the hunt.

And when it was all over, Duke, now Stridler, had established himself as a rich, but hard-working farmer in Cooper's Crossing. He worked out in the fields with his hired hands, just one minor way to win the acceptance of these sunrise-to-sunset Yankees who were normally slow to welcome outsiders into their communities and to accept them as comrades.

Stridler, Fryer discovered, had gotten close to Farnsworth, gubernatorial hopeful Owen Brewster, and others of renown.

The rewards of Klandom might even be greater here in Maine than they had been back in Kentucky.

₭₭₭

"Richard, what do you see in the fire—fancy or fact?"

Stridler's voice, powerful even in a one-on-one setting, jolted Fryer out of his thoughts. He took a step back.

"Sorry if I startled you," Stridler said. He removed his pipe from his lips and studied the burning tobacco in its bowl. "It seemed that you were daydreaming. Perhaps I shouldn't have interrupted. If it was contemplation and not daydreaming—well, cerebration is the lifeblood of success. Idle meandering has never led to accomplishment."

Stridler stopped for a moment, looking over his farm foreman, then added, "As a matter of fact, I've done some of my best thinking right at that couch, staring into the flames until they enveloped all that was around me—all the peripheral things so that I could focus entirely on the central thought. Yes, indeed, Richard, fire is a help in many ways. Right?"

He gave Fryer a wink and sly grin, and Fryer got the message.

"Th-that's just what I was th-thinking about, sir. I was th-thinking about the fire in Kentucky. A-and I guess I was thinking about that b-because of last night."

What bit of good humor had accompanied Stridler into the room vanished. He looked flatly at his farm foreman, wondering.

Fryer's eyes darted here and there, never settling for longer than a moment on any one thing. Dressed in his rumpled clothes, he looked out of place in the mahogany-walled room.

Stridler looked flatly at him, waiting for him to continue.

To his surprise, Fryer did indeed press on. "W-well, w-what I was thinking about was w-what if it all happens again? What if a lot of p-people die? And w-what if they c-come after y-you again?"

"Richard." Stridler held up a hand in interruption. "Kentucky was a long time ago. You came to me a year ago. Yes, you're a passable foreman, but you're here for other reasons—reasons that serve us both. I know you've been a loyal klansman for years, always doing what you're told, never questioning our beliefs, always standing firm against the wailings of the wimps around us."

Fryer started to speak, but Stridler held up a hand to cut him off. "I want you at my side because you *are* experienced in the fight we face. I need men I can trust to do what must be done."

Stridler turned and walked to the bear rug in front of the fireplace and watched the flames lick the air. After a few moments, he turned on his heel and pointed a finger squarely at Fryer. "Yes, people died," he declared, his voice swelling. "They will die in any war. But in the last war, the circumstances weren't right for us. They *are* right this time. *All* the factors are right. Down South, we had to put the black man in his place. We had sins of various kinds. But that wasn't enough.

"This is the 1920s. This is Prohibition, man. Not only is liquor sinful, it's illegal. Not only is illicit sex sinful, it's an outrage. And it is all the more shameful because of those men, like the log-rollers, it attracts to continue its existence. Those men are the crux of the entire issue. They're the reason we will win *this* war.

"Unlike the Negroes, no one forced them to come to this country. They've crossed our borders as aliens. They've come here, they've transgressed on our women. They've taken drink from the devil—devils like that squaw on Pocomoonshine. They've dirtied our Sundays with Catholicism, taking their orders from the Pope on the other side of the world. And they're planning to push us—the people for whom America was meant, the one-hundred-percent Americans—into the center of the country, to surround us. They want our blood, and to prevent that, we must take theirs first!"

Stridler's voice had risen an octave, as if a crowd were before him. He eyed Fryer. The man stood immobile, probably in awe, his hands pushed deep into the pockets of his baggy pants.

Stridler took two steps toward the tousled little man and lowered his voice conspiratorially. "Besides, Richard, our link to the establishment may even go higher here than it did in Kentucky. Senator Brewster—soon to be Governor Brewster— will give us his support in response to the financial backing we've given his campaign.

"Also, certain Sheriff's Department personnel are of the correct persuasion. Right?"

Fryer nodded and offered a grunt of affirmation, but he still appeared ill-at-ease.

I'm going to keep a close eye on my foreman and klavern enforcer.

CHAPTER 12

Matt Whittaker could hear the cries approach the house from out-of-doors—two separate wails of hurt. They drew closer, coming down Harlowe Way from town. Then louder and more distinct as they entered the driveway and approached the front door. One of the cries turned into a gasping sob as the door opened. Matt rose from the chair at Clara's bedside.

As he stepped outside the bedroom, the sound of little feet ascending the stairway accompanied the cries. Then the dirt- and tear-stained faces of his two children appeared.

What sort of disaster could have brought this on?

From the bedroom, Clara, her baby suckling at her breast, called out with alarm, "Matt, what on earth is the matter?"

Willie and Ming Su reached the top of the stairs and, with pained expressions, looked up at him. Willie's shoulders heaved with sobs and his little lungs struggled to suck in air.

Matt knelt and Ming Su plunged into his arms and buried her head into the crevice of his shoulder. Willie followed suit, and Matt held them both tight to him, soothing them, stroking their heads and trying to calm them with soft words.

"Now, now, kids, you're home now. Everything's going to be all right. Your mom and I are right here. Come on into the bedroom and tell us what's the problem."

Matt picked them both up—one in each arm—and carried them to Clara's bedside.

With her free hand, Clara patted the bed beside her, inviting them to sit down. "Come here and tell your dad and me and your new little sister what happened. It sounds like an awful tragedy."

Matt gently set the two children down on the spacious bed and they cuddled up close to their mother. Still snuffling, Ming Su put one hand down to pat the fuzzy-haired head of the baby and wiped tears from her eyes with her other hand as she gained control of her breathing. Willie continued to blubber in gasps, but those sobs were slowing.

Finally, Ming Su drew in a breath and said, "We went down to the Thurstons' to play. But Tommy and Teddy and Mindy told us to go away."

Tears started up again.

"Yeah—and they called me a 'nothin' nigger,'" Willie said. "Told me I belonged in 'frica, wherever that is."

"And," said Ming Su, wiping her eyes, "they said I was nothin' but a Chinaman, and that's a yeller nigger."

"And they told us to get out," said Willie.

"And to never come back. They didn't want to play with us," said Ming Su.

Both children began to cry anew, and Matt caught Clara's eyes with his, no words needed.

Clara nodded her consent, then soothed the children as Matt left the room, his face taut, his jaw set, a steely glare in his eyes.

He would deal with this. In no uncertain terms.

𝕶 𝕶 𝕶

Matt urged on his big dapple-gray horse as they turned the bend in the road toward the Thurston farm. A number of children played in the yard as he rode in, and he saw a handful of men working in the field behind the house. Ian Thurston sat atop a stationary harrower and one of the men was adjusting the land wheel on the contraption.

Matt rode out into the field, tied the reins around the bridle horn, dismounted and strode up to the harrower. All the while, he locked eyes with Thurston, who sat scratching the stubble on his chin.

"Yo, Matt, 'n what can I do for you this fine day?" Thurston said.

"There's nothing you can *do* for me," Matt said, "but you can answer a whole lot for me—beginning with where all those kids out there are getting their ideas about 'Negroes and Chinamen' and all that malarkey."

Thurston stayed in his seat a good couple of feet above Matt. Matt was well aware that his sheer size intimidated some people. He doubled his hands into fists, not caring that his body language didn't exactly invite a friendly exchange.

"W-well, Matt, I thought you might know by now, but if you don't, I guess it's up to me to tell ya' and I got to tell ya' straight out. There's no other way, much as I wish there was."

The other men had stopped their work and strode to the harrower, forming a semicircle around Matt.

Matt guessed they were on Thurston's side of the matter, but he stood his ground as his neighbor continued.

"There ain't nothin' in all of this against you, Matt, not personally anyhow," he said. "We all grew up together, most of us—"

"Hold it right there," Matt interrupted. "Who's this 'we' you're talking about?"

"'We,' Matt, is the Klan," Thurston answered, "the Ku Klux Klan."

"My God," Matt said through his teeth, "I'd heard it, but couldn't believe it. Thought it was just a mean joke or a passing fancy. The Klan in Cooper's Crossing? Pshaw! That's like putting Genghis Khan in a nunnery, Ian! The Klan belongs down South. What's it doing here? And how can it find anyone damn fool enough to join it? We haven't got any of their kind of troubles up here, and we haven't birthed any of their kind of killers up here, either."

"Now, Matt, don't you go callin' the Klan killers." Agitation boiled out of the man. "It's a great social, patriotic, fraternal, beneficiary order—"

"Don't give me any of that guff." He threw Ian a malevolent look. "Social order? What kind of social meetings have you had here in The Crossing? You can call it patriotic, but ingrained in being patriotic is a belief in what this country was founded on, like the principle that all men are created equal. And from what I hear, the Klan doesn't exactly follow that belief."

Annoyance burned across Thurston's face.

"Fraternal, it might be, but beneficial? Come on, Ian, beneficial to whom?"

Annoyance had turned to anger.

"You giving scholarships so some of the kids in town can go to college? I know firsthand how hard it is to work your way through. You giving lots of money to the church or to the poor?"

Anger morphed into rage. Why wasn't it shame?

"What, exactly, are you doing that's beneficial, Ian? Tell me."

Thurston lifted himself out of his seat and stood, towering a good eight feet above Matt down on the ground. His face was crimson with fury. His men surrounding Matt seemed to give him courage. Ian obviously felt untouchable atop the harrower, and he was intent on having his say.

"I don't care what you have to say about it, Matt," he seethed. "Disagree with the Klan all you want, but we need it. This community, this country needs it—to keep America from being taken over. No, we don't have all the same exact problems they do down South, but there's plenty of our own to handle. Look at what's happenin' around you, man. Look at what those damn Canucks are doin'. They're choppin' down our trees, they're fondlin' our women, they're drinkin' illegal moonshine. They're takin' jobs down in the mill towns that Americans should have.

They're up to no good and someone's got to stop 'em. And since no one else is doin' it, it's got to be us, the Klan."

Matt cast a steely gaze at Thurston and shook his head slowly. He was dumbfounded that his neighbor was saying this and that the others agreed. Somewhere, sanity must prevail.

Thurston continued, raving now, "And it don't just stop with the Canucks, Matt, or with the Canucks bein' Catholics—and we all know what the Pope and the rest of his cronies plan for these United States. No, it don't stop with them. And it don't stop with booze-makers like Suzie Cooley—'n we heated her hide good. And it don't stop with fondlin' whores like those down to Ilsa's or other men's wives. Jean Bonneau found that out. And it don't stop with Negras."

Matt scrutinized the harrower, figuring how he could jump up and strangle the man.

"And I'll tell ya' where else it don't stop," Thurston fumed. He wiped some spittle from his chin with the back of his hand and steamed on. "It don't stop at the little Nigras, nor with the little slant-eyed chinks."

That's it!

"It don't stop 'til it gets to your doorstep if you keep the likes of them in your house."

Matt coiled his muscles to leap onto the harrower when Clara's final pleading before he went out the door came to him: "Careful, darling. We need you here. Please!"

Thurston pointed a dirty finger at him and went on: "You were born and brought up a good, wholesome American. Least that's what we all thought. But then you don't have no kids of your own, so you go out and, 'stead of adoptin' yourself a white un, you get a yeller un and then a black un."

"That's enough!" Matt fumed. "Stop your talk right there or I swear to God you'll be unrecognizable in thirty seconds!"

He stepped closer to the harrower and turned his own finger accusingly on the man above him. "The bull's got to stop and it's got to stop right here. Listen to me and you listen straight." Matt spun around and looked at the farm hands. "And you listen too. You're all being boondoggled. People from outside are putting fool ideas into your heads. Just like you were boards and those ideas were nails, they're taking a sledgehammer and driving those nails home until they get all the way through. And you believe them? How you can let it happen amazes me."

With that, a big young man who stood the full size of Matt stepped forward, forehead furrowed. "You callin' us stupid, mister?"

"Take it any way you want, bud. Just think through what they're telling you before you lose your soul."

Matt turned back around to his neighbor. "And you, Ian Thurston, you astonish me more than any of these guys. We've known each other since the crib. Your wife grew up with Clara. You talk about Willie and Ming Su like they aren't human but some kind of animals. Well, I'll tell you, the color of your skin doesn't make the least bit of difference—not to them, not to me, and not to anybody with any sense."

Thurston uttered a curse, but Matt motioned him quiet. "You say klanners are social. How social is killing? You explain to four-year-old Willie how social those klanners were who made him watch as his real daddy was castrated and left to bleed to death. That little boy, who didn't know his skin made him any different from anybody else, will have nightmares for the rest of his life. That's real sociable, now, isn't it?"

Thurston fumbled with words that wouldn't come as Matt showed him his back, parted the ring of farm hands, and stalked back to his horse. He could feel cold eyes on him, but they were staying in their place. And as he swung himself up onto the saddle he knew that something important had been slipped into that conversation. Ian Thurston had let a couple of remarks slip and Matt intended to find out exactly what they meant.

ҝ ҝ ҝ

Jennifer Craig stood in the backyard, hanging a sheet on the clothesline. A brilliant sun shone down on her, but it wasn't hot, rather a fine, comfortable spring day.

Back in the field directly behind the house, Sam was running the tractor, drawing the cultivator behind it. The heavy burden made the tractor's engine roar loudly with the strain. This new engine-powered machinery needed its kinks worked out by those people in Detroit, Sam had said. Yet it was the wave of the future and so they, like other farmers, had invested in it.

But while the tractor droned on in the field, Jennifer could hear something else or perhaps sense it. At first it was just a sound out of place with the machinery and nature. Then it became more discernible—a voice ... a boy's voice ... and it was calling from *inside* the house.

Wait, from inside the house? Yes, from inside the house! My God!

She dropped the sheet and clothespins and ran feverishly for the rear door of the house, unhampered by the baby in her belly. Her body tingled with the excitement, expectation.

My God, dear God, please let it be, please let it be ...

She opened the rear door into the kitchen and ran through it toward the parlor, and the voice became clear. It was calling to her and it was Joshua's.

"Mom. Mom!"

Jennifer ran through the doorway and stopped short.

"Hi, Mom." Joshua's voice was simple and soft. As he struggled to raise himself on his elbows, Jennifer smothered him with hugs and kisses. Hot tears flowed from her eyes, dripping onto his cheeks.

🅚 🅚 🅚

Minutes later, Joshua sat up in bed and looked at both his mother and father sitting on the edge of the mattress. He was still a bit dizzy. When he found out he'd been unconscious for so long, his mouth fell open in disbelief. But when his father told him that Moe hadn't left his side for more than a minute at a time, Joshua broke out in a broad smile.

Yet while they talked of what had happened and of how worried they'd been, and of Pastor Hind's prayer and Doc Walker's visits, and his pals coming over to see him, something was playing in his mind. Where'd he been. What'd he done? They'd pulled off the triple play and then what? Then …

Both his parents got funny looks, then his Mom asked, "What is it, son?"

"Mom, Dad, why haven't you asked me what happened—why I fainted or whatever?"

The burning cross. The chanting figures. The man on the horse. His return, with Moe, to Henhawk Hill. The hand reaching out of the ground in the bushes. He told them the whole horror of it.

His parents listened intently, their eyes opening wider, getting bigger. Like the big globe in Miss Randle's homeroom.

𝕶 𝕶 𝕶

Sam broke the brief silence that followed. "'A fraternal order of intelligent men,'" he quoted with scorn. "My eye."

He stood, laid a hand on Joshua's forehead, then turned on his heel and walked to the doorway.

"Samuel, where are you going?" Jennifer asked. Worry was written across her face.

"To town to tell Sheriff Wright and take him to find the body, whoever it is."

"Don't be too hot-headed," Jennifer said. "Please."

She stood up and added, "I'll call Doc to see if he can come out."

Sam nodded, kissed her, marched quickly through the front door and turned left, straight for the barn. In ten minutes, he had saddled his horse and had ridden a mile toward town. He'd just passed the Whittaker home when he met Matt riding the other way.

His best friend wore a tense, serious expression. Something was troubling him, for sure.

Sam uttered words that played down his spine. "Matt, there's been a murder."

"What?" Matt was wide-eyed. "You're kidding!"

"Wish I were. Joshua came to—"

"Hey, that's fantastic!"

"Yeah, it is. But, boy, did he have a story to tell. It wasn't any nursery rhyme; it was about murder. And that murder was right up there." Sam pointed over his shoulder to Henhawk Hill.

"Oh, my Lord," Matt whispered. "Do you know who was killed? Who did it?"

"No, not specifically. But there was a burning cross and men dressed in white sheets. Sound familiar?"

Matt's forehead wrinkled. "I think I can tell you both who it is and who did it. And maybe I can even tell you why."

Unbelievable!

"Yes and?" Sam hurried the words out.

"I just had a one-to-one with Ian Thurston. Unturned a few stones and had a couple thrown at me, too, and in the midst of it, Ian let a couple of things slip."

Ian! There was trouble.

"He was boasting about the Ku Klux Klan and its 'righteous endeavors' for America and how boozers and womanizers must be vanquished. That sort of thing."

"Yeah?"

"Yeah and right when he was in the middle of his rant he let slip 'burning Suzie Cooley's hide' and 'teaching Jean Bonneau about playing around.'"

"Jean Bonneau," Sam interjected. "Jacques LaBonte said Jean's been missing from the lumber yard several days now."

"Really? Well, I think I know why. What exactly did Joshua tell you?"

Sam told the tale, and punctuated it with, "Boys Joshua's age might have vivid imaginations, but he's never lied to me in his life, and I'd bet my horse for your dog that he isn't now."

"That's it, then," Matt said. "They taught Jean a lesson. The lesson went too far. And he's probably lying up there in that ground right now."

Sam gazed up to Henhawk Hill. He, like Joshua, had spent much of his childhood wandering the woods around Cooper's Crossing. He'd found skeletons of dead deer and rabbits and he'd taken home a wounded bird or two and even an orphaned baby wolf to nurse back to health.

But never had he come across a dead man, and he wondered just how well he would have coped with such a thing when he was twelve. Probably not too well. Thank God, Joshua had pulled out of that comatose state and could, even wanted to, talk about it. Henhawk Hill did look threatening, and Sam wondered just what precisely did happen up there, the part that Joshua had *not* seen.

"It must have been awful." Matt's voice interrupted his thoughts.

"What?"

"What Joshua saw," Matt said. "It must have been horrifying to put him in such a state. And terrifying to tell the story, to relive it."

"Actually, he handled it very well. Maybe it was cathartic. He simply launched right into the story. He said, 'Don't you want to know what happened?' Then, without so much as a blink he proceeded to weave the story with intricate detail. It was like, during all that time when he was in that comatose state, he was wrestling with his fears, with his reaction to what he'd seen. He grappled with them and, apparently, took them down for the count. He seems fine now."

"That's the best news I've had in a long time. Tell you what, Sam, if you can wait for a minute, I'd like to rush in and tell the *good* news (as well as bad) to Clara and then go into town with you."

"All right. Give her a hug for me."

Minutes later Matt and Sam were riding toward Cooper's Crossing. They'd passed the Sherwood, Beatty, and Flanders farms, wondering aloud which of the three were klansmen. They guessed Beatty wasn't but Sherwood and Flanders were. It was so hard to tell. A week ago, who would have thought that any of them, or anyone in The Crossing, for that matter, was affiliated with the Ku Klux Klan?

As they approached town, Frank Thomas' saw mill was visible on the right beyond a field filled with piles of lumber.

Sam turned to Matt and asked, "What was it, exactly, that Ian said about Suzie that made you curious?"

"He was talking about people taking over the country. Frenchmen mostly, but others, too. Corrupt, all of them, and planning nothing but bad things for America. Can you believe it?

"Sadly, yes." Thurston's face flashed before Sam, along with the thought of a rat in the corn crib.

"Well, in the middle of this diatribe he says, 'The whole conspiracy doesn't stop with Canucks, nor Catholics, nor booze-makers like Suzie.' And then he off-handedly adds, 'And we heated her hide.'"

"'Heated her hide'?" Sam locked eyes with Matt and they both halted their horses at the intersection with Main Street. "Doesn't sound like he was talking about a house-warming, does it?"

Matt slowly shook his head. "What do we do first—look for Jean's body or ride up to see if Suzie's okay?"

"Perhaps one of the sheriff's deputies—if we can trust them— can check up on Suzie while we're searching for Jean."

"Good idea."

"For some reason," Sam said, "I fear there's not much we can do for any of the victims at this point."

"Yeah, but we can help prevent future casualties, maybe."

"And there must be a whole lot more of us non-klansmen around. Plus, the law has to be on our side."

"One thing we've got to do, Sam—"

"What's that?"

"Pray."

They did just that, sitting on their horses, their heads bowed.

𝔨 𝔨 𝔨

The street was quiet as Sam and Matt dismounted and tied their horses to the Sheriff's Office hitching post, one of the few remaining in The Crossing where cars were becoming the norm.

They found Sheriff Wright sitting in his cramped office to the left of the front hall. Deputy Frank Tyler sat in front and to the right of the desk.

Sam thought the desk, its size, and its appearance fitting of Will Wright. It was big and cluttered but with a sense of order amidst chaos. Will was a big man whose clothes were always a bit too loose, yet he always knew the law, knew how to interpret it justly and fairly, and knew how he would go about it.

Will sat in a straight-backed office chair, framed by the dying light from a small window behind him. His wooden desk, too large for the small quarters, was laden with papers, some in stacks, others just strewn about in no apparent fashion. His hat served as a paperweight and, it appeared wittily to Sam, as a "crowning" effect to the scene.

Framed photographs adorned the walls. Will shaking hands with the attorney general. Will holding a plaque from the Maine Sheriff's Association. There he was with a couple of state senators. There with several sheriffs from other areas. And over there with gubernatorial candidate Ralph Owen Brewster, who had signed the picture.

Sam scanned the photographs, then his eyes lit on Deputy Tyler. Thirty-five-ish, medium height and thin, he seemed to be perpetually scratching his pock-marked face, but at this moment he was pre-occupied with twisting the end of his long mustache around his index finger.

Sam broke the silence. "Hello, Will ... Frank. If we're not interrupting, we have something important to talk to you about, Will."

Sheriff Wright waved them in. "What's up?"

He leaned forward, his elbows resting on the desk, and looked up curiously at the two men.

Sam hesitated, eyeing Deputy Tyler, and Will interpreted the expression. "Frank," he said, "check out that summons for Mattson and see that it's delivered to him right away? The court date isn't all that far away, and that's been burning a hole in our desk out there for a couple of days now."

Tyler got up from his seat with reluctance and sidled past Matt and Sam into the outer office. Sam took the chair to the left and Matt closed the office door and sat in the chair on the right.

"We've got some disturbing things to talk to you about," Matt began.

ᴋ ᴋ ᴋ

As the three men huddled together in the office, Frank Tyler stood by the closed door, pretending to look at the summons he carried in his hand. But his eyes were not focusing on the summons, his ears doing his mind's work.

ᴋ ᴋ ᴋ

Sam studied the sheriff while Matt related their story. Wright's expressions went from doubtful to interested to disturbed to alarmed and, finally, back to doubtful. But all the while, he kept his composure, contemplating for a full minute, then asking, "You sure you're not jumping to conclusions?"

Sam was about to jump all over that suggestion when Wright held him off with a raised hand. "I know, I know, Sam. Joshua's a pretty solid-minded boy and doesn't go around fantasizing. But if he went through a traumatic experience, there's no tellin' what his mind could've manufactured."

Sam felt his hackles go up but remained silent.

"Because he saw some men carry something down into the woods doesn't mean it was a body," Wright said. "And he might've found some kind of animal. It mightn't have been a dead man at all. Your mind can do funny things, no matter how old or young you are. But if you're a boy Joshua's age, going through the emotional and physical changes of puberty, your mind can cause all kinds of neuroses that can turn your life topsy-turvy."

Sam raised his eyebrows, shook his head and with disgust blurted out, "Come on, Will—"

"Will, you don't really mean that," Matt interjected.

"Now take it easy," Wright said. "I'm just raising possibilities. You're jumping to conclusions and I'm saying those conclusions may not be right."

Sam was about to suggest he and Matt take their concerns to the county district attorney in Farmington when Wright added, "But it's true, some unusual things *have* been happening lately, and I don't like this Ku Klux Klan thing for a minute. The implications are scary. But you and I know the men around this town. They're not a bunch of hate-filled marauders."

Wright stopped, scratched his head and added, "Jacques LaBonte told me he thought something mysterious had happened to Jean Bonneau, though. And Joshua's story seems to confirm *something's* happened. I still haven't heard head nor tail of Jean. So, I'll look into it."

"And Suzie?" Sam asked.

Wright nodded. "Suzie, too. I'll send one of my deputies, John Cotton, out to check up on her. Meanwhile, why don't you two get back to your families? I'll be in touch if I find out anything."

"No way." Sam stood up. "I'm going looking for Jean with you. I grew up all around Henhawk Hill. I know it as well as any man alive."

"Count me in, too," Matt said. "I've got a stake in this, and I'm not sitting at home while you guys dig into it. Murder's not to my taste."

Wright rolled his eyes and heaved a deep sigh. "Okay. But we don't go out today. By the time we get started, it'll be dark." He looked behind him out the window, where the sky was turning a deep shade of pink.

"I'll skip church and get going with you first thing in the morning, then?" Sam asked the sheriff.

"Fine, we'll meet at your place, Matt, at eight o'clock," Wright said.

"Agreed," Matt said.

"Agreed," Sam confirmed.

A thought struck Sam. "How about if I get in touch with Jacques LaBonte and have him join us? He and Jean were close. I'm sure he'd want to help."

"Fine." Wright shrugged, giving up any argument. "Why not? The more the merrier, right?"

Sam flashed a brief smile, thinking that Will Wright was glad he'd have some help going out there in those woods.

I would be, too, if I had deputies like Frank Tyler and John Cotton.

Sam nodded and left the room and the sheriff's office, Matt close behind.

Once they stepped outside Matt said, "I sensed a bit of reluctance. I think that when we were considering who might and who might not belong to our beloved KKK, we should have placed Will in with the Klan."

"No, no." Sam looked sharply at his friend. "Will's just too darn nice. No, that's not it. Will's just too darn fair for the Klan. Their philosophy's based on people being unequal, and I think that would irk Will no end. He wouldn't stand for it."

Matt's mouth twisted. "Well, maybe you're right." He mounted his horse. "But it's something to ponder if things go astray tomorrow."

𝕜𝕜𝕜

Crickets were chirping a loud chorus around the klavern's hall. When someone pulled a car into the field or tethered a horse alongside the barn, the chirps stopped in unison. Then, as the white-robed men entered the hall, the crickets simultaneously began their refrain, as if led by a conductor.

Richard Fryer enjoyed the concert. It soothed him, calmed his nerves. He much preferred it out here in the cool night air to in there where dozens of men milled around in the center of the hall or sat talking in groups in the oval grandstand. For some reason recently, that sort of atmosphere played games with his nerves, made him stutter when he talked.

The fact that he was the klorago, the klavern's inner guard, somewhat mollified his anxiety about the situation. He hoped no one noticed. Keeping watch, away from the klanners, helped camouflage his recent inner turmoil, and that was reward enough, never mind listening to the cricket concerto.

Fryer walked toward the back of the hall. He looked to his right to the fields behind the main house. The corral fences formed a maze in the meadow, the focal point of which was the stables.

A maze, life's a maze.

He looked from the field back to the hall, to the flickering torchlight bouncing off the blood-red walls and ceiling of the hall through the line of small windows below the roof line.

Fryer retraced his steps to the hall and entered. The red tint to everything inside was caused by the light from the flames glancing off the walls. As he closed the second, inside door, Stridler mounted the platform, clothed in his white-trimmed red robes, his hood up.

𝕜𝕜𝕜

Stridler had written notes, but he didn't need them. What was coming was from the heart. The men would see it, feel it. Confidence oozed out his pores.

"Sin! Perversion!" He clenched a fist and shook it as he reached the front of the stand. "The Crossing is inundated with it. We can see it happening. Cooper's Crossing was once a law-abiding town. Many of us who live in and around it are hard-working farmers. We're millwrights, carpenters, store clerks. We're heads of households, paying taxes, fighting inflation, doing life's battle to care for our children and raise them right, to give the best we can to our wives and protect them from bad-mouthed and malicious people. We do battle each day to preserve our way of life and try to improve it. Yet, at the same time ugly forces are fighting another battle against—that's right, *against*—everything we're striving for, everything we hold dear."

Stridler noticed Fryer leaning against the rear wall, peering over the seated crowd. And Stridler wondered about his right-hand man, for an instant.

"Now, I'm calling you, klansmen, to join with our brothers around the country in upgrading this battle," Stridler said. "We must hit sin, corruption, filth, foreign invaders, booze. We must hit it all from every conceivable side. It will take a Herculean effort to outflank this many-faceted adversary."

Stridler paused and let his eyes wander over the assembly of faceless figures, only their eyes peering out from the hoods that fit down to their necks. "We've carried out phase one of our struggle. Now it's phase two, which should strongly pull the tide of public support in our favor—and then, very quickly, on to phase three.

"When outsiders look at our society and check for weakness, for stress points in our armor they soon focus on our children— their young minds, their special susceptibility. Then, they immediately recognize the immense importance and impact of propaganda, properly utilized to their ends, on the youth of

America. They've done that already in Cooper's Crossing and their conspiracy has taken hold.

"Tonight, we'll take our first strides to rid ourselves and our children of this propaganda," Stridler said, "and tomorrow we'll demonstrate for the citizens of The Crossing the generosity of their newest, and greatest, organization."

Stridler pointed to three men seated in the grandstand immediately to his left. Their Klan hats off to reveal their faces, Simon Foot, Garner Fletcher, and Royce Whitney responded by looking over the stands.

"Our klokann here," Stridler said, eyeing them singularly, "has weighed all the strengths and weaknesses, and has mapped out our strategy. And that strategy, for the next twenty-four hours, is what I want to reveal now."

The hall of klansmen hadn't moved, hadn't made a sound since Stridler had taken the podium. They continued to listen intently as he told them, point by point, what their movements would be in the moments ahead as the Klan asserted itself for America and Americanism.

CHAPTER 13

It was midnight. Louis Levesque had been struggling to get to sleep, so he'd put on his bathrobe and wrapped the sash tight around his waist. He'd wandered out onto the porch on the front of his house on Cross Street across from St. Joseph's Catholic Church, which he attended. Levesque was a middle-aged, confirmed bachelor, but he wished a woman were on his arm as he gazed at the dazzling show in the sky.

As a fingernail moon stood brilliant in the midst of a shocking yellow ring, Northern Lights swirled and throbbed, shooting hues of greens and blues across the sky. It was spectacular, as if a master artist had brushed the heavens with strong strokes of white, speckled with crystals of silver.

Levesque stood on one spot, incredulous, losing sense of time. Finally noticing the late hour, he came back inside, but still wasn't able to sleep. So now he sat in a plush easy chair in his living room, preparing lessons for his junior French class. He was reading a book about the French Revolution. Levesque liked to "spice up" his language classes with a touch of history sprinkled here, a dash of French drama there. He interjected stories of the French settlements in North America to give his students a better impression of the impact of the French on America. And he found that playing out a French drama brought life both to the class and to the language.

Just as his eyes were about to close with the weight of the night's silent loneliness, he heard several heavy footsteps on the front porch, then the crack of steel on the steel lock on his front door.

Robbers!

He jumped to his feet, his face frozen, its nerve ends twitching.

A furious force smashed open the door and it crashed into the wall and splintered. Then, twin Goliaths filled the door frame, one draped in a red sheet and the other in white—each with a KKK emblazoned on a hood that covered their faces.

"Look here!" Levesque screamed. "What do you want?" Fear dripped off each word and he realized it, but he couldn't let them know. He straightened his shoulders, steadied his voice and asked with the most resolve he could muster, "What do you mean, busting your way into my home?"

The red-cloaked figure pointed a long finger at him and, in a deep tone that seemed to come from the depths of hell, said, "We want you!"

Then, he and his twin giant moved aside, and before Levesque could react, a dozen white-robed bodies swarmed in and around him. One of them drew out a black hood and slid it over his head.

Darkness! Rough hands grappling him, pulling his arms behind him, tying them together with rope, stuffing something like a rag into his mouth.

But the end didn't come—as Levesque had expected. Instead, he was picked up roughly by a couple dozen hands and carried out the door.

Suddenly, the night air was not so exhilarating. Now it felt thick. Thickness so potent, he could touch it and sink teeth into it. But he didn't have time to ponder that sensation, for he was brutally hauled, dragged, pushed and thrown across his front lawn. Then, he could tell by the gravel under his feet that he was dragged over the street. They were taking him to the wide, sprawling lawn of St. Joseph's.

Oh, help, Father Frank! Help!

The hood was pulled off his head and the pungent odor of hot tar stung his nose. And as he was shoved and dragged by myriad hands, he spotted a black cauldron hanging over a fire.

Oh, my God! No! Father Frank! He must see this cross out his window! The neighbors, too!

He was almost upon the cauldron now and looked inside. A heavy black liquid nearly filled it to the brim. One of the white-robed figures was stirring the liquid with a long, metal rod. The smell permeated the immediate area.

Levesque turned as another white-robbed man arrived carrying a burlap bag, its top open, exposing chicken feathers.

Levesque knew then his fate. As hands stood him up before the cauldron, he screamed into the rag. Anyone nearby would have heard a dull, ragged cry. But the night offered no refuge.

Father Frank! Help!

"Douse the flame," ordered a deep, forceful voice, and the red robe stepped out from the mass of white. The person stirring the tar picked up a bucket of water and threw it on the fire under the cauldron. "Let it cook a while as we tell our anti-American conspirator here our intentions."

"Anti-what?"

Levesque tried to cry out, but no one paid attention.

Erik the Red, as Levesque now thought of him, turned to a couple of others and told them to light torches. A short one stammered, "Y-Yes, exalted cyclops," lit a match and touched it to a torch he held in one hand and another torch the other person held.

The torches flickered, then rose in brilliant flames, enveloping the crowd in light and creating an even eerier scene. For the first time, Levesque noticed the night had turned chilly and he stood dressed in only his pajamas and bathrobe.

The red figure looked directly at him, and Eric the Red unleashed from a dark abyss before unknown to Levesque, attacked the teacher. "You, Canuck, you are vile and gross. You are the closest thing to a criminal, debauching our children."

Levesque stared unbelieving at the man. He shook his head violently and tried to cough out the rag. Again, Eric the Red spoke: "You can't corrupt this proceeding with your traitorous words. Don't dare to think that any of the knights of the Ku Klux Klan would open even one ear to despicable whining from the likes of you!"

The crowd moved in closer to Levesque and a man close to him said, "He ought to die now."

Another said, "But that would be too quick, too easy."

But the Red again rose above the melee. "We don't want him to die. We want him alive to serve as a lesson. A bit different from the lessons he's been teaching our children."

The Red stepped in front of Levesque, directly between the teacher and the cauldron which sat just six feet away, its contents steaming.

Father Frank, help!

A sudden thought, a light of hope, came to Levesque. He thought the sheriff or his deputies must have been called by Father Joseph or other neighbors who must have heard the commotion. They might arrive any moment. But then he wondered why these robed men seemed to be taking their time, why the Red seemed unhurried.

His thoughts were broken by a sudden burst of intensity from the Red whose deep, rich tone rose.

"Levesque, you've corrupted our youth long enough. You've attempted, in every scheming way you could, to lull them into willfully accepting you French-Canadians and Catholics as equals, even as people to envy and admire, to emulate and honor.

"You, teacher, have mentally molested our youths, whose flesh is white, whose blood is American, whose ancestry is pure. And as sure as there is a God above, I'm sure you've planted the seeds of Catholicism, too. You've transgressed too far and you must be punished for this criminal behavior!"

Levesque stood, baffled, thinking back to how he taught his students. He shivered, his knees weakened. It was like a dream. It *must* be a dream.

But again the Red, unwavering, interrupted his thoughts, demanding attention by its very authority. "The laws of our judiciary system do not list what you have done as a crime. Yet to let it continue would be a travesty. Self-preservation is intrinsic to the very nature of a nation. Just because our laws are slow to change when necessary, doesn't mean we cannot act in the meantime."

With a dramatic flourish, The Red turned away and ordered, "Carry out the sentence."

Immediately several pairs of hands seized Levesque, grabbing his ankles and wrists. He was picked off his feet and swept into the air like a hammock.

He was able to spit out the rag and hollered, "No!"

But his voice was shallow, nearly inaudible. He was carried to the far side of the cauldron, the dense thicket of white robes following oppressively close all around him. He tried to kick loose, but it was a faint attempt of little effect.

A pair of stakes stood two feet apart, six feet out of the ground and he was carried to those stakes, where his was set on his feet. His wrists were pulled tight, one against each of the wooden posts, and wrapped taut by rope. He was bound, helpless. He felt his heart beating fast but shallow and wondered if he was about to faint.

Again, he cried out: "My God. Someone help me!" But his throat was hoarse, his cry barely above a whisper.

He looked around the crowd again. *Sheriff Wright, where are you? Deputy Cotton?*

As he scanned the scene, his eyes stopped at the dark form of the church—his church, St. Joseph's. *Father Frank!*

He looked at the steeple reaching toward the heavens and followed its lines downward past a large clock and then some windows near the base of the roof. He followed the lines of the church down toward the front entrance, and there, above the door, in beautiful pastel colors, looking out on the lawn, Jesus hung on the cross. Mists of fog whirled about behind Him and a bluish-white light shone down upon Him from above. He hung there, feeling the pain, with a look of sadness and disbelief but forgiveness on His face. His expression told Levesque: "Forgive them."

But Levesque couldn't cope with that sentiment. Four white robes had picked up the cauldron by a metal rod stuck horizontally through holes in its side, and were carrying it to Levesque's Klan-styled cross.

No!

Levesque strained against the rope. He could sense the blood vessels bulging on his forehead and carotid artery. The rope tore into the flesh of his wrists. He uttered one last, croaking wail as the four men drew up in front of him and lifted the cauldron to shoulder level while a fifth used a metal contraption to tilt the big kettle forward.

He watched the lip of the cauldron as it leaned toward him.

Please pass out. Let me pass out!

The thought passed through his mind that, thank God, they'd let that stuff cool awhile. Otherwise ... And as the thought flickered, the black, viscous liquid poured out of the cauldron.

"Yeah, douse him good." ... "Tar the Cretan." ... Vile blasphemies and jeers about his mother, his heritage, his religion filled the air as the tar oozed over Levesque's head. It covered his head, rolled down over his shoulders and the length of his body, winding its way in twisting rivulets that grew wider and wider until they all converged.

The weight of the tar tugging heavily against him, Levesque slumped to the ground, his body twisted forward, wrenching his bound wrists. As the last drops of tar fell upon him, applause exploded.

From the midst of the white throng the Red's voice rose above the noise, "Judgment, klansmen, bring it on!"

The rest of the nightmare was a blur. The hot tar was incredibly sticky. And when the burlap bag was upended, its feathers didn't flutter but fell heavily upon him, clinging from head to toe. Levesque tried to blow feathers out of his mouth, but they stuck to his lips.

Shame enveloped him. Panic became absolute.

A horse-drawn cart—his horse and his cart—was driven up beside him. The ropes around his wrists were untied and rough hands bullied him into the bucket seat.

Father Frank! Sheriff Wright! Anyone!

Klansmen smacked the horse's hind quarters, hollered giddy-ups and chased it down Cross Street westward out of town.

Their calls were red meat to a carnivore, raw hatred to a demon.

What had he done to deserve this?

The shouts echoed along a corridor of Levesque's mind, a memory that would be preserved in countless nightmares the rest of his life, for certain.

Terrified by the crowd and the torches, hauled from his stable by unfamiliar hands, the horse galloped out into the countryside for several minutes before slowing. The cart jounced along. Levesque lay slumped and dazed, jolted by almost continuous bumps in the highway.

ʞʞʞ

Back on the lawn of St. Joseph's Church, Stridler stood in the middle of the crowd, his robes swirling around him, a smile on his face covered by his hood.

"Good job tonight, klansmen! Tomorrow morning it's phase two. I want you all to meet at Frank Thomas' saw mill at nine forty-five for our procession and donation to God and our community. In the meantime, remember that what has been said and done here tonight mustn't pass your lips to anyone outside the Klan. Not even wife, brother, best friend."

A murmur swept the crowd and its outer edges began to fall away, dispersing in all directions.

Stridler scanned the scene and spotted a figure looking out a window on the second floor of the St. Joseph's parsonage. It was the priest. Did the guy just wake up? Had he really missed such a colorful send-off to one of his sheep?

Stridler stared at him. *Your turn will come—in due time.*

When most klanners had left, a handful remained gathered in the center of the lawn. Nathan Boyd and a comrade had removed his cauldron and Silas Clark his burlap bag. Only the two posts Levesque had been tied to remained, bathed in the residue of the tar-and-feathering. The cart's wheels and horse's hoofs had pockmarked the lawn from the direction of Levesque's home to Cross Street.

"I don't want him coming back," Stridler said, peering westward down the street. "Caleb, keep watch at his house for a few hours. If he comes back, pitch-fork him back out of town. Don't even let him get his clothes. Nothing."

"Got it."

"Klansman Tyler," Stridler said matter-of-factly, "back during the meeting you mentioned something about the sheriff and Jean Bonneau. Just what is it I need to know?"

Stridler and five others listened intently as Frank Tyler told about Sam Craig and Matt Whittaker's visit to the Sheriff's Office.

"I thought Whittaker might be trouble," Stridler declared, "what with those two brown- and yellow-faced aliens he's got running around the house. Now Craig's in it, too? Well, we can handle it."

Stridler turned to the shortest of the figures around him. "But, Richard, how in the world could that boy find Bonneau if you buried him?"

"W-W-Well, the earth was still f-frozen in that th-thick w-woods where the s-sun h-h-hasn't got to it," Fryer responded. "A-And we c-couldn't bury him more'n a couple of f-feet deep.

"It's the kid's dog found it," Tyler cut in. "Mangy mutt. I'll kill it if I ever get a hold of it."

"Well, you messed it up, men. It doesn't matter that we didn't intend for Bonneau to die. It's still murder—or manslaughter at the least."

Garner Fletcher, who with Stridler stood tall above the others, said, "We may have to have Frank take care of it. Plant evidence that a passer-by did it." He nodded Tyler's way. "The sheriff trusts Frank. He's been one of his best deputies."

"Unless," Stridler interrupted, "unless we don't have to worry about explaining it. If they can't find a body, they can't prove a crime.

He looked at Fryer. "Richard, do you, or any of the others of you, remember exactly where Bonneau's body is? Can you lead us to that spot right now? If so, we don't have to worry about Sheriff Wright or any other legal mumbo-jumbo. The whole scene was that Craig kid's imagination. Kids all have wild imaginations."

ƙ ƙ ƙ

Jennifer Craig lay in bed, looking out the window. The skinny moon was a nearly hidden urchin, a glow in the midst of a sky radiating swirls of silver sprinkles created by the Northern Lights. The puffy quilt covering her, made by her mother just after she and Samuel were married and just before her mother died, came alive in the light of the sky. Its golds and yellows glowed, like one of those little fluorescent Virgin Marys down at the Cutters' store.

What a stunning, beautiful night. What a gorgeous time to be alive. She snuggled deeper into the crook of her husband's arm. She felt wonderful, vibrant, happy. At least about her family, if not about the other news Samuel had brought back with him.

Joshua was out of his catatonia and back with them, normal. The baby had been playful, kicking and squirming in her belly.

Not unpleasant when you realized it meant a healthy baby impatient to be born. If only he could be born this moment—to see the beauty of God's creation up in the heavens through this window. God's creation observing God's creation—child and heavens.

Oh, but it wouldn't be long. Soon, darlin', and you'll be out here with us and we can all hold you in our arms and watch you grow and learn and blossom.

Again, Samuel's words came back to haunt her. "Murder, Jen, murder's what we're talking about. I'm sure of it, as sure as I know Joshua did indeed see the arm of a dead man."

She turned to look at her husband. His breathing had been constant, rhythmic, and she thought he was asleep. But when her eyes caught his face, his eyes were wide open and staring at her with a special gleam she knew well. It was a warm look. When she saw it, she had always thought what a miraculous journey it would be to leave her body and take a soul-trip into the loving hallways behind those eyes.

She was sure she'd find enduring love, commitment, honor, integrity, playfulness, hard-working conscientiousness—had she mentioned enduring love?

She knew most of what there was to know about her husband, but far down the corridor of his mind, there were certainly "rooms" that were hidden, suppressed far, far back near the fathomless edge of his character. She witnessed one of them this evening, and though it frightened her at first, it comforted her in an odd way.

Samuel had told her about Jean Bonneau and his affair (something she had expected), and had explained its possible link with what Joshua had witnessed. And he had told her about the KKK meeting he had walked out on. The frightening statements from this group played over again and again in her mind.

Samuel was furious. He'd been tense, on edge, impatient in his wait for the morning sun to begin the search on Henhawk Hill.

All he'd told her had left her limp. It had been so impossible to believe, so incredible and incomprehensible.

If all this were true, where was the perfect, planned pattern God had designed? The country had just recovered from a world war. It was battered and in pain. The rest of the country was recovering well, but Maine was stuck in economic doldrums. There was wide unrest with foreigners in the country.

But why would anyone want to start an internal war? The answers evaded her. And how could you fight the Ku Klux Klan? Preach the gospel, battle them with words? Or an eye for an eye and a tooth for a tooth?

To which Testament should your actions conform? Turn your cheek and wait for another blow?

Samuel, her dear gentle Samuel, had almost hollered, "No!" He wanted to take up the sword. "Either justice and the law handle these guys, or we'll have to resort to the only other cure," he'd said. Venom had seethed through his teeth—so unlike Samuel.

She'd heard him out, had been frightened for herself, him, Joshua, and indeed all their friends in The Crossing. She'd tried to soothe him, cajole him, calm his distraught temper. It had taken hours but now it seemed she'd been successful.

"Oh, darling," she whispered. "You've been so patient for so long. Another six weeks and the baby will be born, so there *is* light at the end of the tunnel."

Samuel flashed a smile and put his hand on her belly. "Worth the wait."

CHAPTER 14

Joshua squirmed in his seat. The hard, mahogany pews always made him uncomfortable, but he was especially ill at ease this Sunday morning. He'd been in bed so long his fanny hurt, what his Dad called bed sores.

He leaned forward, adjusted his position and wished he could simply go walk to the back of the church and stand up through the service. No one would mind, would they? God would understand.

Todd and Tommy had walked by and bopped him playfully on the head or shoulder. They'd know, too.

He stirred again. This was going to be a lo-n-n-ng service. It was going to dr-a-a-g. He just knew it. Boy, wouldn't it be his luck? He'd have to just sit here for an hour, an hour and a half. And by the time the service was over, his bottom would hurt twice as much. It wasn't bad enough what happened, but in the meantime, he'd missed the last couple of baseball games.

He pictured himself standing by the bench when everyone else was sitting. Coach Coombs would ask, "What's the matter, Craig? You being anti-social? These are your teammates here, you know."

And he'd say, "Yeah, well, Coach, you see, my fanny's sore."

Laughing stock. That's what he'd be. Joshua Craig, from hero to dunce.

How embarrassing. Something a twelve-year-old kid didn't want to be exposed to, that's for sure.

Joshua looked from the back of the polished pew in front of him up to his left. A long, narrow stained-glass window reached from near the ceiling down to about waist-high. It was a bright day outside and the sun's rays splashed the scene with a brilliant light. Doves darted and soared through the celestial blue sky while a sunset (or was it a sunrise?) glistened crimson and purple on the horizon. In a field just below the horizon, a shepherd, resting gently on the curved handle of a crook, stood watch over a small flock of sheep. The pasture around him was a shimmering, emerald green.

Lie down in green pastures. The phrase came to him out of nowhere.

He continued it, thinking of the well-known psalm he'd learned right after the Beatitudes. "He leadeth me beside still waters. He restoreth my soul: He leadeth me in the paths of righteousness for His name's sake. Yea, though I walk through the valley of the shadow of death ..."

Joshua stopped and shuddered.

His mother's hand enveloped his, warm and comforting.

"The shadow of death."

"Go away." Joshua said it audibly, surprising himself.

Obviously startled, his mother looked quickly down at him. "What did you say?"

"Oh, Mom, I didn't mean you. Honest." Joshua squeezed her hand and flashed a faint smile. "I was just thinking of somethin'. I didn't mean to say anythin'."

His mother put on a smile, but Joshua detected it as an imitation, just as his was. He didn't want to trouble her by telling her what was troubling him.

ﰮ ﰮ ﰮ

Jennifer inhaled deeply and looked keenly at her son. He'd seemed subdued, and rightfully so, since regaining consciousness yesterday. She'd thought coming to church would help. Even seeing his friends didn't seem to ignite a fire in him. He was restless, ill at ease, so maybe it wasn't such a good idea.

Besides, Samuel wasn't here. He was out on that search in the woods. Pastor Nathan wasn't here. That crew-cut young man up in the pulpit was taking his place today. And she felt edgy herself. She couldn't understand why. It was a beautiful day, sun shining, birds singing.

A lot of women in church were without their husbands. There was Missy Fletcher without Garner at her side, Nancy Foot but no Simon, Gladys Chamberlain but no Cecil, Mary Whitney but no Royce, and others—ladies with children at their sides but no husbands.

But there's no reason to be uneasy or sullen. Absolutely none. Come on, snap out of it!

The organ did the trick, springing to life and grabbing her attention. Joyce Oberland had been playing the soft, liturgical, come-hither chords of pre-service music. Now the heavy beats of "A Mighty Fortress Is Our God" filled the church. The congregation stood in unison, joining the organ at the beginning of the first stanza:

> A might fortress is our God, a bulwark never failing; Our helper He, amid the flood of mortal ills prevailing: For still our ancient foe doth seek to work us woe; His craft and power are great, and, armed with cruel hate, on earth is not His equal.

Jennifer and Joshua had raised themselves to their feet along with their neighbors.

𝕶 𝕶 𝕶

Joshua disliked the song despite the fact that famous Martin Luther guy had written it ...

Did we in our own strength confide, our striving would be losing. Were not the right Man on our side, the Man of God's own choosing: Dost ask who that may be? Christ Jesus, it is He; Lord Sabbath, His name, from age to age the same, and He must win the battle.

Joshua took his eyes from the next words. He didn't like the images his mind conjured up ...

And though this world, with devils filled, should threaten to undo us, we will not fear, for God hath willed His truth to triumph through us: The Prince of Darkness grim—we tremble not for him.

Joshua drew a curtain across his mind, closing it to the final stanza. He wanted to leave, he wasn't sure why.

Then the hymn was over and that minister, Pastor Hind's replacement, was standing at the pulpit, black robes flowing around him. He motioned everyone to sit.

"Good morning, friends. I'm Reverend Clark Utheridge." His voice seemed awfully loud to be coming from such a little man, smaller than Principal Smart even. "I'm here for only today in Pastor Nathan's absence, but I'm glad to join with you in a special celebration and service.

"Christ has called us to be His church, to celebrate His everlasting rule and, by our actions, to help maintain the relevance and prevalence of Christianity in our society."

Special celebration? I wonder what's this all about. I sure wish it was Memorial Day. Then school would be about out. But it isn't.

"People of Cooper's Crossing—we're all sinners, but we must strive, continually, to reduce that daily portion of sin that we're perpetrating. We must persistently and tenaciously reduce that great chasm that separates the purity of our souls from that of Christ the Lord."

Didn't sin when I was unconscious. Joshua giggled to himself.

"Destruction of sin is the divine method of pardon."

"Destruction of sin"? The phrase stuck with Joshua like a leech clinging parasitically to his mind. "Destruction"? Joshua pictured a sledge hammer slamming violently into a wooden wall, a giant Tyrannosaurus Rex ferociously crushing a squirming animal in its powerful jaws, a fierce fire turning a house into cinders.

Joshua grimaced, then looked up. The minister was leading a general confession now, his head bowed to the rostrum before him: "... we are sorrowful and grieve before you that we are so lofty in our promises but so lowly in our practices, so fond of sitting idle and lackadaisical toward work, so overflowing with good intentions yet so far from fulfilling them, so egotistical in propriety yet so timorous in adversity."

Idle? Lackadaisical? Egotistical? Don't know what "timorous" means, but am I supposed to admit to that other stuff?

"And, Lord, it is especially sad that we so desire a truly Christian and Protestant America, yet are so lazy when called upon to drive out the evils threatening that dream."

Aren't we already a Christian America?

"O God, we ask you to grant us forgiveness through Jesus the Christ, our Lord. Amen."

That part I can agree to. "Amen."

The minister scanned the congregation. "It is this final lament—a desire for a Christian, Protestant United States, void of evil—that I want to address today," he said. "To guide us toward that end, let us sing hymn number 138: 'Onward, Christian Soldiers.'"

Oh, good!

Joshua suddenly came alive. He let go his Mom's hand, reached for a hymnal and began to leaf through it toward the hymn. The numbers on the pages dimmed as a cloud shaded the sun which was shedding light through the stained-glass window beside him.

The congregation rose to its feet collectively as Mrs. Oberland's organ turned that imaginary corner back to the opening of the first stanza:

> "Onward, Christian soldiers marching as to war,
> with the cross of Jesus going on before ..."

As Joshua put his heart into his favorite song, there came a noise in the back of the church and a scuffling of feet. The noise metamorphosed into the sound of steps on the hardwood floor. The din grew louder and drew closer, and it seemed to be coming from three directions rather than one.

Joshua looked over his shoulder, and though the taller adults behind and around him blocked most of his view, he caught glimpses of white sheets moving forward down the sides of the church and center aisle.

Were they marching?

> Like a might army moves the Church of God,
> brothers, we are treading where saints have trod;
> we are not divided, all one body we, one in hope
> and doctrine, one in charity...

Joshua stiffened. The muscles in his cheeks quivered
What's happening? Who are these people?

> ... Gates to hell can never 'gainst that Church
> prevail; we have Christ's own promise, and that
> cannot fail ...

Joshua sensed his mother tense beside him. Her arm reached over and encircled his shoulder, drawing him close to her ...

... Onward, then, ye people, join our happy throng,
blend with ours your voices in the triumph song;
glory, laud and honor, unto Christ the king; this
through countless ages men and angels sing.

The song ended with a drawn-out "amen," and as Joshua and the others in the congregation sat down, whispers hummed through the pews.

"What is this?" one man said from the back of the room, the statement more challenge than a question.

A "Shush!" from the man's female companion quieted him.

A strange sensation of fear was in the air, something Joshua had never felt in church before. Alien and scary.

Suddenly, with everyone seated, dozens of white-robed and hooded figures stood between the front pew and the pulpit. The night at Henhawk Hill flashed before Joshua; he looked at the robed men and the sight gave him the shivers.

The three columns that had marched to the front had merged before the minister, in front of the gleaming wooden cross which stood eight feet high as a sentinel on the white wall behind the pulpit.

Facing the rows of ghoulish figures stood a large person in red who was a head taller than all the others except one who was right beside it. While the robes worn by the others were white with red trim, this red-clad figure had white trim on its robes.

Kind and nice, God-fearing, and color-coordinated, too.

Joshua recalled the red-and white-clothed Lewiston baseball team he and his dad had watched play the previous summer.

The red-robed one moved along in front of his charges and stepped up onto the pulpit to where the minister stood behind the podium.

More whispers from the congregation. Ada Cutter stood up and declared, "I want to know—" but Mr. Cutter pulled her back down.

The red figure held out a leather satchel for the minister and said, "For the church and for carrying out the word and deeds of God, we're giving the Cooper's Crossing Community Church one hundred dollars."

The words poured like a rich baritone horn, like the instrument the music teacher wanted Joshua to play. The minister took the bag and stepped back from the lectern, allowing room for the red figure to stand behind it.

Large, strong hands rested on either side of the top of the lectern.

I've seen that ring before, an upside-down V.

"The Klan." The baritone horn rang out. "The Ku Klux Klan is here. It's here in The Crossing. It's here to protect you. It's here to protect this church, the institutions God supports and the land He created."

A low buzz filled the church. It sounded like the beehive he nearly stepped on one day in the blueberry bushes.

"Yes, *we* are here now—a civic organization, charitable and benevolent—compassionate, that is, to Christians and to Americans."

Joshua's mom began to stand up but, without reason, he held tight and she stopped herself.

"God shed His grace on thee, America. And the Klan is here to see that that statement will always ring true. God shed His grace on a land of morality, on a people He has chosen to particularly bless, a land of white Anglo-Saxon Protestants."

Several people throughout the church spoke up now, but they were quashed by the potent, autocratic baritone enveloping the congregation from the pulpit. That horn was like God speaking— or the devil.

"Don't be frightened," it advised. "We're here as friends, as protectors. To deal with morality, that aspect so important to a healthy community that is being corroded by bootleggers, roadhouse hussies, extramarital goings-on. We're here to drive out carnal indulgers, to preserve American ideals and morals. We're here to protect the home and land, the chastity of womanhood, and to sustain the blood-bought rights and liberties of Anglo-Saxons."

The baritone drowned out sporadic objections from the captive audience.

We can't leave!

A strange state of limbo enveloped Joshua. A hazy brown gauze. Everything seemed foggy, a blur like just before he passed out on the kitchen floor the other day.

"Our enemies live right here in The Crossing, some of them unseen until recent days," said the baritone. "We have exposed some of them. We will expose more in the near future. And we will rid our town, just as the Klan will rid the nation, of these vermin."

As if brandishing a sharp-edged sword, he added, "Bear with us. Support us. And we will support you in many more ways than money. *We will help preserve your Christian souls!*"

The baritone's hand slid from the rim of the podium to the large Bible on top. It turned near the end of the book and quickly found its place. Then he declared: "As Paul the apostle wrote in his epistle to the Romans in chapter twelve: 'I beseech you therefore, brethren, by the mercies of God, that ye present your bodies a living sacrifice, holy, acceptable unto God, which is your reasonable service.'"

The figure moved out from behind the lectern. His right hand rose—yes, Joshua had seen that ring before—and pointed to the white-robed aisle to his left, and as it passed over the other ghoulish forms before it, baritone thundered: "Present your bodies as a living sacrifice unto God. Paul asked that of the Romans two thousand years ago. Now the Klan asks it of you today!"

With a quick turn, the red-robed figure stepped briskly off the podium. And as he reached the church floor, the organ played the first notes of "The Old Rugged Cross.

𝔨 𝔨 𝔨

In sync, the rows of white robes began an orderly procession back to the entrance of the church. Many in the church stood to sing. Joshua took his mother's lead and remained seated.

He looked up at her, understanding that she didn't know what exactly to do. If this song were to acknowledge or accept what these men were doing, then Joshua was sure she wanted nothing to do with it. Joshua's mind was flickering in and out of a sort of daydream, absorbing some of the surroundings and noises of the present...

"On a hill far away stood an old rugged cross ..."

(He was looking up the hill at the huge cross that blazed in the sky and white-cloaked bodies moving around it.)

"The emblem of suffering and shame ..."

(A scream shot into the night air, and a few minutes later several of the figures were coming down the hill in his direction, carrying something.)

"For a world of lost sinners was slain ..."

(Lit by torches, they were coming toward him, weaving their way around the trees and through the brush.)

"So I'll cherish the old rugged cross ..."

(They were just yards away from him now; his feet wouldn't move.)

"so despised by the world ..."

(My God, they won't move.)

"Has a wondrous attraction for me ..."

(Like a locomotive hissing clouds of steam but not budging ...)

"For the dear Lamb of God ..."

(They're getting closer. Come on, feet, move!)

"To bear it to dark Calvary ..."

(Oh, please—please!)

"stained with blood so divine ..."

(In panic his feet finally, suddenly, sprang to life and he bolted down the path and away.)

"A wondrous beauty I see ..."

(But now the scene changed. He was back in the woods, Moe growling in a thicket. He could hear his dog but not see him.)

"For 'twas on that old rugged cross Jesus suffered and died ..."

(Moving closer to the dense mangle of bushes, for some reason he couldn't open his mouth to call his dog, but could hear him digging—a low, menacing growl coming from him.)

"I will ever hold true, its shame and reproach gladly bear ..."

(Muscles tensed in his legs, then thrust forward like a tightly wound spring, propelling him through the thicket toward Moe, the breaking branches crackling in his ear.)

"I will cling to the old rugged cross ..."

(He crashed through the bushes and landed on the leaf-covered earth; a moment later, a nauseous smell reached his nostrils at the same time he noticed a red bandanna on the ground.)

"And exchange it some day for a crown."

Joshua's shriek cut through the air like a bolt of lightning, cleaving its way through the fog of tension that filled the church.

CHAPTER 15

"It's *got* to be right in this area somewhere." The jagged edge of frustration was evident in Sam's voice. They had been searching for about two hours, pushing spring-bare branches out of their faces and stumbling now and then on the rough, branch- and twig-covered floor of the woods. Matt and Will Wright flanked Sam, and Jacques LaBonte was beyond Will—each assigned a slice of woods about twenty yards wide to search. They had made a couple of quick sweeps through the area in hopes that they would find their quarry.

The sun shone so brightly through the branches that it transformed the ground into a puzzle of many-angled black and white pieces. That sharp contrast made it difficult to see even distinctly different objects.

When, finally, a rash of clouds—which had been drifting in from the southwest—passed in front of the sun, Sam said aloud, "Just what I've been praying for! That sun ought to help!"

"Amen," Matt agreed.

⚜ ⚜ ⚜

Jacques looked up from where he was standing toward the plateau of Henhawk Hill. Before beginning the search for Jean, they had all gone to the top of the hill and, sure enough, something out of the ordinary had happened there.

The young grass had been trampled. Tracks of a wagon wheel were rutted in the earth, having traveled up the hill when the ground was moist. And there was one spot of particular curiosity. A small pile of hunks of charcoal lay undisturbed. The remains of two thick sticks of wood lay in its midst. Mighty peculiar, they'd all thought, Sam adding that it added credence to Joshua's story. No one had disagreed.

Calculating how the klansmen would have come down the hill if they'd been walking from the cinders, Jacques focused on a clump and bushes. They must have stopped fairly close to the trail, he thought, because that was where Joshua said he was standing when the klansmen were nearly upon him.

Jacques noticed several sets of footprints heading down the hill and they all followed them until they reached the cluster of bushes. It was obvious something had broken a lot of the short, tight bare branches.

Slowly he walked toward the thicket, one thought heavy upon him like an unseen weight. What if Jean is in there?

He'd missed Jean—as a dear friend as well as a great foreman. Mon Dieu, they'd all missed Jean. Even-keeled, that was Jean. Never low and glum. It could be rainin' out and you could be feelin' that way inside, but when you got to work there would be Jean with a whole different attitude. Gloom took flight, frowns disintegrated and ill temper turned its tail and ran. And it didn't take no time neither, by golly.

When Jean first arrived in The Crossing from New Brunswick he could hardly speak a word of English. But Jacques, too, was French-Canadian, and they communicated just fine, thank you. It didn't take long to find out that Jean was a hard worker, and not only at his job in the sawmill but also at joining the community. He studied hard to learn English, forcing himself to use the language, and burn the nighttime oil.

Jean had hardly been there a week when he organized a house-building for a mill worker whose home had burned to the ground. And when one of the men discovered that Jean had bought some land on the outskirts of town, the whole crew, along with a bunch of loggers who were in town, surprised their new friend by building a nice cabin on that land.

And every Sunday when Father Lajoie looked down on his parishioners while saying Mass, he was sure to see Jean.

He'd quickly earned the respect of his fellow workers, and when Jacques promoted him to foreman, the move was roundly applauded.

Then he fell prey to the appetite of the flesh. Worse yet, Jacques thought, it was with a married woman—and a woman whose husband, Jacques would bet his last dollar, belonged to the Ku Klux Klan.

Jacques approached the circular thicket. The branches stuck out in the air like a porcupine ready to unleash its arsenal. But its prickly armor had been dented, not in just one place, but in three or four. In fact, on the back side of the bushes it looked like a small army had plowed through.

Jacques protected his eyes in the crook of his elbow and plunged through to the center of the thicket and looked down. No hand sticking out of the ground. No red bandanna. Apparently, no Jean, but obviously something amiss.

The soil had been overturned, its orange color betraying that it came from several inches deep in the ground. Someone had taken twigs and old leaves, some of them stuck together with unthawed ice, and swirled them around on top of the broken-up dirt in an aborted attempt to conceal the disruption.

Jacques bent to his knees, brushing some of the twigs and leaves aside, and reached his hand down into the soil. He dug deep down. Nothing. He tried another spot, and another. Nothing.

Were you here, Jean? Were you? I think you were.

He stood up and called, "Yoo-hoo! Hey, fellas, over here!"

k k k

Sam and Matt looked in the direction of the call, but saw Will, who was close enough to finally discern exactly where Jacques was standing.

"Over here," Will called, waving his arm.

Matt and Sam hurried through the woods to Will and followed him as he stepped out to the east.

When they approached, Jacques said, "Come on in from the other side, fellas. Looks like a herd of cattle came through that way."

The men all walked around and crammed into the open space. "Looks like something's been in here, all right," Matt said.

"Yeah. But is there anything buried here?" Will asked. "That's the important thing."

"No, there's nothing here—now," Jacques responded. "If Jean was buried shallow—and I just know it was Jean, with that red bandanna and all—then he isn't here now."

"Maybe he got carried away by some hungry animal," the sheriff said.

"Sure, an animal with two legs," Sam retorted. "Come on, Will. Something was here and it didn't just up and disappear. Someone came and took it away."

"And now," Matt broke in, "the question is, who did it, and why did they come back—"

"Unless they knew Jean had been found and they had to dispose of the evidence," Sam said. "Okay, Will, whattaya say we solve this mystery?"

Will pointed at Sam. "Don't you dare believe that I went and told someone about this!"

Sam shrugged. "Really?"

"Listen, I didn't even tell any of my deputies. And I only told my wife this morning just before I left. She thought I was going to church with her—until she saw me get these old hunting clothes on. No one else knew we were coming here but us."

"Hold it. Hold it." Matt held up a hand and bowed his head in concentration. "Sam, we were alone in Will's office, but we weren't alone in the building, were we?"

Sam thought it through, then, "You're right. Tyler was there."

"Stop right there, fellas." Will's voice rose a half-octave. "Don't get carried away. Frank's a bit bigoted, I admit. But this is like charging him with murder or at the very least with being an accessory to murder, with concealing evidence, and hindering an investigation. These are pretty heinous crimes."

"Okay, then, how else do you explain it?" Matt asked.

"Listen, Will," Sam said, "it's obvious now that Joshua *did* see something. Right on this spot. It also seems fair to say that whatever it was that those people in white robes were carrying was buried right here. Now, Joshua said he saw a person's hand and a bandanna. If it were something other than that why would they come back and take it away? And if it was a man, and they found out somehow that we were coming to search for it this morning, they'd get their butts out here and carry it off somewhere else to dispose of it. If you've got another answer, I'd like to hear it."

The sheriff hesitated. His eyebrows knit together. It was obvious he was struggling. Sam would feel the same as Will if it had been Matt or another close friend.

Finally, Will said, "I-It's just so hard for me to accept this. I've lived in The Crossing all my life, fifty-five years now, and I think I know the people of this community pretty darn well. Sure, we've had barroom brawls, even a murder every several years. But I can't believe a whole segment of the population has gone loco like this. Even one of my deputies."

Will rubbed his chin with the back of his hand.

Sam nearly blurted out his opinion of Tyler—a bigoted bully if he'd ever seen one—but thought better of it.

"But," Will said, "I guess I've got to resign myself to the fact. I didn't want to tell you men this right now, not until I get to look into it more. But about three o'clock this morning, Father Lajoie came knocking at my door. The poor guy was shaking, stuttering, scared to death. Looked like he'd seen a ghost.

"Then he winds this tale about Louis Levesque, the French teacher at the high school, being tarred and feathered on the church lawn and then run out of town in a cart."

Sam's jaw dropped in disbelief.

"Oh, mon Dieu." The words escaped from Jacques' lips on a wisp of breath.

"Incredible," Matt said. "They're taking it all the way, aren't they? Tar and feathering, murder—"

"So, what did you do?" Sam asked.

"I went over and checked it out," Will answered. "Sure enough, there were tar and feathers stuck together on the ground and some charred wood where they'd heated up the tar, and there were wagon-wheel tracks on the lawn. I went to Levesque's house, but he wasn't there. I thought I saw someone by some trees on his lawn, but when I walked out to check it out, nobody was there.

"But then I figured this search was more pressing and decided to carry it out and then investigate the Levesque incident. Father Lajoie couldn't make out any faces because they were all wearing white robes and hoods—except one guy who was all in red. I'll tell ya', I really didn't believe this Klan thing would catch on like it has."

Sam shot a look at Matt and Matt nodded. It looked like their fears of Sheriff Wright being involved with the Klan were unfounded.

That's one comforting fact.

"It all fits their *modus operandi*," Sam said. "According to my brother, that's what's been happening down South—standard procedure."

"Whatever it is, we haven't found Jean and it doesn't look like we're going to," Jacques said. "They'll have hidden him someplace where he'll go undiscovered forever."

"It's hard to prove murder without a body," Will said.

"The whole affair gives me a sense of claustrophobia," Jacques said. "It's like I'm in a tiny room filled with evil and that evil's trying to cover me like a blanket, cramming its way in, suffocating me, and leaving no way to get out. It's a claustrophobia worse than standing in this little place here."

Jacques skirted around Will and Matt and stepped out of the thicket.

Sam followed on his heels, with Matt and Will close behind.

The woods had been especially quiet since they'd arrived for the search. Sam suddenly felt like an alien, even in these woods he knew so well. Men, some men anyhow, had proven themselves aliens—to nature, to its Creator and to His laws.

Animal killed animal for survival, for food, to keep a balance. No question of beliefs, or ideology, or dogmas, or religion was involved.

But men, at least some men, operated on different principles, or lack thereof. Balance of nature had nothing whatsoever to do with their actions. Rather, what they did was driven by hate. Founded or unfounded, their motive was hate, and that was despicable.

Sam and the others walked back down the path toward the road. No one spoke, each apparently caught up in his own thoughts.

"Jean was about the best friend I've ever had," Jacques said softly, breaking the silence. "There are going to be a few people—not just the men who work for me—who're going to be mightily upset when they hear he's dead. They're goin' to want retribution."

Will stopped short and laid a hard stare on Jacques. "You don't want to start a riot, my friend. This has got to be handled within the confines of the law, and besides Joshua's testimony, we have no legal proof of what happened."

Sam stepped between the two men. "To get proof like that, someone in the Klan, or someone who was there the night it happened, will have to talk. And if they were there, they were a party to the murder. I'd say our chances are slim to nil."

"I agree with Sam," Matt said. "Who's going to admit being an accessory to murder?"

"Someone who's scared or who has a conscience," Will replied matter-of-factly.

"I don't think there are many of that type wearing robes and hoods," Jacques said between clenched teeth.

Again, the conversation died until they approached Harlowe Way.

Sam spoke up, "Not that I don't trust John Cotton, Will, but I think that after stopping in at home I'll head up the Alamoosook to Pocomoonshine. I'd like to take a look in on Suzie Cooley myself and see if I can find the log-drive crew."

"Fine with me, but what are your intentions?" Will asked.

"The kettle's brewing, and I think some funny-dressed cooks are preparing a strange concoction."

"Want me to come with you?" Matt asked.

Sam waved him off. "Clara needs you at home right now. I'll be all right."

"Darn right, you will," Jacques declared, "'cause I *am* going with you."

Sam didn't complain, just looked back over his shoulder and up at Henhawk Hill and frowned. It has never looked so foreboding before.

𝕶 𝕶 𝕶

Sam was making sandwiches in the kitchen, with Jacques drinking coffee at the table, when Jennifer entered the front door. Sam heard the door open and close and called, "In here, hon."

Jennifer arrived in the doorway, distress written all over her face.

"Hello, Jacques," she said softly, then looked at Sam.

He stopped spreading mayonnaise on slices of homemade bread. "What is it? What's the matter?"

Jennifer stepped toward him and sucked in her breath. It was her way of trying to control the emotion welling up inside her, like the day her Dad died. But it was no use and in a moment, as Sam came to her and held her in his arms, she began heaving sobs.

It took several minutes, but, between moans and tears, she finally got the whole story out of what had happened at the church and of Joshua's scream that had punctuated the sordid event.

"Where is he now?" Sam asked.

At that moment, Joshua appeared in the kitchen through the back door. "I've been scrubbing down the horse, Dad." He looked at his mother. "Oh, come on, Mom, you didn't tell Dad and make a big fuss out of it, did ya'? Geez!"

"Doesn't sound like a *little* thing, son," Sam said.

"Well, those guys in those hoods were the *big* thing," Joshua replied. At that moment, he saw Jacques.

"Jacques, Jacques!" Joshua cried and ran to him. Jacques stood, leaned toward the boy and when Joshua hugged him around the neck, the big man picked him up off the floor with his powerful arms.

"Oh, boy—phew," Jacques said. "I won't be able to lift you up much longer. I won't even be able to get you off the ground. Joshua, you—are—growin'!"

"And I'm better with the fishin' pole, too!"

Jacques laughed. "That an invitation?"

"You always say this is the best time of the year."

"I hear those trout up in Meddybemps Stream are so big and they're bitin' so hard that they'll steal your pole away if you're not careful. Why, I hear tell one man—and he's a big guy, weighs two-fifty—got old Grandpa on the line. He hooked him up at Squapan Ridge and that fish hauled him right into the stream after him. By the time the guy washed up on dry land, he was a mile downstream by Oxbow Bridge."

Joshua laughed a high-pitched squeal at the tale. Sam, back making the sandwiches, joined in.

Jennifer chuckled, then in a sober voice said softly, "Joshua, I think Jacques has other, more important things to do than to take you out in the woods fishing."

"Now, Jen, what could be more important than taking a young man out into God's forest and to the best places to catch the most tasty fish in Maine?" Jacques asked.

Jennifer laughed. "I swear, Jacques, if you aren't the nicest friend a boy could have. If only you and Rosie could have had just one."

Jacques chuckled. "Well, having four girls in the house can be pretty pleasurable, too. Which, by the way, leads me to you, young lady. I expect for Rose and me to have a special audience with Baby Craig when he or she arrives."

"I expect Rose will arrive with a cool towel for my forehead." Sam smiled at his wife's ease with his friends, all of them.

"You've also got a Samuel Craig special," Sam cut in, "chunky chicken sandwich with cheese imported from Wisconsin."

He set down a glass of milk and a plate with a huge sandwich on it in front of Jacques. "Joshua, why don't you go upstairs now and change out of your Sunday best?"

"Okay, Dad."

﷼ ﷼ ﷼

After Joshua hopped down and ran out of the room to the stairs, Sam sat down at the table with his own sandwich.

He locked his eyes on Jennifer. "We're just grabbing something quick to eat before heading up to check on Suzie Cooley and track down Jigger and the boys on the drive."

"Why? What's happened?"

"We didn't find Jean. But I think we found where his body'd been laid."

She flashed a questioning look at him.

"We think someone got wind of what we were up to and moved his body."

"Oh, my!" Her hand shot to her mouth. "So, Will Wright is one of them?"

Sam shook his head. "I don't think so, but I believe Deputy Cotton is."

Jennifer leaned against one of the chairs at the table, then pulled it out and sat down with a sigh. "This is getting worse and worse," she said. "How will it ever end?"

"Differently than we hope, maybe," Sam said. "But now's the time to put a stop to it. That's why we're going now, not only to check on Suzie but to warn the river-drivers. I have this odious feeling, a sense that something macabre is going to happen right here at The Crossing."

"There were a lot of people at church this morning who were scared and disgusted by what happened," Jennifer said. "If only more people had as much gumption as Ada Cutter. Maybe if we could get all those people together we could *do* something."

"What about the pastor?" Sam asked.

"I don't know the pastor who stood in for Nathan, or where he came from, but he was part of it. Nothing like this would have happened if Nathan were in town."

"Nathan! Of course!" Jacques broke in. "He's the perfect choice to get everyone together and put an end to this. If ever there was anyone who could do it, he could."

Jennifer shrugged. "We'll find out soon. I think he's due back tomorrow."

"Let's just hope that the cavalry's not too late," Sam said. "I don't want to put a damper on your hopes, but a lot can happen between now and Monday, especially if this pace continues."

ʞʞʞ

Despite Joshua's anguished requests to go with the two men, Sam told him to stay home with his mother. If she went into premature labor, he'd be able to get Doc Walker. That man-of-the-house mission had obviously done the trick. Joshua was happy to oblige.

Sam, Jennifer, Jacques, and Joshua held hands in a tight circle and Sam prayed, "Lord, thank You for Your presence here today. Lead Jacques and me and grant us discernment to solve the mysteries of what's happening around here. Amen."

Sam kissed Jennifer, winked at Joshua and pulled himself up onto his horse. With a snap at the reins, he and Jacques galloped north toward Pocomoonshine. Strange that they didn't see Deputy Cotton on their way. Perhaps he had passed by while they were in the house.

A few miles up the road, Sam turned to his friend. "Jacques, you were in the infantry in the Great War. Did you ever get used to killing anyone?"

His friend's eyes narrowed. "No, never. Pulling the trigger the first time when the sight was on another man? That was the hardest moment of my life. Yeah, it got easier. But the gut-wrenching knowledge that you've killed or at least injured, someone? It never stops—at least not for me."

"A bunch of us in this town fought in that war and every one, to a man, says basically the same thing," Sam said. "And yet look at what's been happening right here, with our own neighbors and friends. It's unbelievable!"

"Believe it or not," Jacques rejoined, "like it or not, it's true. I pray to God it's short-lived. But hate like this comes out of a mighty dark place in men's hearts, and where there's darkness, men know not what dangers lurk."

Men know not what dangers lurk. Mulling over the thought brought a shiver to Sam's soul.

They were about a mile up Alamoosook Stream from its confluence with Limerick River and thus, about six miles from The Crossing where the Limerick merged with the Androscoggin River.

"From here on into town the drive's a cinch," Sam said. "Upstream a couple miles there are some bad rapids that can cause a jam, but once you get by them you're home free."

"You're right, and they must be pretty close to here now," Jacques said. "Yesterday we got a few lead logs that bear Andre LaRoche's brand."

"Good. There—there's the path to Suzie's."

The two men turned left off the road and into a woodland path. Riding high on their horses, they had to turn away tree branches that threatened to smack them in the face. The aroma of young fern filled the air, the dominant smell along with a hint of a skunk's sharp odor.

I'd like to spray Stridler a time or two.

"You know most of these lumberjacks, too, don't you, Sam—as well as Jigger and Andre, I mean?" Jacques asked.

Sam shrugged. "Andre's crew has changed so much in the past few years. A lot of the old crew have gone west to Michigan, Minnesota, Oregon, British Columbia, where there are more virgin forests and taller trees."

"Yeah, I remember when Jigger went out there," Jacques said. "He was gone two or three years, or maybe four, and then one spring he came in on a drive to my mill. When I gave him a big greeting and asked why he returned to Maine, Jig said, "I'm goin' to stay a Mainer 'til hell freezes one foot thick. Michigan may have its Saginaw River and Portland, Oregon, its North End, but I'll choose Maine's Penobscot and Androscoggin rivers and Suzie Cooley's potion any day.'"

They shared a laugh. But then Sam added soberly, as he pushed a branch out of his face, "I question, though, what's going to happen to Jigger—and others like him who've lived the life of a lumberjack for so many years—when the last of the river drives comes down."

"He'll lie down and die," Jacques answered somberly.

"It's coming, you know. Modernization is catching up to the woods. It's like a slow death. Years ago, when the peavey and the sorting boom were invented, they helped make the logger's job more efficient and his life easier. Today, inventions are making his job extinct and his life a memory."

Sam thought back on his time in a lumber camp. These men, these lumberjacks were his friends, and the lives they lived, the fourteen-hour-a-day, six- or seven-days-a-week labor of the woods that they battled through during the cold, hard Maine winters made them a mighty different species of man.

Some among their ranks even attained legendary status. Not to the eminence of Paul Bunyan, perhaps, but still a sort of mythical place as heroes in immortal folk tales. Ed LaCroix, Dave "The Moose" Dillman, Roaring Jim Boyle, Black Bill Fuller.

Yet, some of the stories about Jigger towered over those of the other loggers, and Jig was still alive.

The banging of hammers on nails close by caught Sam's ear.

"Sounds like it's coming from up around the bend," he said. "But it can't be just Suzie. There sure is more than one hammer at work."

They came around a stand of fir trees and "Whoa!" Sam exclaimed.

The makings of a brand-new cabin stood before them. The walls were a good eight feet high and there were frames for windows all around. There was bustle all about. Beyond the structure, the black crust of Suzie's old home stood stark against the forest background.

"Well, I'll be," Jacques said.

Sam couldn't help himself. He broke into an adaptation of a familiar tune:

> Come, all you sons of freedom and listen to my theme. Come, all you roving lumberjacks who run Alamoosook Stream. We'll cross the Androscoggin where the mighty waters flow. And we'll roam the wild woods over and once more a-lumberin' go.

A flock of lumberjacks stopped their hammering, their chopping, and their hauling and came around to the side of the cabin where the two visitors approached. Andre LaRoche raised his hand to lead them in refrain: "And once more a-lumberin' go. We will roam the wild woods over and once more a-lumberin' go."

Sam and Jacques brought their horses to a halt and dismounted. Sam laughed, then sang:

> When the white frost hits the valley, and the snow conceals the woods, the lumberjack has enough to do to find his family food. No time he has for pleasure, or to hunt the buck and doe. He will roam the wild woods over and once more a-lumberin' go!

"A-ha, Sam, Jacques!" Andre stepped forward from his crew. "Friends, it's good to see you," he said, adding with a smirk, "But you two should be singing the last verse of that song: 'When our youthful days are ended and our stories are growing old, we'll take to us each man a wife and settle on the farm.'"

The moment he married Jennifer flashed in his mind and, with a smile, Sam joined in, as did everybody: "We'll have enough to eat and drink, contented we will go. We will tell our wives of our hard times, and no more a-lumberin' go."

Laughter echoed in the clearing all around as the crew of lumberjacks surrounded Sam and Jacques. As hands were being shaken and backs patted, a shrill whistle pierced the noise. Several of the crew turned and looked toward the cabin. The others followed suit. Jigger, extracting his index and little fingers from his mouth, sat atop the wall at the corner nearest the men, his legs dangling on either side of the cabin. "Why is it, *mes ami*," he called down, "that you all find it so easy to leave Jigger stranded up here in the clouds?"

With a cackle, he stood up and leaped through the air. Sam gasped. Pierre Bonneau sprang forward as if to catch Jigger. But, to the amazement of everyone and no one, Jigger landed on a branch of a tree about ten feet from the cabin and grabbed the tree trunk. In a few seconds, he had shimmied and swung his way down to earth. A flurry of good-natured cuss words greeted him and some of the slaps on his back were a bit beyond the edge.

Sam slid through the men toward Jigger. "My God, Jig, how have you lived so long, anyhow?"

Jigger took Sam's hand. "I have a lot of good friends praying for me, that's how," he said, laughing. "And your God—and mine, now—saved my life the other day. But that's another story."

"I want to hear it," Sam said.

But Andre interrupted. "What brings you two out here? You couldn't wait another day for us to arrive? We'll wind up the drive tomorrow, Jacques.

"We'd be there today," Jigger said, "but a bunch of men dressed in funny clothes jumped Suzie two nights ago, and burned her cabin down."

Startled, Sam turned to look for Suzie. "Is she okay?" he asked.

"Suzie?" Jigger asked. "Angry black bears and prowlin' coyotes ain't been able to drive her from this mountain. So, a bunch of crazies won't, will they, Suz?" He turned to the Indian woman who had quietly entered the gathering.

Suzie laughed and hugged him. "This land is me," she said. "Bone of my bone. Nothin' can separate me from the place I love."

"Much like God and us, huh?" Jigger replied.

Sam gaped at him; so did Suzie.

Boy, has this man changed. I've got to find out what on earth happened to him.

Before he could ask, Jacques said, "Andre, we came out because we thought something might have happened to Suzie and because we had to see you *before* you got into town." He looked at Sam and added, "You'd better tell them."

Sam didn't relish the chore. *After all, how do you tell a group of men like this about another group of men—no, a mob—like* that? *Contemptible, quick to chastise, adept at flogging an innocent and later holding a grudge—and a killer grudge at that.*

He'd worked hand-in-hand with some of the crew and with others exactly like them—from similar rural areas, families, and backgrounds. Some carried well-worn and tattered Bibles in their back pockets at all times and could quote from the Scriptures as well as from their wide selection of ballads. True, the ballads oftentimes didn't reflect the godliest thoughts, but they were sung in fun and entertainment, not pious belief.

These were men of distinct character. Loaded with faults— some drank too much and told too many naughty tales—they were ferociously *good* people in a certain sense of the word. The chameleon-like Jigger was a fine example. Vain, reckless, and adventurous, he was also self-reliant, trustworthy, chivalrous and—yes, in his own way—gallant.

They engaged in more than their share of fights, but seldom, if not rarely, held grudges. No, those battles, usually one-on-one, were most often amusement, sport, a diversion from the anguish of the elements they worked in, the blistering heat in the summer, the relentless cold in the winter, the annoying and downright painful bites of the mosquitoes and black flies that infested the woods.

It took more than an ordinary man to withstand the rigors of the lumberman's life and remain sane.

Sam didn't savor the task of telling the lurid story, but he must and he did. Joshua's sighting of the burning cross. The initial, informational meeting he himself had walked out on. The children's rejection, full of defamation and recriminations, of Willie and Ming Su Whittaker. The pernicious tar-and-feathering of the French teacher Levesque in front of the Catholic Church. The incredible presence and declaration in The Crossing's

Community Church. And, most heinous, the suspected killing of Jean Bonneau.

Until the end, they all stood motionless, listening, each one obviously dealing with the revelations in his own way. But when Sam mentioned the suspicions of Jean's murder, a universal moan echoed in the woods.

Several muttered, "*Oh, mon Dieu*." Several swore. Huge Yvan Rousseau brought his ax high into the air and, disgust written on his countenance, flung it, whistling through the air, toward a pine tree twenty feet away, where its blade was buried.

"That's it, Sam. This is where we draw the line!" Jigger exploded. "Maybe the sheriff can't do anything to them, but we can. I don't care what they call themselves. They can add more K's to that foolish name for all I care. The Klippedy Klappedy Kluds. And it don't matter what they believe in, 'cause nobody's got the right to do things like this. And to claim God's on their side?" Jigger slammed his hammer to the ground. "Hogwash! To claim right's on their side? Hogwash! And to declare it's race against race, religion against religion, or any of that other folderol is just plain bull." Jigger snuck a peek at Suzie. "Excuse my tongue, Suz."

"I've heard worse and I've said worse—when the culprits weren't half as bad as these," Suzie said.

"So, Sam, Jacques," Andre said, "you don't want us to come to town? Is that it?"

Sam shook his head. "That's not it. After all, you've got to get your money and Jacques has got to get his lumber. We came to warn you, to prepare you. Your arrival in town could bring this whole thing to a boil. God knows, it's beyond simmering now."

Jigger cut in. "Sam, we won't start a war. But if they pitch their front lines in our path, we can't run away. We'd never be able to show our faces in another town again."

"I'm not asking for you to run, just to be prepared."

"The obvious solution, then," Pierre said in his unique French-Indian accent, "is for us to sneak into Ilsa's, confine ourselves to her quarters. Not an unpleasant thought, even for a man like me who loves the outdoors."

Laughs of approval met his suggestion. But Jigger spoke up. "We'll do nothing of the sort. We'll finish Suzie's cabin and, when we're done, I'm going to tell you men about Gideon and his wee little army."

A loud moan, but no one disputed him.

ʞ ʞ ʞ

Sam and Jacques remained at Pocomoonshine for a couple of hours, helping wherever they could, catching up on the latest stories of the woods. Sam and Jacques caught the woodsmen up on the news of the day.

Jigger kept them on edge with his tale of salvation from the river. The churning water, the blow to the head, the logs blocking his return to the surface, the face of death. Then Christ's hand of salvation.

Jigger, a saved man? Phew!

Not only that, but what a relief to hear that Deputy Cotton had indeed checked on Suzie that morning. Cotton had seemed horrified at the attack and had questioned Suzie at length about her experience, how the people were dressed, what they'd said, if she recognized their voices, if any of them wore anything on their hands or had anything particularly novel for footwear that she'd recognize if she saw them again.

But, the nightmarish experience had been too overpowering for her. In the end, she'd gone blank, her thoughts had been claustrophobically trapped in a tomb.

"Sounds like the sheriff and *one* of his deputies are on our side." Jacques shrugged.

"Now we have to contact the other people in town we're sure of," Sam said. "But you know what, Jacques, I have a feeling our secret weapon is going to be Nathan Hind."

"Yeah. I'll bet the Klan was just waiting for him to leave town so they could march into the church."

"He's getting back tomorrow. He's the key. He's the one person who can turn this thing around, who everyone will listen to."

"Don't feel too safe about that, my friend. I think there are those who are beyond the reverend's words."

Sam made a face. Stridler's mug flashed before him, "You may be right."

As they prepared to leave, Jacques told Jigger he'd have an order of floorboards for Suzie's cabin ready when the crew arrived, probably late Monday afternoon. "God be with you," he said.

"And with you, also," Jigger replied.

The whole crew turned from their jobs and waved a good-bye to Sam and Jacques.

ʞ ʞ ʞ

Jennifer had watched Sam and Jacques ride up the road and around the next bend, out of sight. She hoped Suzie was all right. The lumberjacks, too. Hers was a universal feeling. She prayed everyone everywhere was all right. The whole world around her seemed to be coming undone, like thread on a cuff. The only place she felt safe, really safe, was here in her home.

Other people had said it. Clara once told Jennifer that her home was like a "home" to everyone who visited ... a safe, peaceful haven. Once people stepped inside the door, it was like the house took them under its wings—warm, loving, secure.

When she came back inside the house she could feel it herself, as always. Even in church we're not safe, she thought, but here we are. How bizarre.

There was Joshua, changed into jeans and a button-up shirt, pouring milk into a glass on the kitchen table, with Moe at his side. He didn't seem to be suffering any ill effects from the morning's experience. Her first thought when he screamed in church was that the fiasco had jeopardized his mental health, that in his state of shock he'd been walking a narrow line between sanity and mental oblivion.

She was wrong. Doc Walker had checked him after church and said Joshua "passed inspection." Right now, he seemed as strong as a rock, unbothered by any thought of the past. She prayed it remained that way.

She drew closer to him. "How about some chocolate chip cookies, hon?"

Before Joshua could answer, the knob to the rear door to the kitchen turned and the door flew open. Jennifer turned at the sound. Two white-robed figures stomped into the kitchen.

Moe growled, snarled and sprang at the one on the right. He closed his jaws around an arm and sunk his teeth in. The man hollered and in a split second, the other one brought a gun barrel down hard on the dog's head. Moe fell to the ground and lay still.

Joshua shrieked and ran to the dog.

My house!

"How dare you!" Jennifer roared. "What're you doing?!"

"Don't worry, lady," said the man with the pistol." The voice was gruff, filled with disdain. "The dog'll be all right. And so'll you and this snivelin' little brat here. And so will that one, too." He pointed at her stomach. "That is, *if* your man keeps his nose outta places it don't belong."

What!?

He grabbed her by the neck and forced her back up against the wall. "You better listen and listen good, lady, if you want your little 'uns, and that hubby of yours, to be safe. You tell 'im to lay off and lay off *now!*"

She gagged and grabbed at his wrist. It felt rigid like steel.

From the corner of her eye she spotted Joshua. Rising from Moe's side, he charged the man and jumped on his back, pounding him with his fists. "Let my mom go!" he screamed.

The hold on her throat loosened. But the other goon wrenched him away by the scruff of his neck and threw him to the floor.

No!

The man holding her snarled. She turned her head to avoid the smell of peanuts and beer on his breath.

He let go. "You hear what I said, woman?"

Jennifer looked first at Joshua, sprawled on the floor, then sharply at the eye holes in the hood. Her voice boiled. "You *dare* come into my house. You *dare* threaten a woman with child and a boy. What kind of animals are you? How can you think what you're doing is right? How can you do what you've done here and then live with yourselves? I may not know who you are, but *God* does."

The man took a step back, as if slapped. But he recovered, pointed a finger at her and that ugly voice shot back. "You'd better not dare sleep if you don't do what I say. If you and your man force us to return, it might be any time of the day *or* night."

He spun and stomped out the rear door, his companion at his heels.

Joshua pushed himself up and rushed to his mother. "Are you all right, Mom? You all right?"

"I don't know dear, I don't know."

She took him into her arms—a young boy who was nearing her height now, but nevertheless still a boy, and he was faced with adults' hates and transgressions.

Moe's whine grabbed her attention. He was moving, wincing with pain.

"Oh, Moe," Joshua called, and he rushed to his dog.

Jennifer looked down at her hands. They were shaking uncontrollably. She put her right hand to her chest. Her heart was beating like a runaway horse. She felt her belly. There was no movement. She gasped.

ᚴ ᚴ ᚴ

Jennifer and Joshua spent an unsettled afternoon at home. Moe lay recuperating, moaning and pawing at his head but apparently not permanently injured. Joshua had wanted to read about the Battle of Jericho, about David and Goliath, about Daniel in the lion's den—everything about fighting. The stories, or rather their outcomes, had comforted him, more than Jennifer could have done.

Like all boys his age, he was impressionable. Jennifer knew she and Sam just had to make sure Joshua was exposed to the right impressions.

She and Joshua had then taken the cue from the warm spring sun and had settled into Adirondack chairs in the back yard, Jennifer with her knitting—booties for the little one, Elisa or Seth. Since they didn't know which it would be she was using greens, blues and yellows—as neutral as possible, and Joshua with his knife, whittling a horse exactly like the one he dreamed of having, the one his father had promised as a present when he graduated from high school—a whole six years away.

She tried to forget, as she hoped Joshua could. But, no matter how busy Jennifer kept her hands, her thoughts kept wandering north to Suzie Cooley's, south to The Crossing and the church, and right back to her own home, once her refuge, and those awful men.

Once she turned to Joshua and asked him what was on his mind. He was reluctant. She persisted. He hemmed and hawed. She persisted. He aw-shucked. She persisted. It's what mothers do.

Finally, he blew out a breath, threw back his shoulders in defeat and said, "I keep seeing that hand, Mom. That dead, stiff hand. Stickin' out of the ground."

She stood and leaned down, hugging him closely and praying for God's peace on her child.

ﬂ ﬂ ﬂ

Sam waved goodnight to Jacques and turned his horse into his driveway.

"Tomorrow then, Jacques," Sam said.

"Tomorrow," Jacques agreed. "I'll check in with Sheriff Wright on my way home to tell him about our afternoon."

The western sky was streaked with a pallet of reds, one of the shades simply too close to that of blood. Beauty diluted by reality. Just like Henhawk Hill. Just like his beloved Crossing?

As Sam swung his leg around to dismount, Moe greeted him with a bevy of barks, a busy tail and wiggly hips. Sam smiled, but the smile turned sour when he noticed the cut on the side of the dog's head.

His dismounted, chest tightening. *What have we here?* He put a hand to the wound and Moe flinched.

At that moment, Joshua crashed out the back screen door.

"Dad! Dad!" A sudden burst of tears and his son hurried to his arms.

Holding his boy, Sam heard the door squeak open again and looked to see Jennifer standing there. Worry and relief were written on her face.

His eyes asked the question.

Her response was to rush to his arms. There he stood, his arms wrapped around the ones he loved most, his mind in a fog. What in the world happened while he and Jacques were gone?

ᛕᛕᛕ

Livid? Livid!?

Sam ground his teeth at Jennifer's words. She was quote-unquote "livid." Him? He'd tear those men apart.

My wife. My son. Our house! Terrorize them, I'll terrorize you!

Tonight, he'd stay with his family, protect them, comfort them. Tomorrow, watch out.

They lay in bed, Jennifer's head on his chest.

"I was worried about you out there in the woods," she said.

"Ended up, the place to worry about is with the people in town." Sam smoothed her hair. "Imagine. Even the church!

204

Nathan's going to go be outraged. His church is his home like this place is ours."

"And God's home. Can the Lord's feelings be hurt?" Jennifer's face twisted with the inner pain.

"Well, He feels love, hate, disappointment, grief ..."

"So, yes."

He kissed her forehead. "I'm so proud of how you stood up to those men," he said, his voice quiet. "And Josh, too."

"What a kid."

"And what a dog."

She nodded. "Our hero."

Sam ran through a list of the men who could have done this, who would have known that he was not home. What men, so filled with hatred, would endanger the lives of Jennifer, Joshua and their baby?

"Don't worry, Jen," he said, trying to sound as reassuring as possible. "Everything will work out. The Lord works everything to the good. He'll watch over the righteous and that includes us."

Jennifer stretched up toward him and presented his favorite lips in the universe. It was a kiss to savor, and at such an unsavory time.

CHAPTER 16

It was near midnight on Sunday. Fear struck Richard Fryer in the solar plexus—pure, supercharged terror. Dozens of frigid tendrils raced down his spine, making his tiny facial muscles quiver.

My God, he's doing it again. The nightmare from the past, the horror down South, was being replayed here in Maine, given fresh, new breath by Robert E. Lee Stridler, alias Simon Duke. Oh yes, Stridler was in true form tonight—a prime performance worthy of a big city, like back home.

Yep, tonight turned up the intensity of the crusade one more notch. In a couple a days, Stridler had confided to him that afternoon, when things cooled down a bit, he was going to drop the real clincher on klansmen.

There'd be little left of the Catholic Church in The Crossing after this announcement. The Pope, always an easy target, had arranged the purchase of strategic high ground overlooking West Point and Washington, and two antique cannons on the front lawn of Georgetown University, found to be in perfect working order, were pointed directly at the capitol.

Fryer'd gasped when told *that*. Yet, who would believe it? he wondered. Then, he recalled the reaction several nights before when Stridler had told the hall full of klansmen that every time a boy was born to a Roman Catholic family, the father added a rifle and ammunition to his church's arsenal. Whoa! Even Stridler had a difficult time keeping control of the would-be mob after that. It was like a jockey holding back a stallion straining against the bit.

But here he was again, sitting atop a statuesque Arabian, speaking to a throng of white-robed figures surrounding him in Frank Thomas' lumber yard. Not more than a hundred yards away stood the object of Stridler's derision: Ilsa's Inn.

As Stridler spoke out, Fryer's eyes flicked about nervously. He wondered as to how many of the men present had themselves visited Ilsa's. *Before their transformation to sainthood, of course,* he thought, snickering sardonically.

Heck, he himself had snuck upstairs once or twice with one of Ilsa's girls. In fact, he liked Ilsa, a classy lady despite her profession, a woman who possessed "presence." When she came into a room, no matter how many or who was in it, everyone took notice. Her wit could light up a room of the dullest men.

However, tonight's not your night, Ilsa. My boss is juicin' up this crowd, juicin' it with one hundred-proof rhetoric.

The Voice, as he considered Stridler, was gaining momentum. Its force was innate, yet grew with energy from the crowd. That energy built and built until you could hear it, a swirling hum, a consuming wind. Whatever was in its path should beware destruction. In the middle of this force, like the quiet eye of a hurricane, was Stridler, calmly harnessing the energy, ready to unleash its fury.

"Sterilization!" the Voice intoned with conviction, his fist raised. "It's the ultimate solution. Sterilize all those people—the blacks, the Canucks, the yellows—and in one generation's time we've vanquished the problem!"

Cheers rang out from each and every white robe that surrounded Stridler. His grip was as tight as a vise.

"So, we know at least some of the problems facing America, and we know some of the cures. We've tackled some isolated evils directly affecting the lives of our neighbors in and around The Crossing. One battle at a time, we'll win this war for the heart and soul of our country."

Stridler paused to catch his breath as well as give time for his message to sink in. Then the Voice plunged on, "To protect the moral fiber of the community we must crush every vice. Booze and bootleggers like that one at Pocomoonshine. Moral degenerates—"

Didn't mention Jean Bonneau. Smart.

"Foreigners and their alien beliefs, like that French teacher. And, tonight, a whore house and sinners. Klansmen, we are standing a stone's throw away from a tabernacle of immorality, a den of iniquity that is corrupting not just every man who enters it but every soul walking by."

Stridler's outstretched hand guided everyone's eyes to Ilsa's and he added, "So, do we just stand here and denounce it, or do we destroy it?!"

"Destroy!" was their unified answer.

Oh, how easy that was! Like drawing "Momma" from a child.

"Light the torches," Stridler commanded, "and follow me against this blatant sin!"

Flashes of light sprung from gasoline-and kerosene-soaked rags that clung to torches and in a moment the lumber yard, the dozens of white-covered figures all around Fryer, were illuminated. Any passer-by would be frightened into a run by the eerie sight. But Main Street was empty. Midnight Sunday, a perfect time to execute this particular cleansing.

ҡ ҡ ҡ

Sunday night was also a mediocre business night for Ilsa Neilsen. Fridays and Saturdays were her busiest times. Tonight, she didn't have to hurry about. Fewer clients meant fewer needs to be met, fewer demands on her time. She could relax in the giant parlor and listen to one of her girls play the Strauss Waltz on the grand piano. Beautiful.

The room was luxurious, Ilsa's favorite. She lay back against heavily stuffed silk pillows that littered the seat of a deep-blue, velvet couch long enough for five people. The couch afforded her a view of the entire room. To her right was a wide archway allowing entrance from the front hallway.

The room was divided into three conversation areas—one across the room from her where a large, marble fireplace sat filled with snapping logs and sparkling flames; another to her left in front of a huge bay window looking out upon Main Street; and a third where she sat. A deep, oyster-white carpet ran from wall to wall and a gorgeous wallpaper of golds, silvers and whites accented the scene.

She was alone, sipping slightly chilled sherry. Two couples sat by the fire—two of her girls with a Cooper's Crossing lawyer and his out-of-town friend. Three more of her girls stood talking by the archway, giggling, with bright smiles lighting their pretty, young faces.

Several couples had retired to rooms upstairs. The guests were a grain salesman in town for the night, a young pharmacist who had recently arrived in town to open a drug store, a farmer from up near Mooselookmeguntic Lake who was returning home from a visit to Lewiston, a man who owned a clothing store in another community down the river, and a man who worked at LaBonte's lumber mill.

Her two maids were finishing up the dishes left from the dinner Ilsa hosted for the handful of guests who fancied joining her and her girls.

The voices in the room and the whir of the fireplace created a low, relaxing whisper. Ilsa wrapped her fingers around the stem of the Riedel wine glass and closed her eyes. The pillows surrounding her were comforting, and her mind yielded to thoughts of her success.

But those memories, as always, brought bad with good. When she was a young teenager in Norway, her parents had drowned. She had been left in the care of her aunt and uncle and had been taken to live with them and her cousin, Erik, in his late teens.

The unhappy situation grew intolerable when the cousin made advances upon her. At first, he joked and laughed like he was kidding when she turned him away. But then, as she turned fourteen, and then fifteen, he was at her constantly, putting his arm around her shoulder or about her waist, and rubbing her back or placing his hand on her knee as they sat side by side at the dinner table.

Finally, it happened. Ilsa was sitting at her vanity table, dressed in a light cotton nightgown for coolness in the hot summer evening. She was brushing her long, golden hair and counting softly to herself, "… thirty-four, thirty-five ..."

"Thirty-six." It was Erik. "I'd say these were a fine thirty-six." Suddenly his arms were around her from behind, his hands cupping her breasts. He sneered and added a foul comment.

The rest of that memory was a fog. His picking her up from her chair. Her kicking and beating him with her fists. His overpowering strength. Her cries for help in an empty house.

Ilsa shuddered as she recalled her nightgown being ripped from her, the stinging backhand he landed to her cheek when she fought, the blood trickling into her mouth. She winced as the memory of the struggle came to life. The pain, the shame, the exhaustion that left her too limp to continue the fight when he brutally raped her.

Her one victory had come when he relaxed against her afterward. She sank her teeth viciously into his shoulder, leaving deep teeth marks that drew blood before he could pull away. His fierce blow to her other cheek had nullified her brief moment of revenge, but her revenge still felt good to this day.

The next morning, she had quietly packed her belongings and secretly left her aunt and uncle's house, withdrew her inheritance from the bank and traveled to France. Then to England. And, finally, to America to begin a fresh life—only sixteen but now a woman. That was in 1897. She had no sooner fallen in love with a young man whose family owned the Boston clothing store where she worked than he was killed following Teddy Roosevelt into battle at El Caney.

His parents had made overtures about accepting her into their household. It was a sort of appeasement. For them, it would bring someone their son had loved into their lives. For her, it would mean a family of some kind at least.

In the end, she had declined their offer. She was still but a young woman of seventeen. She still had her entire life in front of her. Didn't she?

But, then again, she had no formal training. Times were difficult where she lived. Her inheritance had run out. No job meant no shelter, no food. Desperation had set in, and when she looked at her thinning body in the mirror one day, she saw an answer. She did possess something. The devil on one shoulder argued with the angel on the other. It was a lengthy debate. Several days passed. A number of meals missed. And the devil won. Sell your one asset or avoid starvation, she convinced herself.

Yes, she had become expert at justifying that decision. This was not a sordid profession. It was not demeaning, or wicked, or anti-Godlike. She had overcome the devastating rape and discovered the "true depth of meaning and feeling" pleasure could entail.

There was not nearly enough love in the world, and though there were men who harmed women and men who killed one another, there was still hope for a better world. Her part in it was bringing enjoyment was the best way she saw in bringing about that peace.

Her part in the scheme for peace was small, true. Her house might touch upon the lives of but a few, but she was trying to do her small part, to bestow a bit of comfort on troubled lives, to soothe some little-loved souls.

She had always acted like a lady and treated men, all men, like gentlemen, and most had responded in kind.

Since turning to this life and later investing her money in this home, Ilsa had always been a "good citizen." She had learned the language, earned her American citizenship, obeyed the laws (except, of course, against prostitution—such an ugly word). She kept a clean property and hired only well-mannered girls. And thus, the law had left her untouched.

Reverend Hind and Father Lajoie had repeatedly dogged Sheriff Wright to uphold the law and shut Ilsa's down. But Wright had turned a deaf ear to them and others who complained. He'd told Ilsa that if she kept low-key and her girls "clean," he'd leave her alone. He added that he'd appreciate her keeping the lumberjacks off the streets and well-restrained when they arrived in town on a drive.

It hadn't been easy. No, none of it. But she'd come through it all. Relatively sane, relatively uncomplicated despite the sometimes insane, sometimes very complicated world she inhabited. Being the girls' confidante and adviser, their boss and their friend, could be terribly difficult and draining. Yet the rewards could be thrilling. She had persuaded a few girls to leave the profession, and talked more than a handful out of having abortions. Life, she said, was precious.

Ilsa felt happy. Content. She stretched languidly on the couch and again sipped her sherry.

She opened her eyes and looked around the room again, savoring its peaceful intimacy and fellowship. Everyone's face was lit with enjoyment. No animosity invaded this world she'd created. That sort of thing was alien to her environment, a world away from Norway and her cousin.

Yes, this is my home, my womb, Ilsa thought, and a smile began to curl her lips.

Just then, Crack! Shards of glass sprayed the room around her. Then a lit torch crashed through the window, flipping end over end.

Ilsa shrieked.

The torch landed in the empty couch in front of the window. The girls and men in the room turned at the sound. One quick-thinking man ran to the couch and buried the flame with one of the seat cushions.

Ilsa jumped to her feet and looked out the window. A mob of linen-clothed forms swarmed in on her home. "Girls!" she called. "Run upstairs. Rouse the others and get them out the back. They've come to destroy us!"

She hurried to the stairway behind the younger women and the two men. She was halfway up the stairs and the others were at the landing when the heavy front door burst open behind her. The others ran down the hallway, but Ilsa stopped. Gracefully, she turned, straightened her back, took a deep breath, and with the elegance of Queen Maud of Norway, whom she'd met as a child, began to descend the stairs. Elegance mattered, even in détente.

She determined to confront whatever entered the doorway. But she was flabbergasted when a huge, shining Arabian horse carrying a red-cloaked, hooded figure clopped into the entryway. The spectacle stopped her in her steps. Her mind raced.

Stall for time so the girls can escape through the back stairway and the rear door. Who were these demoniacs to invade her nest, anyway?

"Stop this! What kind of maniacs are you!?" Ilsa's tone was both emotional and condescending. She steeled herself to keep some degree of composure, then stepped down the final two stairs.

"We're the Klan of Cooper's Crossing," bellowed the red-robed figure as others in white robes pushed their way through the door. "We're charged with upholding the morals of the community and, therefore, with ridding it of evils and evil persons—and that includes you and *this place*, whore!" The hate dripped off the last word, and Ilsa cringed at its nastiness.

"Whore?" she rejoined. "Whore, you say? I say you are the whore. And you, and you!" She pointed at the horseman and then at those who had entered around him. "You all define that word. Lewd. Sinful! Vile! You're whoring now, prostituting your very souls! Following a false prophet and bogus principles!

"And you," she asked, nodding at those in white robes, "are you familiar with the history of the Ku Klux Klan? Because I am. Have you asked your leader here how much money he has made from your 'initiation fees'? Or has he not offered that information? Why not—"

A shout from the one in red cut her off. "Enough, woman! We're here to cleanse this place and that is what we intend to do!

"Spread the fire, klansmen, spread the cleansing fire," the horseman called. Taking a torch from one of the men, he rode right at Ilsa. She turned to flee, but a hard blow above her ear knocked to the floor. She managed to mutter "Mur. Mother," before losing consciousness.

𝕶𝕶𝕶

Stridler looked down on the madam and spit. *Offensive trash. The fires of hell await you.* Snapping the reins, he rode down the hallway, holding his torch high, prepared to set the rear of the house on fire while the others tended to the rest.

By the time he reached the rear of the house, Ilsa's girls and their companions had vanished. Stridler bent to his horse's neck and peered out through a window into the darkness. The forest was thick back there.

So, they think they can escape the sentence of the Klan of Cooper's Crossing.

𝕶𝕶𝕶

"Hank Green, you smell of smoke." Harriet Green's nose twitched as she stood inside the barn, watching her husband a few feet away unsaddle his horse. She startled him. He spun around at the sound of her voice.

He blurted, "Harriet!" Then, "Hello, honey. Didn't hear you come in. I suppose I do smell of smoke."

"We saw the light in the sky from a fire. Was it downtown?"

"Ilsa's burned down."

Concern ruled his face and a dark tone his voice. If she had to guess, he was in the midst of deep introspection.

Something white on a nearby bale of hay grabbed her attention. She looked. It was a sheet.

My missing sheet!

"What?!" escaped her lips and Hank held up a hand to stop her right there.

Hank locked eyes with her. Twin tears were flowing down his cheeks. The seconds of silence ticked off.

"So—you went to fight the fire?" she prodded.

More silence.

Alarm bells went off in her head. "Hank?! What is it? What's happened?"

Finally, he replied, his voice shattered, "We have to talk."

Now fully troubled, she rushed to him.

"Oh, God, Harriet. Oh, God." Hank grabbed her shoulders and pulled her close to him. "I've made a big mistake. We all have made a big mistake."

Harriet pulled back enough so that she could look him in the eye. "Who is 'we all' and what was your 'big mistake'?"

Hank sat down on a bale of hay, she settled down next to him, and he proceeded to tell her a harrowing tale of arson and terror.

"I can't believe we all did that. I'm an evil man. A very evil man!" He dropped his head to her shoulder and wept.

This was awful! This whole Klan thing. The man she loved. There had to be a reason.

"No, darling, you're not," she said. "Ever since your brother died you've been depressed. You've been under stress and pressure and haven't been yourself." She motioned toward the sheet. "This isn't you."

Hank unabashedly wiped tears from his eyes. "What do I do now?"

"You go to the sheriff to get right with the law and you go to Reverend Hind to get right with God."

"I don't know if I dare, Harriet. There's no telling what they'd do to me—and what would happen to you and the kids, for that matter. I'm afraid."

Harriet held her husband's hand. They talked until daylight, from the barn to their bed, from a distressing wakefulness to a troubled sleep.

CHAPTER 17

Late Monday morning, Nathan reached the top of a hill a couple of miles south of The Crossing. Black wisps of smoke curled into the air over the village.

Strange. That wasn't coming from the location of the dump on the outskirts of town. What could it be?

"Dear God," he pleaded, "put Your angels around our town. Protect Your people, Lord!"

Nathan planted his feet on the floorboard and snapped his horse into a gallop. As he drew nearer to town, it appeared the smoke rose from the center of the village. He took a deep breath and prayed that the source wasn't the church—or parsonage.

Putting yourself first?

Shamed, he apologized to God and prayed especially that no one was hurt. He rode past Stridler's farm. What was the strange red barn-like structure that stood behind some trees off the road near the main house? And why hadn't he noticed it on his way out of town?

He spotted the KKK sign and frowned as images from his youth crashed in on him. Trouble lurked ahead.

When he reached the intersection with Main Street, he looked to his right and across the street. That was when the foreboding became real, startling his senses.

Two or three dozen people stood on this east side of the street watching the last charred beams and braces of Ilsa's Inn teetering. A large heap of rubble lay where an elegant house had stood when he left town. The guts of the house lay black and bared to the sun. The cracked remains of beautiful crystal and vases, the blistered and crinkled strips of once-luxurious wallpaper peeked out from the debris.

Once every few moments a board or frame fell into the ruins, sending up a puff of sickly looking smoke. It looked as if nothing had been saved. A sad thing.

Nathan had never approved of the house. He'd preached against the goings-on inside it. But he knew and, oddly enough, liked Ilsa Neilson. And every soul was worth saving—for God, and for him.

Nathan looked around the crowd to see if Ilsa was there. As he did so, Jennifer Craig and Ada Cutter approached him.

"Good day, ladies." His voice was low, sad.

"Hello, Nathan." Jennifer smiled weakly.

"Mornin', Reverend," Ada said. "I guess this isn't the best welcome-home present we could have given you."

"No, I guess it isn't, Ada." He eyed one of his favorite parishioners. "Say, is Ilsa around? Is everyone okay?"

Ada looked at the ground. "No, Reverend," she said slowly. "Ilsa isn't around—not unless you call being in there 'being around.'" She pointed at the smoking rubble.

The words took Nathan's breath away.

"Oh, my Lord." The words were barely audible. He stepped down from his buggy and slowly crossed the street to the remains of Ilsa's Inn. He reached the edge of the charred mess and looked deeply into it. "Ilsa," he said so quietly that only he and God could hear, "I pray you bowed your knee."

He stood still for several minutes, the eyes of all those gathered upon him. He recalled a conversation he'd had with another pastor at the conference in Boston.

"The Klan in Maine's not like down South," the pastor had said. "There's no violence, just a stand against the Catholic invasion, against foreigners taking our citizens' jobs, against Jewish control of finances."

Nathan had seen this back home and the old saw "A tiger doesn't change its stripes" came to mind.

"You know Reverend E.V. Allen from Rockland," the pastor said.

"Of course."

"He was the first to join the Rockland Klan. It must be all right."

"Really?" Nathan had met Allen. What this proved was "you can't tell a book by its cover."

Oh, too many clichés. Actually, too much reality.

He came away from the conference struck by the number of clergy backing the Klan—a minority, for sure, but still …

And there was talk of the Portland KKK buying the Rollins mansion on Forest Avenue and building an auditorium to seat six thousand and a dining hall to seat sixteen hundred. Up in Bangor, the Klan was buying an auditorium. All this in Maine where there was but a handful of Africans? Yes! People had seen crosses burning from Sanford to Bath to Pittsfield to Aroostook County.

Suddenly Jennifer interrupted Nathan's thoughts. "Nathan, there's something more we must tell you immediately. It's urgent."

Nathan squeezed his eyes tight, then opened them to look at this fine lady he so admired, her forehead creased, her mouth turned down. Inner turmoil, or was it even agony?

"Go ahead, Jen. Spill it out, dear."

Jennifer retold the Klan takeover of Sunday's church service and the threat at her home.

Nathan's mouth fell open. *Here? In my own town. My own church. My very own church!*

Stridler's face, smirk fully loaded when Nathan was leaving town, flashed across his mind.

Holding his rage, Nathan turned to the people lined on the other side of the street. His words crisp and authoritative, he said, "I'm asking you, all of you, to be my couriers. I want you to carry the message all about town and into the countryside that there will be a special, crucially important meeting at six o'clock today at the Community Church. It is for all faiths and it is absolutely a life-and-death matter that everyone attend.

"Are you with me? Will you help?"

"Yes!" came the loud chorus of several men and women alike.

Nathan looked at Jennifer and Ada. "There's a lot we must do, ladies." He looked at his watch. "We've got just about seven hours to get ready."

As they walked across the street, talking quietly to one another, Nathan sensed eyes upon him and looked up. It was Stridler. Dressed in riding garb and sitting atop a young Arabian, he looked like a noble European equestrian, bizarrely out of place in Cooper's Crossing, Maine.

I'll be darned if I'm going to be impressed by that get-up.

"Going on a fox hunt, are you?" Nathan asked.

Stridler chortled.

"Good one, Reverend! Ha-ha." He leaned toward Nathan. "Not today, but it appears you *do* have plans. May I ask what your important meeting will concern?"

Nathan stood straight, chin up, hands on hips. "You know full well. I don't intend for you and your kind to take over The Crossing. Not without a fight, I don't."

"Listen, Reverend." Stridler's tone was so condescending that it must wilt most men, Nathan thought. "I'd like to give you a piece of my mind—"

"No, you'd better not," Nathan snapped. "You can't afford it."

Stridler showed a dramatic look of hurt, then asked, "Pastor, Pastor. So cruel. Doesn't the Bible say, 'Turn the other cheek'?"

"In Luke 22, Jesus told His disciples to arm themselves with a sword. Don't dare to use the Bible against me," Nathan countered. "You'd be waging a losing battle."

Stridler sat forward in his saddle and chuckled. "I don't think my battle is being lost, *Mister* Hind."

"You know, Stridler, there've been a few times over the years when I've wondered what the presence of some men on earth is for, and I think I've finally figured it out. It's the devil's errand, to devastate it. There are some sins that are not easily washed from your hands, some that are not easily forgotten, and one that is unforgivable. You? You have engaged in all three kinds. Everything you stand for is anti-Christian—from your white Anglo-Saxon Protestant banner to your stance against Catholics and foreigners."

"My dear reverend," Stridler said with reproach, "we antagonize no man's religion more than they do ours; it's an honest plan for equal recognition. We are not anti-Jewish; any Jew who can endorse the Christian religion can get in. We are not anti-Negro or anti-Oriental; many other fraternal organizations do not admit them. We are not anti-foreigners; we simply require that our members be native-born Americans.

"And, dear reverend, I feel compelled to tell you that scores upon scores of ministers have joined the Klan all across the country, and many of them are taking positions as kludds and klokards, that's chaplains and lecturers.

"So, you see, your complaints are really very minor."

Nathan clenched his fists, the anger boiling in him like lava surging in the veins of a volcano.

"Mr. Stridler," he said, his voice now a monotone, "by taking over my church you violated both it and me and, most of all, God Almighty. You are assailing the intelligence of the entire town and the whole country. You are raping people's minds with your propaganda, and with what consequences? Indeed, it appears your actions have led to the death of a woman in this fire. That counts for murder."

Nathan whirled around and walked to his carriage, leaving Stridler sitting on his mount. He refused to look back, but could feel the man's eyes upon him. He was like an evil playwright, probably contemplating what wild and curious twists he could spin in his plot to destroy the fellowship in this wonderful town of Cooper's Crossing.

Nathan wondered if he had ever met anyone so Machiavellian. That speculation lasted for about three seconds. The answer: No way, not close.

Jennifer stepped up to his carriage and said, "I'll be taking the call to meeting to the farms along Harlowe Way. God bless you, Nathan."

He smiled back at her and heard Ada, who was now across the street in her store. "John," she said, "there's going to be some excitement tonight!"

Amen to that.

ꝅ ꝅ ꝅ

No sooner had Nathan entered the rectory than the knocker sounded on the front door. He opened it and before him was Alice Whitney. A tall, graceful lady, Alice had long, wavy blonde hair that swirled around a fine-lined, beautiful face accented with large emerald eyes. She was a striking woman, yet, at this moment, a look of anguish caused a crack across the perfect picture.

Carrying a sense of urgency, she slid quickly through the doorway and past Nathan, toward his study on the left of the hallway.

"I must speak to you—privately and *now*, Reverend," she said.

Nathan followed her into the study, motioned for her to sit on the black leather couch in the mahogany-paneled room.

"What is it, Alice?" he asked softly.

"It's a lot of things. It's been building." She lowered her eyes. "But I'll only tell you about the most important, something that concerns more than just me."

Nathan sat quietly, nodding, letting Alice Whitney tell her story. A woman in her mid-thirties. No children. Unhappy with her marriage to Royce. Her material needs were taken care of by her wealthy farmer husband, but there was no more love, no caring. She hadn't been looking, not actively, but it had happened nonetheless. With Jean Bonneau. A gentle, kind, genuinely loving man. Everyone had seemed to love him. And so had she.

They'd been quiet, discreet, planning how she would divorce Royce and marry Jean. Something he'd do even though he was a Catholic. No one had known about them. Or so she'd thought. Then ...

Alice shakily undid the top buttons of her blouse and folded back a lapel, turning to show the sight to Nathan. Above her breast, an ugly welt in the shape of—

"It's the letter 'W,'" she said. A tear escaped the corner of her eye.

Nathan flinched, cringing from the pain that must have accompanied being branded by a hot iron.

"Royce's message," Alice's voice cracked. "It stands for 'whore' as in *The Scarlet Letter*."

Nathan leaned forward and took her hand. "You poor girl."

"Yes, poor in the only way that counts. Royce won't let me go, won't let me leave him in spite of it all. It might further expose his wife's 'tarnished reputation' to public scrutiny. And, Nathan," her look was one of anguish, "I think something terrible has happened to Jean, too."

"Why do you say that?"

"I haven't heard from him since that night. I rode out by his house a couple of times and there was no sign of anyone. I've heard that he hasn't shown up at work since the night this was done to me."

Nathan sighed deeply. *Yet one more nail in the coffin—the Cooper's Crossing coffin.*

CHAPTER 18

Jigger sat up, holding court in his normal fashion but this time about a polar-opposite topic. They'd made a quick day of it. They'd left Suzie behind with her new cabin and memories of her old one. They'd negotiated the churning, violent waters where Alamoosook Stream and Limerick River met, and had maneuvered the logs easily down the Limerick. Several men had gone ahead downstream to Jacques LaBonte's mill to guide the LaRoche crew's branded logs to their destination.

Now, the entire crew had crossed over the river to LaBonte's and sprawled, exhausted, on the green grass on the edge of the lumberyard. A perfect audience, too tired to leave.

Jigger had always believed in a Creator, he was telling them, but One who had made the world and then let it clip-clop along like a windup toy. But since his encounter with the angel and deliverance from the grip of death in the Alamoosook, "I've seen the light," he said.

"He's right here watching over us," he declared. "Otherwise, why'd He send an angel to rescue me?

"I've been livin' in the woods all my life, but now everywhere I look I see God. In the fir trees and birches, in the broom, the fern and the bushes …"

"That's what my people believe," Pierre said of his Indian heritage.

"No-no. I don't mean I see God 'in' the trees. I see His hand, His creativity *in* the trees. He's out there, not down here in the acorn. He created the process that produced that acorn. He's the Creator, not part of the creation."

Jigger pulled a hand-sized Bible from his hip pocket. "Look here. My Uncle Charles gave this to me years ago, and it's been in my bags ever since. I just pulled it out last night while we was restin' at Suzie's and opened to this here.

He read: "I was there when He set the heavens in place, when He marked out the horizon on the face of the deep, when He established the clouds above and fixed securely the fountains of the deep, when He gave the sea its boundary so the water would not overstep His command, and when He marked out the foundations of the earth. Then I was the craftsman at His side."

"The 'He' there is God and the 'I' is Jesus. And that was Him who reached down into the river and lifted me out."

Every eye stared back at Jigger. These men he'd caroused with from beer hall to cathouse, these men who he'd give his life to save. He had to convince them he wasn't the same man.

Andre broke the moment, pointing toward the village. "That smoke we noticed earlier is still there."

Jigger followed his direction. When they got within sight of Cooper's Crossing this morning, they'd noticed smoke but were too busy preventing the logs from continuing downstream to worry about it. The Crossing had a fire department. The town could handle it.

The sun was setting now. Jigger pulled an old, gold watch from a pocket. Almost six o'clock. About time for a savory supper at a Crossing restaurant, a meal they'd all been dreaming of for months.

Jacques, busy overseeing the sleuthing of the logs out of the water, walked over to the crew. He looked troubled.

"What's the matter," Jigger joked, "logs too big for your wee little saw blades?"

The men laughed, but Jacques' expression grew even dimmer.

"Friends," Jacques said, "take a look past the railroad trestle and over the main building of the Thomas mill. At this time yesterday, you could see the roof of Ilsa's Inn. You'll notice it isn't there now."

Jigger followed Jacques' directions. A short, stunned silence hung over the crew.

How can this be?

Reality set in and Jigger hustled to his feet, wide-eyed. "Are you tellin' us—"

Monty and Pierre had both rose up beside Jigger. "*Mon Dieu,*" Pierre sighed.

Now everyone stood. Andre said softly, "*That's* what was burning."

"Yep," Jacques said solemnly.

"How are the girls?" Jigger asked. "Anybody hurt?"

Jacques didn't reply.

"Jacques," Jigger pushed, "who was hurt?"

Jacques shrugged, then answered, "Ilsa." He looked Jigger square in the eye, anger mixed with pain. "She's dead, Jig. Burned alive."

A blow squarely to the stomach with the blunt end of an ax head. That's what it felt like. Excruciating mental pain, accompanied by a physical ache. It was like when Papi died.

Why'd you save me, Lord, and not Ilsa? I know we're all sinners, but I'm a worser one!

ꓘ ꓘ ꓘ

The clock on his desk in the anteroom behind the altar at the back of the church said six o'clock. Nathan took three deep breaths, concentrating on relaxing every muscle. He reached for the glass of water and swirled the last of its contents around in his mouth before swallowing.

"Father God," he prayed, "I've failed You and Your people, or this evil would not be in our midst. I've not been looking with spiritual eyes and seen the spirits of anti-Semitism and hate battling for the minds of Your people in this town. Please forgive me, Lord. Give me Your wisdom and discernment. Consecrate my mind to Your purpose. Anoint me to speak Your words boldly. And, Father, give these people ears to hear and hearts to act upon what You have to tell them. I need to thank You again for Your mercy and grace, O Lord, for Your humble servant and for the people of Cooper's Crossing. Amen."

The door to the rear of the church opened. Frank Lajoie, the St. Joseph's priest, The Crossing Congregational Church Pastor Harry James, and Baptist pastor Daniel Osbourne looked in.

"You ready, Nathan? The church is full," Daniel said.

"I'm coming."

Nathan walked to the door and peered inside. The church was indeed jammed, standing-room only. Indeed, people were standing in the aisles and two deep along the walls.

There were obviously more females than males. But, still, there were a number of men—and well-respected ones at that. Doc, with Alma at his side, sat in the front center pew and looking as calm and comfortable as if he were in his own living room. Selectmen Shawn Mason and Tom Bradley sat together halfway back in the center row of pews. There were Matt and Clara Whittaker, with their children, and Sam and Jennifer Craig over there on the right with Joshua. And Ada and John Cutter, and Fred White, forever the liberals' spokesman, and many others, many with their children.

Center-right sat his housekeeper, Hannah, her lips tight together with her best friend, Katherine.

And at the front, double-doored entrance Sheriff Wright on the right and Deputy Cotton on the left.

Nathan ascended the three stairs to the right of the pulpit and stood beside the lectern. Frank, Harry, and Daniel all followed him and stood behind him—a united front.

"The—devil—is—here!" Nathan spat out each word. Like daggers, they hurled out at the assembly, sharp edges piercing their targets.

"He is all around us—alive, crawling on his serpentine belly. Vile, wretched, seething with hatred, he is living around and among us."

Nathan spread his gaze out over the crowd. He had their attention. "He has found a home, a refuge in our midst. Believe it or not, in the midst of the people of Cooper's Crossing! And we—must—vanquish—him!"

The power of the Holy Spirit swelled up inside Nathan, pouring out with every word, mounting in force with every moment.

"Most of you, and perhaps all, know what has been happening here in The Crossing. Violence has been perpetrated—from minor name-calling to tar-and-feathering and fire."

Nathan hesitated. Dare he say it? Yes!

"Possibly even *murder*."

Gasps.

"Right here in this church, while I was out of town, the supposed 'saviors of our souls' marched to this very pulpit and declared they were here, in God's house, as the 'protectors' of our morality. Hrummpf! 'Protectors'?"

Declarations of "No!" greeted this question.

Nathan moved to the lectern and opened the huge Bible. "This is what their leader read, dear ones. The twelfth chapter of Romans. It begins like this: 'I beseech you therefore, brethren, by the mercies of God, that ye present your bodies a living sacrifice, holy, acceptable unto God, which is your reasonable service ...'"

Nathan raised his eyes and looked at Jennifer Craig. "But he didn't read on, did he, Jen?"

She shook her head.

"No. He'd rather the Ku Klux Klan sound holy and not like a group that would do something that could scare a young boy to death or nearly so."

Joshua squirmed in his seat and glanced sideways. In the pew to Joshua's left, Tommy Mullen sat with his parents, and in front of Tommy, Abe sat, nervously squeezing his baseball hat into a ball. All good boys. Joshua had felt the assault, but his good friends were affected.

"Let's see what our friend, the kindly exalted cyclops, omitted, shall we?" Nathan dropped his eyes again down at the Bible. "Let's jump down just a few sentences to verse nine: 'Let love be without dissimulation. Abhor that which is evil; cleave to that which is good. Be kindly affectioned one to another with brotherly love; in honor preferring one another; not slothful in business; fervent in spirit; serving the Lord.'"

Nathan looked up and scanned the church. All eyes were on him and the silence was almost pungent.

"Let's go on further: 'Recompense to no man evil for evil.' And further: 'If it be possible, as much as lieth in you, live peaceably with all men. Dearly beloved, avenge not yourselves, but rather give no place unto wrath; for it is written, vengeance is Mine; I will repay, sayeth the Lord.'

"And further still: 'Be not overcome of evil, but overcome evil with good.'"

Nathan gently closed the cover of the Bible and stepped to the side of the lectern. The air was stagnant and warm and the people sat and stood elbow touching elbow; but Nathan had their rapt attention.

ᛟᛟᛟ

A bit of a breeze made things more comfortable outside the church. From Klan Hall on Stridler's estate, a throng of white-robed horsemen approached Main Street from the south. At the front of the ghostlike figures was Stridler, riding tall and confident, buoyed by the unified response to his orders given a few minutes earlier.

Quiet as church mice, just as I asked. Stridler smiled. *And once we reach the other side of the bridge spanning the Androscoggin River to LaBonte's mill, then ...*

There they would rid themselves of yet another major evil. Those vermin had to be destroyed, those foreigners and Catholics who were planning their invasion, who had taken American jobs and were storing arms in preparation for driving the white Anglo-Saxon Protestants out of their land. Sheriff Wright wasn't doing it. The Maine and federal governments weren't putting a stop to it.

Waiting for elections? That was not his style. Never was, never would be.

No, the Klan had to ride in a united, armed front. Maine was an outpost, like the granite beneath its surface, a vital and strategic area. Simmons had declared it must be won over for the Klan, and it would be. It would be a cornerstone for the entire nation. More than that, The Crossing klavern would be the spearhead! And who was seizing that spearhead? Robert E. Lee Stridler, aka Simon Duke. His father would be proud. His uncles would be envious of his father. His cousins would be jealous of him.

Would be? *Will* be!

₭ ₭ ₭

"Yes," Nathan said, "God created man in His image. But the minds of some men have become infested with evil. Good men are God's men. They make the space they fill positive. They spread an influence of kindness, honesty and decency to those around them. The non-God-fearing man? He's negative, burdensome, prideful at odds with the world, and ultimately at odds with God.

"That lethal mixture is exactly what we have here in The Crossing and what we must contend with. I have asked God's forgiveness for being blind and lax, for being asleep at His wheel in not recognizing what was happening, spiritually, in our town." Nathan motioned to the men behind him. "Pastor Falmouth, Reverend James, and Father Lajoie have all joined in this battle.

It's time to unleash the Spirit of God. It's time for us all be bold together, to face this evil together—"

ℬ ℬ ℬ

The horsemen turned onto Main Street and crossed the bridge to the west side of the Androscoggin River, just a short distance now from the bridge that crossed over to LaBonte's point of land on the north side of the confluence of the Androscoggin and Limerick rivers. The streets were deserted.

Odd, thought Stridler as he scanned the village.

Smoke still rose from the remains of Ilsa's. That brought satisfaction. There was word Ilsa's "girls" had all fled south, out of town and out of sight. That brought a smile. Word was, Ilsa's charred remains had been discovered.

Too bad, so sad, she was seldom fully clad.

ℬ ℬ ℬ

At LaBonte's, Jigger and the others hung on every word as Jacques told them of Ilsa's fire. One of his men had been in the house and had escaped with the girls. He'd told Jacques that he thought Ilsa had died in the blaze. She never came out of the building, the man said. They didn't know if she'd just stubbornly stayed inside, like a captain aboard a sinking ship, or whether she'd been hurt and couldn't get out.

"It would have been just like her to 'make a statement' by staying inside," Jacques said, using air quotes.

"Bold as brass," Andre said.

Jigger buried his face in his hands and wandered off toward the front of the yard, trying to make himself believe that it was all a dream. Suzie Cooley and now Ilsa? This stuff only happened in books. Make-believe atrocities for imaginary people. Not Suz and Ilsa.

Utter opposites in every way, but two people he liked. Each a complex person in her own way, both having antagonized the Ku Klux Klan enough to commit arson, if not murder.

Ilsa'd had too much spark and spirit to die. How could anyone want her dead? It made no sense, even if someone didn't like how she made her living. She'd never hurt anyone. She was a soul worth saving. Now that was too late.

Dreams, Ilsa once told him, reveal our soul, our innermost thoughts, our loves, our fears. Was this, then, a dream revealing a fear? It was so agonizing. Could it be real? Apparently so.

ƙ ƙ ƙ

Nathan wiped perspiration from his brow and continued his diatribe. "At our conference in Boston, the Klan was a leading topic of discussion. As you may know by reading the papers, it has come alive all across the country. And I feel compelled to share this editorial from an Oklahoma newspaper."

Nathan unfolded a newspaper clipping and read:

"'The Klan is the beatinest thing that ever came down the pike. It's a fraternal order for the promotion of strife, an empire for the promotion of democracy, a criminal conspiracy for upholding the law, a peace crusade by violence, and a new sort of Christianity that would flog Christ for being a Jew and a foreigner.'"

Nathan set the clipping aside. "In the late-1800s in the South, where I was raised, the Klan disposed of Negroes who were disrespectful, or committed crimes, or belonged to military or political organizations like the Loyal and Union leagues, or who bought land and prospered, or who talked about equal rights. Its method was violence. It intimidated judges and juries. It exiled, mutilated, flogged, tar-and-feathered, and hung and shot those with whom it didn't agree.

"Those atrocities are long past. Are we to stand idle while they're given new life?"

The clergy behind him called out a ringing, "No!" that reverberated through the church. It gave Nathan courage, especially since Matt Whittaker and Sam Craig's voices were among the loudest. Two highly respected men. Two bold men. Two powerfully built men.

"Satan has his way with some men, working through them," he said, "but God works even more powerfully through the Spirit-filled, born-again believer. So, should we remain complacent and refrain from battle?"

"No!" came the resounding response.

He recited: "'So God created man in His own image, in the image of God created He him; male and female created He them.'

"Friends, before we were Americans or Frenchmen or Irishmen, before we were Protestants or Catholics or Jews or Hindus or Muslims, before men became any of those things that divide us in bigotry today, we were men and women, all of us, created by God. 'In the image of God created He him.'

"That is the basic, the essential, the eternal truth by which we must live. For if we don't, we may very well die instead—by the sword of Satan."

ᛣ ᛣ ᛣ

Morose, Jigger treaded slowly through a small maze of planed lumber stacked in piles several feet wide and six or more feet high. He stared grimly at the ground and kicked the dirt into miniature dust clouds.

He had so much to ask God. His new faith was filled with so many unanswered questions—*probably because I never thought to ask 'em*, he thought wryly.

Do you go to heaven if you have a good heart but don't believe in Jesus? That was the one foremost on his mind right now. *I don't think so.*

Stepping around the corner of a stack of lumber, he noticed movement over on the bridge.

He narrowed his eyes and what he saw was clear—and frightening. A mass of horses was moving slowly and quietly over the bridge toward the yard, the riders cloaked in white, their faces hidden behind sheets hanging down from pointed hats. A few carried torches held high despite the sun still hanging in the sky.

That can't be a good sign.

Jigger stepped back behind the stack of lumber. The meaning of what he'd seen registered in a fraction of a second.

Holy crow!

He turned and ran toward his companions, saying to himself, "Blue-eyed, bandy-legged, jumped-up ol' whistlin' Joseph H. Mackinaw." He leaped over one final four-foot-high pile of lumber and landed right in the midst of his friends, who had been joined by the saw mill crew.

"They're here, boys! They're comin'!" Jigger said.

"Who's here?" Andre asked. "Who's comin'?"

"The Klan. They're ridin' over the bridge right now—and they're carryin' torches!"

"Oh, no, we've got to stop them!" Jacques cried and raced off around the other side of the main building of the mill toward the bridge.

"What are we waitin' for?" Jigger roared. "Grab your peaveys and let's go!"

They all found their long, wooden-handled instruments and followed. The sharp, curved steel edges that handled lengths of trees could do major damage to human flesh and bone.

"Some of you go 'round the other side of the building and some circle around down to the left and get behind them so they can't get back over the bridge," Jigger said.

"Obviously, our own retreat is not on Jig's mind," Pierre said to Monty with a chuckle.

Jigger pointed at them. "I heard that and you're right!"

The men began to disperse and Jigger turned and led the charge directly along the path taken by Jacques. Monty, Pierre, Yvan Rousseau and two mill workers followed him.

𝕶 𝕶 𝕶

Sheriff Will Wright scanned the church intently while listening to Nathan.

They're upset. Don't get a Down Easter upset, or watch out. Pastor or not.

Pastor Hind's voice was riding a high, scorching wind through the church: "'The tongue of the just is as choice as silver; the heart of the wicked is of little worth.'"

Will felt a tap on his shoulder. He turned to face Richard Fryer. Fryer was breathless, his face red, his right cheek twitching.

Distraught. Flustered. Never a good thing.

"I've got to see you, sheriff. I've just got to see you right now," Fryer said, his eyes darting toward the inner sanctum of the church and back again.

"Okay, Fryer, what's it all about?"

"Alone." Fryer motioned to the outdoors. "It's gotta be alone."

Will followed Fryer to the front lawn and noticed a bundle of white linen folded under his arm.

Fryer led him down the street eastward toward the parsonage. They were a good thirty yards down the street.

𝕶 𝕶 𝕶

When Jigger turned the corner around the warehouse Jacques was approaching the front entrance to the office structure. That's where the horsemen would enter onto the premises from the bridge.

Seconds later, they turned the corner to hear Jacques bark, "Whadda you people think you're doing on my land?"

"Well, we're not here to *buy* anything," declared a deep Voice from behind the red robes. "Perhaps to take but not to buy."

"The only way you'll take anything is over my dead body," Jacques shot back.

"We'll take that as an invitation, LaBonte," the Voice answered. "Here and across America, the Ku Klux Klan will continue to reclaim *our* land for *true* Americans!"

With his attention focused on Jacques, the figure in red was obviously surprised when Pierre stepped out from beside Jigger and stepped out of the shadows into the wide-open front driveway before all the horsemen.

Pierre shouted, "'True Americans,' eh? Well, the only *true* Americans are the Indians. And bein' half Indian, I guess I must be more entitled to this land than you, don't ya' think?"

The man in red spurred his horse toward Pierre and drew up within a couple of feet of him. Then, with a sharp metallic *zing*, he drew a shining sword from a sheath beneath the folds of his robe.

"It was white Anglo-Saxon Protestants who made this country what it is today—not heathens like you," The Voice seethed. And the sword took deathly aim at Pierre's jugular.

ƙ ƙ ƙ

Finally, Will said, "Fryer, this had better be important because I really should be back there." He pointed to the church. "Someone's got to be around to keep things from getting out of hand in case those people decide to react with a violence of their own."

"Th-Things are already out of h-hand," Fryer said, his shoulders now twitching along with his cheek. "It's h-happening all over again. Just l-like l-last time."

"What are you talking about— 'again,' 'last time'?"

"J-Just l-like it happened years ago, where we l-lived in Kentucky. F-Fire. K-K-Killing."

239

Killing?!

Fryer's eyes flicked back and forth as if ricocheting off phantom objects. Perhaps ghosts from those years ago. This man was becoming unraveled, losing control. Best to get as much of the story Fryer had to tell as he could before he went over the edge into Never Never Land. Or was it Wonderland? He could never get those two straight.

Oh, what a story Richard Fryer had to tell.

ƙ ƙ ƙ

The sun was now so low on the horizon that it glowed a bright gold in Jigger's eyes as he tried to see what was happening with Pierre and that large fellow in red robes about fifteen yards away. Then the glitter of the sun's rays hit the drawn sword and shot off the blade into the late-day air.

Jigger didn't know exactly what it was, but something in his mind told him sharp and clear—weapon. Without hesitation, he hoisted his peavey and flung it like a spear. Its pointed metal tip sailed in a spiral, straight and true, and smacked the sword from the grasp of the man in red. Startled, the man's horse reared up on its hind legs. The man swore, then grabbed his reins with both hands, his sword pointing skyward.

Pierre grabbed at the horse's reins, but just missed.

"Drive them outta here!" It was Andre, calling from the far side of the building.

"Get 'em, men," said another voice from the left, near the bridge and behind the horsemen. That was Ernest Plourde.

Jigger figured the dozen lumberjacks and a half dozen mill hands were triply outnumbered. But they surrounded the horsemen and began whirling their peaveys high over their heads in circular motions like wooden lariats. Jigger looked down at his bare hands.

No peavey. No problem.

He and his comrades closed in on the horsemen.

ᚕᚕᚕ

Stridler settled down his horse and released the reins with his right hand to wing his sword at that indolent Indian. But the lumberjacks rushing to form a circle around he and his klansmen drew his attention away. For the first time, he felt unsure.

"They-they can't do this," he shouted, spinning his horse counterclockwise and scanning the situation. He raised his sword high. "Don't let them surround you, klansmen. Fight back!"

ᚕᚕᚕ

Jigger heard the call to battle and thought the horsemen had the advantage. But he and his friends were too fast, their exhaustion a forgotten discomfort left behind with the rambling waters of Limerick River.

They rushed onward, some flinging their peaveys. Many jumped high, grabbing fists full of robes and pulling horsemen to the ground. Shouts and howls of pain filled the air. Horses' hoofs kicked up flurries of dust around men wrestling on the ground.

Jigger searched for someone to take on one-on-one. It appeared none of the klansmen had guns. They probably expected only to burn down the mill. No bullets, just flames.

The lumberyard was a battlefield. Fists flailed, connected, men fell and got up to fight again.

Jigger chuckled when Ernest Plourde raised one klansman's robes over his hood, blindfolding him and wrapping him up helplessly. Ernest then grabbed another and, seizing each by the neck, brought their heads together with a crack.

Ouch!

The man in red had backed away from Pierre and was riding through the mob urging his charges to "Kill the scoundrels."

Pierre was trying to get to the man, but there were too many others, both robed and plaid, blocking his way.

So, swinging his fists in powerful blows, he knocked klansmen off their feet like leaves in a hurricane. But he got no closer to the man in red.

Through the horses, the dust and men clutching and battling one another, Jigger saw the man in red turn a whip onto his horse and flee over the bridge.

In the same instant, in the midst of the fray, one of the horsemen broke loose and headed, with flaming torch, toward the main building of the mill.

Jigger lurched quickly toward the rider's path. He angled and rushed to cut him off. He couldn't quite reach him but he was able to catch hold of the cinch on the side of the horse's belly.

Big mistake.

Jigger's hand was caught and twisted in the cinch, wrenching him with acute pain. A bone snapped in his left wrist and he cried out in agony. But the horse rode on and the rider thrashed Jigger's forearms with something hard.

Jigger's legs were dragging on the coarse gravel, the horse's hoofs pounding the ground just inches away. Would he get crushed by those powerful hooves?

Saved from the river for this?

Jigger squinted through eyes nearly shut with shooting pain. Finally, he managed to undo the cinch strap with the fingers of his free hand. Mustering a surge of strength, he yanked, and the saddle slipped off the horse's back. Jigger, the horseman and the saddle plunged to the ground, the torch falling from the klansman's hand.

Jigger rose to a crouch, ready to jump on the klansman, when a flare from the torch caught the man's robes. Billowed by the pocket of air beneath the robes, the flame shot up toward the man's head. He screamed and waved his arms to stomp out the fire. But it was a losing battle.

In full panic, he started to run for the river. But that was too far. He'd burn alive first.

Jigger bolted toward him.

ꝃꝃꝃ

When he heard the scream and saw the flames, Pierre loosened the deadly full-Nelson he had on his opponent. Around him, in the midst of riderless horses, entangled bodies, grunts and groans, everyone turned.

There was Jigger, one wrist at an obviously unnatural angle, running and pouncing on the ball of flames. After knocking the man to the ground, Jigger ripped off his own shirt and batted at the flames while kicking dirt onto them.

The fire died under the assault and the man lay still, face down, deathlike. Pierre looked around. Everyone stopped fighting. Punches were pulled in mid-blow. Yvan, who held an enemy high over his head, gently set him down on the ground.

A large klansman who sat atop Monty and was about to deliver a jaw-breaking right, stopped, his fist inches from its target.

ꝃꝃꝃ

Wincing from the pain from his broken wrist, Jigger knelt at the side of the klansman. Was he dead?

With his good hand, he turned the man onto his back. His robe had burned entirely and the clothes beneath were charred. Jigger laid his head on the man's chest and listened.

A faint thump-thump, thump-thump.

Jigger lifted his head, smiled broadly and lay back, sprawling on the ground. A feeling of satisfaction radiated over his body.

There was a brief silence, a deafening stillness, as if the world was mute.

That's odd!

Jigger turned on his side, then leaped to his feet to see what was happening in the fight.

Apparently forgetting their place and their intentions, the men on both sides were making their way toward him.

One especially big klansman leaned over the burned klanner. He took off his hood. It was that banker guy, Fletcher. He turned to Jigger and declared, "You saved his life."

Jigger frowned, looked down at the unconscious klansman and shrugged. "Yeah, I guess so." He paused, then added, "Why do you reckon I'd do a thing like that?"

"I know!" The voice came from behind the crowd. Heads turned. Jigger peered between them and spotted Nathan Hind. Hind stood, hands on hips, puffing. And behind him, running over the bridge, came a crowd of Crossing residents. A couple hundred of 'em.

 KKK

Nathan gulped for air, taking a moment to calm his pounding chest. He looked about at the swarm of disheveled white robes, grime-faced lumberjacks and, beyond them, that famous little fellow, Jigger Jacques. What a sight!

Finally, he mustered, "I can answer it, and I think we all can. But first—" he turned to Doc Walker and said, "Doc, can you look after that man on the ground?"

Doc, carrying his ever-present medicine bag, stepped out of the middle of the crowd of church-goers and rushed to the burned klansman.

Nathan turned back to the klansmen, lumberjacks, and mill workers. "I've just returned from Boston where each and every one of these tales of Catholic arsenals, and cannons atop a hill at Georgetown University, and French-Canadian takeovers was proven a lie. Bigotry? Hatred? Fighting? There's no reason for it. We're all God's people and this is all God's land."

He pointed at a circle of white-robed men. "And your man, your god, Robert Stridler, has been exposed by his own right-hand man, Richard Fryer. Years ago, Stridler carried out this same siege of hatred, this set of lies—in Kentucky, where he is wanted for manslaughter."

A sudden whuff, a mass intake of breaths, met this declaration.

"Men of the klan, you've followed a lie," Nathan said. "And we know who is the father of lies: Satan. You've been taken *in*. Now's the time to get *out*. Our Lord forgives a repentant heart. Please, as a messenger from God, I pray that you lay down your weapons, dispel your fears of one another, and return to your homes and your old lives."

From the middle of the crowd, Pierre blurted, "Yeah, I'll even relinquish my claim to being the only true American here!"

His guttural laugh was infectious among the lumberjacks and klansmen. Nathan could only guess at the joke.

CHAPTER 19

Suddenly, pulling the hood from his head, Cecile Chamberlain pointed to the south and shouted, "Smoke!" A swirl of smoke curled above the trees in the fading sunset.

It originated along the east side of the Androscoggin River just south of Main Street. This was not Ilsa's. It was another fire altogether.

Sheriff Wright, standing on the bridge, called out, "Is that the Stridler place?" He turned to the group who had arrived behind Nathan from the church. "Hey, Fryer, do you think that could be Stridler's house or barn?"

Nathan, with everyone else, looked around the lumberyard. Fryer wasn't there.

Fletcher stepped forward. Speaking to everyone in general, he said, "Where's Bob? Where's Stridler?"

"He's one of you. He's your leader, isn't he?" Nathan asked.

"Yes, he is. But he's disappeared—apparently," Fletcher said.

Sam, from the front of the crowd, said, "We'd better get out there. Now!"

Nathan, Sam, Matt, Will, klansmen and clumsy-riding lumberjacks grabbed riderless horses and mounted them, heading back past the throng on the bridge.

⚑⚑⚑

"I'd rather be riding a log than this thing," Pierre shouted to Jigger as they raced down the road toward Stridler's farm.

"And you call yourself an Injun?" Jigger chortled as he fought off a grimace from the searing pain in his wrist.

Pierre laughed—a hoot that, for some reason, didn't seem out of place.

ᚻ ᚻ ᚻ

The fire was brighter, higher and louder the closer Sam got to it. He was the first to arrive and, indeed, it was the Stridler farm. He pulled the horse to a halt on the front lawn.

Startling!

Flames licked at the house from all sides. Inside the large windows that surrounded the downstairs rooms, fire crawled all over velvet curtains. But further inside, it seemed more of a blaze.

Others rode to Sam's side.

"What about water?" someone asked.

Matt piped up, "They're bringing the pumper now."

"They'll be too late," Sam said. Flames had just burst into the second floor.

Where were Stridler and Fryer, anyhow?

Another horse pulled up with and unleashed a mind-curdling whinny. The horse was frightened by the fire. Nathan looked down almost apologetically.

Sam nodded to him.

Nathan lowered himself from his mount and said, "We'd better check out the house as best we can to see if Stridler or anyone else is inside there."

Something caught Sam's attention on the span of lawn to the left of the house. It was Fryer, flaming torch in hand, running toward the Klan barn a short distance away.

"Burn, damn you, Stridler!" Fryer screamed. "I'll burn your hide, you monster. You said 'fire cleanses,' huh? Well, I'll cleanse you!"

Odd. This is the first time I've heard Fryer speak without stuttering.

Fryer stumbled forward and, beside Sam, Will ordered, "Stop him!"

ᚳ ᚳ ᚳ

Matt tossed Will and Sam the "I'll-go" look. He took off at a sprint along with Charlie Owen and several others, but the little man reached the barn ahead of them and bolted the door behind him.

Matt crashed into the door and it didn't budge. "He locked us out," he said. "Try around the other side and I'll try to break this door down."

Charlie and the others ran around the corner of the barn while Matt kicked a heavy boot into the door. It didn't budge. He put his weight on his hind leg, then sprung the other leg forward at waist height. The door croaked and gave a bit. He slammed it again and it cracked and gave a bit more.

Fragments of shouts from inside. "… cleanses all! … Burn, bur …! Murd-er …"

Then the snapping, crackling sound of a fire inside grew loud.

Matt took several steps back and ran at the door, his shoulder serving as a battering ram. Pain shot across his shoulder blades and down his arm. The door was not cheap, that was for sure.

Something inside the barn burst. An explosion of some sort? Then he felt heat on the door.

Too late!

"Darn!"

Charlie returned from the other side of the barn. "It's no use, Matt," he said. "We can't get in!"

Matt looked at the main house. It was now an inferno. Smoke seeped out of the seams of its roof and flames were scorching up its walls, aiming toward the darkening sky.

Matt turned back and called through the door, "Fryer, come on out of there! Don't be crazy, man!"

There was no response. The strange little man was going to stay in the barn to die.

But what of Stridler?

𝕂 𝕂 𝕂

Sam, Nathan and about a half dozen lumberjacks and klansmen had run into the house. Flames were everywhere, searing the walls, eating away at the overstuffed furniture, gnawing at woodwork. The searing brightness reminded Sam of a place he had seen in a dream: the fires of hell.

Now to find the devil.

Upstairs was out of the question. Stridler wouldn't stay up there in this firestorm. Besides, the smoke was stifling. Sam ripped off his shirt, grabbed a handful of the material and held it over his mouth.

He hurried through a doorway to his right. A sitting room. A couch and three chairs in a near circle. Two large windows facing the front yard. A small fireplace with inlaid porcelain pieces bordering it. s scuttled along every piece of furniture, climbing the draperies in front of the char-blackened windows. Stridler wasn't here.

Sam coughed out smoke violating his lungs.

It's a furnace!

He rushed to the back of the sitting room into another, large room. A huge mahogany desk, its surface bubbling from the fire crawling over it. Walls of books, their bindings aflame. Another fireplace, its burning wood now consuming a bearskin rug that, strangely, Sam thought, had been thrown onto it.

A number of framed photographs had been smashed while still on the wall. Senator Brewster and Stridler shook hands, smiling for the camera. A book lay in the middle of the floor. Pages had been torn from it and were scattered, shredded around the floor, some burning into ashes, others awaiting incineration. Sam picked up the book and looked at its cover: *The Klan Rises*.

He flung it savagely into the fireplace.

"He's not up here!" The call came from upstairs.

Will's voice, from somewhere downstairs at the back of the house, responded, "You'd better get down here, or we'll be draggin' *your* body outta there!"

Sam coughed again as smoke curled around him. He bolted out the back door of the room and into a dining room. A table and chairs, a bench along one wall, a gigantic, curved, glass hutch in the back corner. Fryer had apparently skipped this room, thinking it too unimportant to waste his time.

Ten feet away a door opened. Nathan came panting from a stairwell. Covered with soot, his hair array, he looked like a chimney sweep. He shook his head. He was out of breath. "Cellar," he exhaled. "No one there."

Sam and Nathan raced into the kitchen. Men were choking and coughing toward the front of the building. Sam called in that direction, "Is Stridler out there? Anyone find him?"

Someone coughed the answer: "Nothing."

His voice panicky, Will screamed from the side lawn, "All right, everybody out! Get outta there! Those walls could go any second. Do you hear me in there? Get out!"

"We're coming, sheriff," Sam called.

Nathan had slipped by Sam and out a rear door to the back lawn. Sam couldn't see a thing toward the front of the house. He hoped everyone *could* get out unharmed. He turned and rushed out the rear door.

As Sam ran down the stairs and onto the lawn, there was Nathan, striding purposefully toward the stables in the rear pasture. The house fire illuminated the lawn, but the barn was barely visible. Sam sprinted to catch up to him.

Coming up beside him, he said, "I think you're onto something, Nathan. I'll bet that's where Stridler is! If he's escaping, he'll take that Arabian."

"Or the roan that he rides in competitions," Nathan said.

Sam frowned. "Right."

They sprinted, half-climbing, half-jumping over the fences on their way.

Stopping outside the stable, Nathan turned to Sam. "Remember," he said, "if Stridler's in there, he's desperate and he could have a rifle. Be careful and listen to the Spirit of God."

Sam nodded.

The stable had a large double-door at each end.

"How about you take that side and I'll take the other?" Nathan said, pointing to the left.

Sam nodded.

Not arguing with the man of God.

𝕶𝕶𝕶

The men reached the two side doors to the long stable at the same time. Nathan put his hand on the door handle. A creepy feeling ran down his back, curling the hairs on his neck. Harried voices from around the house punched into the quietness even from this distance. The sound was amplified for some reason.

Out here, the horses were uneasy in their stalls.

It was dark in the building and opening the double-doors only allowed dusk to invade that blackness. Nathan felt along the inside of the door frame.

A-ha! A light switch.

He flicked it on. Two dim bulbs on either side of the center walkway lit up, hanging high on cords from the ceiling. Several horses snorted and turned in their stalls to see their visitors. Rustling sounds, hoofs on wood. The bulbs cast a paltry light on the walkway near them but barely protruded into the center of the stable. Equipment used for training horses hung from wooden beams and cast heavy shadows into the hidden stalls beyond.

To Nathan's left was a small tack room filled with saddles, harnesses, brushes, buckets and other equipment.

The stable was well kept, even fresh-smelling. He and Sam were in a world removed from the house, where men's hurried shouts rung out in the night air. The fire engine had apparently arrived.

The horses quieted down. It was as still as a tomb.

Nathan looked at Sam at the far end of the stable. Sam motioned, Let's start the search.

One stall at a time, left to right, they began working toward the middle. A horse stood in nearly every stall. Beautiful, powerful animals, they could hide a man standing behind them. Freshly strewn hay was everywhere, deep enough for a person to hide beneath.

Dark shadows dominated. Even close to the light bulbs, it was difficult to see into the corners of the stalls.

You'd think this place would have a lantern at least.

Of course. Stridler's taken the lantern. He's got it and he may be in this next stall, or the one beside it, huddling with the lantern—and a gun.

The stillness became heavy, disarming. One at a time, Nathan found the stalls empty of any two-legged creature. He'd come out of a stall into the walkway, look up and see Sam emerging and sharing a shake of the head.

Then, as Nathan reached the point where the dim light turned to utter darkness, rustling sounded in the next stall. At that moment, he realized he had no protection. If Stridler were armed—and he surely was—Nathan was a sitting duck.

How fitting! A man Stridler surely disdained, standing unarmed before him. The exalted cyclops' last triumph, taking down a nemesis. *Right-o.*

Nathan searched around for something to use, a stick of wood perhaps, or a rider's crop. A halter hung from a beam behind him. As he reached up to grab it, something scurried behind him. He spun back around. Something shuffled in the hay not more than three feet away and Nathan hunched down on his haunches, ready to defend himself.

An icy tendril raced down his spine and he flinched at its chill. This sensation must be something like being in the trenches in The Great War.

Out of the shadows burst two big tom cats, one chasing the other. They blew by him like he wasn't even there and ran down the walkway. Nathan heaved a sigh of relief.

"What was that?" Sam called from the far side of the shadows.

"Couple a cats." Nathan reached back, grasped the harness, and twisted it tightly in his hands. Stridler *had* to be here, crouching, ready to make a break on the Arabian or roan. He couldn't have had time to get away before they all arrived. But which stall was he in?

Only four pair of stalls were left between the men. It was much more difficult to see into those stalls. Nathan and Sam both had to open the gates and walk in. Nathan turned a bewildered horse around so he could check the back corners. Nothing.

Now there were three, even darker, sets of stalls. Nathan peered into the next stall. In the pitch-dark he could nevertheless make out that the horse was white. The Arabian.

Nathan removed his belt, rolled it into a coil, and tossed it into the stall, waiting for a gun to fire at the noise. The horse snorted, but that was all.

Nathan sidled into the stall, keeping his back against the partition between it and the one next to it. He reached for the horse. It was saddle-less but lathered from the race here.

Nathan side-stepped around the stall, kicking in front of him as he went but trying not to startle the horse.

A blow from one of those hoofs could crush a man.

Slipping out of the stall, he continued on to the stall across the walkway in the same manner. Again, nothing. He stepped out into the walkway. Sam, his figure a black silhouette against the distant light bulb, shook his head side to side. Nathan sucked in a breath and pointed to the two centermost stalls. Sam nodded agreement.

Nathan took the stall facing the house, while Sam stepped into the one across from it. Nathan reached in to touch the horse. It spun quickly around, uneasy at the unfamiliar touch and, obviously, the pervading tension.

"Shush, boy," Nathan whispered, and moved the animal to the side and around the stall. If anyone were there they would be badly injured by those heavy hoofs. But there was no one.

Father God, Stridler's got to be in one of these two stalls.

Back when he had looked out at these stables from the burning house, the feeling that Stridler was here was just so strong that he firmly believed it. How could he not be? Could he have ridden out here, removed the saddle and other paraphernalia from the Arabian, saddled up the roan, and slipped out the back? Certainly not. Nathan and the others were so close behind him.

"Nathan." Sam sounded defeated. "Anything?"

"No."

"There's not even a horse here. Guess we lost him."

"*Modus operandi*," came Will Wright's voice. Will was at the north door. Jigger, Matt and Pierre were at his side, along with Garner Fletcher.

"That stall you're standing next to is where he kept his favorite horse," Fletcher said. "Worth a fortune in stud fees."

"My guess is, he also has a fortune stowed away in some bank far from here," Nathan said.

"Probably so," Sam agreed.

"Same thing happened to him down South," Will said. "Fryer told me all about it just before the big fight at the mill. Fryer had a change of heart. Conviction, he called it. Shame, I call it.

Anyhow, he had a lot of misgivings, and I guess he decided to do something about it himself."

"Yep," Jigger said, "that fella was a loony, but it looks like the Lord used him in the end, don't it?"

Sam let go a sardonic laugh and looked at his friends, "Yeah. 'Fire cleanses all,' the man said."

Matt put his arm around Sam's shoulders. "Well, we gave it the old Cooper's Crossing High School try."

"Go, Cougars," Sam said, his voice dim, depressed.

Nathan asked, "What happens now, Will?"

"We'll put Stridler on the Wanted Lists. Some authorities somewhere might find him. As for the klanners still here and what's going to become of them—"

"I think I might be able to shed some light on that," Fletcher broke in. "We're going to have to fess up to all the carnage we caused. There'll be jail time. It's going to be trying for our families. But I think things, eventually, will get back to normal around The Crossing. It's all over now."

Nathan had walked slowly back into the stables and looked into the empty stall in the middle. He turned, his thoughts in a world of the unknown. He looked back at the others and asked, "But, *is* it all over, gentlemen? Is it *ever*?"

CHAPTER 20

Exchange Street was one of Jigger's old haunts, especially this time in the evening. Bars, cathouses, bars—a whole row of all a lumberjack could want down a half-mile stretch of downtown Bangor, Maine. Several men waved to him or slapped his shoulder on their way into the bar Up a Tree. That was "two glasses and he was up a tree" as in intoxicated, not "this whole business has me up a tree" as in confused. Anyhow, Up a Tree had been his favorite bar east of the Mississippi for years.

At one time, Jigger had dreamed of Ilsa's being next-door to Up a Tree. Heaven, he'd thought then. Hell, he knew now.

Jigger inhaled a deep breath. *Give me the words, Lord, and I'll be Your man.*

A sudden jolt of energy took hold and he winked and nodded at Pierre beside him. The force propelled him through the door, into the middle of the dark wood-paneled room, up a chair and onto a table.

"Lumbermen! Friends! Do I have a story to tell you! *Oh, Mon Dieu!*"

⁋⁋⁋

Jennifer Craig looked out the window and smiled, content. She rocked back and forth in her grandmother's red rocking chair and marveled at the brilliant good looks of the Lord's land in the autumn. The trees were a bright rainbow of beauty. Somewhere out of sight from this window, Sam and Joshua were working the fields, plowing the remnants from this year's harvest back into the ground for next spring. Next year's crops would grow rich and strong because of this year's decay.

Jennifer thought—and, she thanked God, it was the briefest of thoughts—about this year. About the rapid rise of the Ku Klux Klan and its hasty fall. The Klan had died that late-spring night when that French-Canadian lumberjack Jigger saved the life of a burning klansman, and when a crazy little man set fire to Robert E. Lee Stridler's mansion and the Klan hall.

It was perhaps a miracle that, with such stunning quickness, the klansmen saw the waywardness of this "cause" and of what Stridler (or, they had learned, Simon Duke) had filled their minds.

All the men who'd taken part in the cross-burning the night Jean Bonneau accidentally died and in the terrorized nights of Suzie Cooley and Louis Levesque, had stood trial *in toto*. It seemed a quarter of the town was on probation, a handful in prison.

But reason now prevailed. The old community unity—a blessing of immeasurable value—was being restored, though in many cases with some circumspection as men and women on opposite sides of the Klan phenomenon revived their relationships. The nightmare had ended, though the scars might remain forever in some people's minds. And what of Jean Bonneau's friends and loved ones?

But, yes, it was a miracle, she thought, and not the only miracle in her life lately. She softly touched the cheek of the sleeping baby girl in her arms, kissed her forehead, then again looked out the window and smiled.

ᛚᛚᛚ

Joshua and Moe stood atop Henhawk Hill, right on the spot where the flaming cross had stood that spring day.

Winds had blown, rains had fallen and grass had grown so there were no remnants of the cross and no evidence of trodden-down ground.

Joshua hefted his bat in one hand and in the other an old baseball, its cover gone and now wrapped in bulldog tape. He tossed the ball in the air, swung the bat and smacked a long fly ball over the edge of the hill deep into the forest. If he had been on a baseball diamond, the hit would have been a homerun over the centerfield fence.

He smiled then knelt down beside Moe and patted his best buddy on the head.

"This place is ours again, boy," he said and nuzzled his head in the big dog's ruff.

ᛒ ᛒ ᛒ

Norma Jean, a clerk in the exclusive men's clothing store, straightened the shirts on the table and looked over to the section where the men's suits were on display.

That tall, broad, distinguished gentleman who'd bought the Macomber estate on the outskirts of town was holding up a black suit to his inspection.

You didn't often see a man of that sort in this northern Minnesota town. He was so self-assured, so well-dressed, so—cultured. Did they call that debonair? He even smoked his pipe with aplomb.

And that *Voice* ...

ᛒ ᛒ ᛒ

Reverend Nathan Hind sat on a blanket upon a shady hillock overlooking the Androscoggin River, an apple in one hand and a novel written by the Scotsman George MacDonald in another. Difficult reading in the old English, but well worth it. MacDonald's writing helped him handle the daily slings and arrows that sometimes flew his way in the wake of the KKK fiasco.

He'd had to deal directly with fallout from the turbulent times since the climactic confrontation. Yes, the KKK had flamed and died, it seemed overnight, but its residue was evident all around. Even today.

Manslaughter, arson, tar-and-feathering—these were difficult challenges in the realms of forgiveness and clemency.

Many, even among his congregants, admitted they were able to forgive but not forget.

If that were how God dealt with sinners, we'd all be in trouble. As far as the east is from the west, so far has He removed our transgressions from us when we repent.

Time would tell. Demons still had to be exorcised. Some people had needed their muddled minds cleansed regarding skin color such as that of Ming Su and Willie. Hank Green and others still seethed over their relatives' lost jobs in such mill towns as Rumford, Lewiston, and Biddeford—Hank all the more because of his brother's suicide. Here and there, businessmen still put out signs: "Job Available. Jews Need Not Apply."

Hard feelings had far from dissipated, but at least those men and women who sat under Nathan's leadership and had harbored ill will toward one another were working out their feelings, face to face.

As for the repercussions of the jury trials, well, Nathan had dealt with them with varying degrees of success. And failure. Some still manifested dark hatreds and resentments. Others had been totally transformed, set free by the Holy Spirit.

The determining factor was always how close the person was to "putting on the mind of Christ," walking as Jesus walked, forgiving as He forgave, even those who had demanded His execution.

Nathan thought of the Scripture from the second chapter of Ephesians: "For we are his workmanship, created in Christ Jesus unto good works, which God hath before ordained that we should walk in them."

Workmanship, in Greek, meant "grand, epic poem."

"Think of that," he said aloud to the blue jay that landed next to his half-finished sandwich. "We're God's creation, His great epic poem, His work of art. We should look at ourselves in that way. Just as we should look at all the things that are happening as if looking at a landscape painting."

The blue jay didn't seem to care much what he was preaching, instead taking a nip from the sandwich Hannah had made for him. Unfazed, he continued, "It's easy to see the Klan's hatred and lies, its oppression, and be afraid of it. Yet, *every single* part of the landscape is created to make the picture as a whole. You can't recognize just how dark a thing, a thought, or a person is unless and until you expose it to the light. Don't you agree?"

The blue jay cocked his head, as if pondering the question, then took another poke at the sandwich.

The End

About the Author

Having won wide acclaim for his first historical novel, *Midnight Rider for the Morning Star*, and for another historical novel, *True North: Tice's Story*, a *Publishers Weekly* Featured Book, Mark Alan Leslie has leaped from the world of journalism, where he has won six national magazine writing awards.

His mystery/thriller, *Chasing the Music*, was released in 2016, the first of a new series featuring archaeologist Kat Cardova and black-ops veteran Max Braxton.

Leslie was a newspaper editor for fifteen years and a magazine editor for twelve years before forming his own media-relations company, which operated for thirteen years before he dove full-time into writing books.

Leslie lives in Maine with his wife, Loy. The couple has two grown sons and four grandchildren.

He is available for speaking engagements and book signings and can be contacted at: gripfast@roadrunner.com

Endnotes:

Rarely will you find even a history buff who is aware of this disturbing chapter in Maine history, when the Ku Klux Klan gained immense ground in this northeastern-most state, growing a membership estimated as high as 150,000 of its 750,000 population. Its targets: Jews, Catholics and French-Canadian immigrants.

The KKK backed Ralph Owen Brewster, who won the governorship in 1925, Maine State Senate President Hodgdon Buzzell of Belfast and politicians who won mayoralties in Saco, Auburn, Westbrook, Rockland and Bath.

The first daylight KKK parade in the country was held in Milo in 1923 and hooded Klansmen marched in Portland, Gardiner, Brewer, Dexter, East Hodgdon, Kittery and Brownville Junction among other places.

The first state convention, held in the forest outside Waterville in 1923, drew 15,000. That same year the Klan bought the Rollins estate on Forrest Avenue in Portland, building a 4,000-seat auditorium and a dining area seating 1,600.

The national KKK targeted Maine because it was considered a bellwether state in national elections ("As Maine goes, so goes the nation.") And so it sent the charismatic F. Eugene Farnsworth north to sway the crowds.

Farnsworth spoke in large open halls and sometimes and his speeches were reprinted in full in local newspapers.

In 1928 the New York Times called Newport and Kennebunkport "old Ku Klux capitals."

The Klan largely disappeared in Maine—and nationally—by 1930, after helping to defeat Al Smith, a Catholic, in his run for the presidency in 1928.

Scandals involving bribery, adultery, embezzlement and bootlegging led to its rapid decline and, in Maine, many left the organization once its goals were widely known.

The organization reportedly had only about 225 members statewide by 1930.

Enjoy Chapter One of
True North: Tice's Story

True North: Tice's Story
A Novel
Mark Alan Leslie

Chapter One
The Year of Our Lord 1860

Tice stood at the banks of the swiftly flowing Ohio River, contemplating his future, or the end of it—the man with the gun chasing him close behind. Try to swim the river, he'd drown. Stay here, he'd get whipped half to death, or maybe all the way to death. That's what happened to runaway slaves.

Struggling to catch his breath, he thought, Lord, how'd Your boy get here? What on earth I done?

Like flipping the pages through a fast-moving picture book, the last hour or so of his life spun before his eyes. The day had begun so quietly, so drearily, like always.

There he was, maybe nineteen, twenty years old, standing with hoe in hand in his Massah's field, reflecting on his short life. This day like all the others. Still hackin' away in the dirt, still pickin' cotton, still sleepin' on a board.

He swung the hoe and joined in singing with the other slaves:

"Swing low, sweet chariot—"

Tice stood working in the cotton field, hoe in hand, singing with his fellow slaves, the words of the spiritual distracting him from the monotony of the chore that would consume his day. Singing helped. Sometimes the less you had on your mind, the better. Sometimes when you're not thinking of your Momma— God bless her soul—or your Pappy—I hope you're still alive!— the quicker the day goes. But today was different ...

"Comin' for to carry me home—"

Tice's arms were swinging the hoe, his mouth was forming the words. But lately, his mind was on his Pappy and the freedom his father had whispered about to him a few summers ago, before being sold by Massah. Pappy had remembered that freedom with happiness.

"I looked o'er Jordan 'n what did I see—"

Tice continued working and singing, making his way across the field with the others under Massah's watchful eye. He had to keep up, do his share, or Massah would whip him, sure.

Just then, Massah gave a random crack of his whip, a frightening reminder of what he did to those who displeased him.

Tice struggled not to look toward the edge of the field, to the road where he'd met a stranger not two weeks prior.

The man had seemed to appear from nowhere, leaned down from his horse toward Tice and said quietly, "Young man, if you can ever escape, do so by crossing the Ohio River just south of the ferry and ask for the Randolph house. That's my place. Do that and we'll get you free. Remember that? Randolph?"

"A band o' angels comin' after me—"

Tice had nodded. Randoaf. He thought of another slave, a skinny old man the women called a "randy oaf."

He didn't know what that meant, but, as the man hurried off, Tice repeated, "Randoaf."

Since then, Tice had worked as usual. But the thought of escape stayed in the forefront of his mind, the taste of Pappy's freedom inhabiting his dreams at night.

"Comin' for to carry me home."

Tice blinked hard twice, shook his head and nearly lost his grip on the hoe as he scolded himself. Freedom 'n such is fool thinkin'.

Suddenly, the whip smacked the ground by his feet and an icy hand laid firmly on Tice's bare shoulder. It sent a chill down his spine and cut the hymn short in his throat. His friends all around him in the cotton field took notice and stopped singing as well.

Clutching the neck of the hoe in his hands, as if to drain the life out of the wood, Tice turned an eye toward the firm grip and knew from the white, square-fingered hand whose it was.

"Yes-sir, Boss," Tice said, turning toward the man who owned him and another hundred slaves who toiled the fields as well as the plantation that spread for a mile in any direction. Tice dare not look his boss in the eye, so he focused on the man's chin.

"You're one of my strongest workers, Tice," Julius Lykins said, "so I need you to go down to the village, to the railroad station."

"Yes-sir, Massah Lykins."

"A shipment's arriving on the train. Morgan'll be down there, along with Gilly, waiting with a wagon. You get down there and help them unload."

Tice nodded.

"The shipment should arrive about the time you get there if you head out now. If you don't get there in time, you'll get the sting of this whip, boy." Lykins pushed his horse whip in front of Tice's eyes.

Tice cringed. He'd felt that sting before and had the welts across his back to prove it.

"Well, get on down there, boy. I expect you, Morgan and Gilly back here in an hour or so."

Tice handed his hoe to Elijah, his friend standing nearby, and started to quick-step out of the field toward the road to town.

"Clock's ticking, boy," his master said.

Tice started jogging.

"Tick tock!"

Tice set out in a full run, his hardened bare feet unaffected by the hard-packed dirt as he reached the road to the quiet Kentucky town of Maysville.

"Gotta get there or feel the whip. Gotta get there or feel the whip," Tice repeated to himself. As he ran, his brief life flashed across his mind. He was born on this plantation and knew nothing else. His Momma died of fever when he was a boy. A few years later his Pappy was sold to another plantation who knows where. He had no brothers or sisters, except brothers and sisters in the Lord.

An' here I is, still livin' for nothin'—'cept my relationship with my Lord. Here I is, runnin' into town for my Massah, goin' to load my Massah's stuff for my Massah's plantation, for my Massah's farm animals maybe, or my Misses's parlah.

The hymn lingered in his mind.

"If you get there before I do—"

Someday he'd have a manshun, he thought, a big old house in the sky. But until then, he was hoein' 'n pickin' 'n runnin' 'n loadin' here on earth for a man who beat him 'n his friends for fool reasons, or no fool reason t'all.

Tice was a speedy runner when need be and soon he looked up to see the rail station ahead. Sure enough, he could see the steam from the engine floating skyward, drifting side to side— same as he'd like to do. He began to sprint, not wanting Morgan, his Massah's foreman, to get upset with him. Morgan packed a more powerful whip than his Massah when his Massah wasn't watching.

"Comin' for to carry me home—"

Shortly Tice reached the train and saw Morgan talking to a man wearing a funny-looking hat. Gilly, another slave, stood behind Morgan. The man motioned to another fellow, who reached up and tugged at a rope on a door on the train, then slid the door open. Tice ran to Morgan's side and lowered his eyes to Morgan's chin.

"Let's get to it, boy," Morgan said. A burly man, Morgan twisted his handlebar mustache with a forefinger and thumb. "Hop up there and hand down the boxes to Gilly. He'll pass 'em to me and I'll load 'em up on the wagon."

"Yes-sir."

Tice sprang onto the train. Box upon box filled the rail car. What was in the boxes, he didn't know at first. Soon he discovered, though, from the sheer weight of them, that the cargo was dishes, plates, pots and pans and such items for the mansion. This'll mean the manshun's old pots and pans for us-uns, maybe.

In short order, Tice passed the last box to Gilly, a big fellow slave Tice hardly knew—indeed, nobody hardly knew 'cause he hardly spoke. A grunt here and a grunt there defined Gilly.

Loading the boxes onto the wagon and then strapping them down with rope, Morgan turned to Tice. "Gilly'll ride with me. No room for three. You'll hafta walk, boy. But don't ya' be dallyin'."

Tice liked that idea. He'd step along the side of the road where it was grassy and cooler under the shadow of the trees. He began the walk back and watched the wagon disappear ahead of him. As he stepped one foot in front of the other, a thought began to ferment in his mind. An exciting idea. An educated person who knew about epiphanies might call it one of those.

He looked up. Morgan and Gilly had disappeared over a rise in the road. Tice stopped in his tracks and repeated to himself, "Randoaf."

He glanced around him. Was anybody watching? Maybe the workers at the train station? No. Anyone ridin' or walkin' down the road? No.

"Tell all my friends I'm comin' too—"

Quickly, he set his feet to motion toward the plantation. Then, a hundred yards up the road, looking again to make sure no one was watching, Tice veered into the woods, eastward toward the Ohio River.

Pushing branches out of his face, Tice plowed through a woodland. "South of the ferry. Randoaf." His destination was etched in his mind. He knew the river. He knew where the ferry left Maysville and floated over to Ripley, Ohio, north of the Mason-Dixon Line, separating slave states from free states.

"Comin' for to carry me home."

As he hustled towards the land of freedom, doubts about that very liberty filled his mind. Sure, he'd be free. But where would he sleep? What would he eat? What work would he do—could he do? Who would be responsible for all this—all of him? First his Momma, then his Pappy and always—yes, always—Lykins saw to it that his hunger, thirst and shelter were taken care of. Now Momma was gone, Pappy was gone and he was leavin' Lykins.

Oh, Massah. Tice thought of more than one whipping at the hands of Lykins. At that memory, he hastened his steps, remembering Lykins saying he expected Tice back to the plantation soon. When I doesn't arrive, Massah'll be furious 'n he'll come lookin' for me, and he'll have that whip in his hand. Oh, that whip!

Several minutes later, he pushed another branch out of his face and came to a meadow. Nothing planted here. No cotton. No tobacco. Tice hesitated and looked around slowly, wanting to make sure no one would spot him if he made a mad dash across the field.

"South of the ferry. Randoaf," he muttered aloud as he sprang into the meadow at a speed that even surprised him. "South of the ferry. Randoaf."

Hay in the field tickled his ankles, but his focus remained on the river. Just then he heard a loud voice hollering, "Hey, you!"

It was a white man's voice. "You there!"

He pretended not to hear the man and continued to run.

"Stop your runnin', boy!"

Stop? Could he stop now? Doubts flooded in again.

He hesitated. Yes, he could stop. Maybe that would keep him out of trouble. Maybe the man wouldn't tell his Massah. Then he wouldn't have to worry about food on the table, a roof over his head, chores to do. No. No worries. He slowed down but didn't look in the direction of the voice.

What should he do? What would Pappy do? he asked himself. Then again he remembered his Pappy talking to him about being free until neighboring tribesmen raided his village, tied them up, then sold the whole village to a white man on a boat. Tice remembered the smile on his Pappy's face when he talked about being a free man, and he speeded up his pace again.

"Comin' for to carry me—"

"Stop or I'll shoot!"

Chills went down Tice's back. His knees almost buckled. Shoot? The man had a rifle? Well, maybe dyin' wouldn't be bad, neither, Lord—compared to hoein' someone else's fields for the rest of my life. He hurried on as fast as he could and finally reached the end of the pasture. No lead bullet was fired, only a missile of fear.

Tice dove into the forest, landing on the ground and rolling into a bramble bush. "Ouch!" he screamed, looking down in pain as blood began to leak out of his right arm. He gingerly pulled his arm away from the bush and touched his forearm. "Ow!"

He heard the man call to someone else, "Hurry up and tell Mister Lykins that I think one of his slaves is runnin' away toward the river! I'm chasin' after him!"

"Chasin' after him," Tice repeated. Oh, no. Hurry, he told himself. South of the ferry. Randoaf.

He pushed himself off the ground to his feet, got his bearings and ran off. How long could he go? How long had it been? Was Lykins missing him already? If not, that man was going to tell him. Fear rippled through him like tendrils of ice as Tice thought of the consequences of being caught.

"Dear Momma," he called out. "Dear Pappy. Save me."

"Dear Lord!" he said louder as he came to a hillock, "Where's my band o' angels?" He looked up and the top of the hillock appeared a mile away even though it was only probably fifty yards. "Oh, Lord, help me!"

Tice clambered up the mound. Was this the Blue Ridge Mountains? he wondered. He'd heard stories and thought they were far beyond the river. Was his mind workin' okay?

Just when his legs gave out, he reached the top of the hill. Falling to the ground, he looked up and saw the river in the distance. He took a few seconds to rest and draw his breath, knowing he couldn't wait long; the man was chasing after him. The man! Tice turned to look behind him. The man was nearing the base of the hillock!

"Stop right there!" The man scowled and pointed a finger at Tice. "Stop there and it may spare you a beatin'!"

Tice shook his head. He knew that weren't true. Not true t'all. I's long past bein' spared no beatin'. A beatin's a comin'. A bad beatin'—if'n I gets caught. If'n.

The thought of the whip spurred him on, giving him a second wind, and he hustled down the hill, ducking away from alder branches along the way. He reached the bottom and skirted around another bramble bush. Gotta get distance. Gotta get distance 'tween me 'n him. A long way. He didn't see that the man had a rifle, but maybe he did.

Suddenly he splashed through a brook, his toes hit a rock and he fell to the bank of the brook, screaming in pain. He grabbed for his big toe. Had he broken it? He sat up and held his foot. Blood seeped out of his big and second toes. He put his foot back in the water, hoping the coolness would help numb it.

But he couldn't wait, couldn't linger a second longer. The man must be nearing the top of the hill by now and might spot him. His Pappy's face flashed before him. "Git ov'r it, son. Buck up! Git up and run!"

"Yes, Pappy," Tice said aloud. He lifted himself out of the water, stepped up to dry ground and set out running again as fast as he could while trying not to touch ground with those two injured toes.

And here he was, several minutes later, wheezing for breath, a sharp pain in his ribs, standing at the riverbank, fixated on the spring runoff streaking past in a maniacal race downstream. Yep. The choice: certain death or certain torture. Here was his future, or the end of it. Try to swim the river, he'd drown. Stay behind, he'd get whipped half to death, or maybe even all the way to death.

Struggling to catch his breath, Tice said aloud, "Dear Pappy, save me!"

Other Books

by Mark Alan Leslie

Chasing the Music, published by Elk Lake Publishing, Plymouth, Mass., 2016

True North: Tice's Story (A Publishers Weekly Featured Book), available at www.amazon.com and

www.barnesandnoble.com, 2015,

Midnight Rider for the Morning Star, published by the Francis Asbury Press, 2008. Second printing 2014. Available at Francis Asbury Press, P./O. Box 7, Wilmore, Ky. 40390

Putting a Little Spin on It; The Grooming's the Thing!, published as an e-book and available at www.amazon.com and

www.barnesandnoble.com, 2014

Putting a Little Spin on It; The Design's the Thing!, published as an e-book and available at www.amazon.com and

www.barnesandnoble.com, 2013

Walks with God: A Devotional, published as an e-book and available at www.amazon.com and

www.barnesandnoble.com, 2010

Fired? Get Fired Up!, published as an e-book and available at www.amazon.com and

www.barnesandnoble.com, 2009

Coming Soon

The Last Aliyah, to be published by Elk Lake Publishing, Plymouth, Mass.